MW01134691

It couldn't happen here!

Terry, wide-eyed and gun ready, faced the doorway.

It was Pratt! In his hands he held a green smock. There was blood on it and a smoldering anger filled his eyes. His voice cracked.

"It's Emaline's. It was in the back window of their car."

"Dang, Pratt! You're gonna get yourself shot!"

"Something's happened to her." Walking up to Bub, who had just gotten up, Pratt slammed him across the mouth, knocking him back to the floor. It was enough to jar Bub's cell phone from his pocket. It skidded to a stop under the drying rack. Pratt stooped to hiss at Bub. "Where is she?"

Terry grabbed Pratt.

"Hold it, Pratt!"

Pratt threw him off and, red-faced with rage, grabbed Bub by the shirt collar and yelled in his face.

"Where is she? What have you done to her?"

Gavin and Terry both grabbed Pratt and managed to drag him off.

"Pratt! Stop it!"

"So help me…!" Pratt shuddered.

Other books by Mark Herbkersman:

Novels in the Henry Family Chronicles:
Prodigals Blood
Revenge on the Mountain
The Branding of Otis Henry
Gideon's Redemption

Book of short stories:
The Christmas Train

Eric!
Thanks for being a
blessing Home!
Mark

Saving Winston Corner

By

Mark Herbkersman

Copyright © 2019 Mark Herbkersman
Kindle Direct ISBN: 9781794228818
Cover by Joy Herbkersman

DEDICATION

With deep thankfulness for Carol, Don, Wayne, Rusty, Rick, David and the others who stroll in and out of the coffee circle at the truck stop.

You keep me up to date, bring joy, information and dumb jokes.

Sometimes the conversation reaches a cliff and goes over the edge. Only us coffee drinkers know what that means.

Those of you reading this – don't ask us what that means. Just leave it alone.

All you need to know is this group inspires me and brings joy to my heart!

ACKNOWLEDGMENTS

Wow! It is hard to believe this is my sixth book! It is a totally different genre from my others, but it took the same teamwork to bring it to this point. Once again, I am compelled by my heart to give thanks to those who helped make this possible.

It has been a fun journey in many ways. I have purposely placed friends in this book. It is a small way to honor the blessing they bring to my life. Greg and Janet Schmeisser are real people and friends of very many years, but they do not run a restaurant and I don't even know if they like bratwurst. Dave Burris is the perfect breakfast companion. We have some secrets. The real Birdhouse Johnson is Rusty Hunt, and there are not many as talented. Others are composites of various people you could know as well as me. Most are imaginary for the most part.

To all those persons, remembered or not, who encouraged my creativity over the years, in whatever format it took. To the authors I've read who ventured from the ordinary and gave me courage to do the same.

Special thanks to Joni Murphy and Juanita Sheward, who have given of their time to make this dream come true. Both have shared their thoughts and guidance and have read the manuscript too many times.

Butch Baker, retired County Sheriff, has been a blessing to me in many ways through the years. He granted me his expertise and contributed to making this a better book.

Thanks to Panera Bread, for Cinnamon Crunch Bagels and coffee on Wednesday mornings.

Christy Luellen, who gave a final edit to the manuscript and contributed to its quality.

My daughter, Joy, who spent hours designing the cover and putting up with me when I changed my mind!

My loving wife, Marilyn, for allowing me to sneak off and write. I appreciate the sacrifices she goes through for me.

To God, who blesses me over and over.

A MESSAGE FROM THE AUTHOR

Does Winston Corner really exist? Yes. Take your map, run your finger along any interstate or state highway outside the bounds of the cities and go about an inch or more to each side of that main road and see all the names. Winston Corner goes by a thousand different names and dots the map from north to south and from sea to shining sea. Nestled in the cornfields and in the mountains and in the sand, the names may vary but the people are the same. It's a special way of life.

Shopping of any real substance is a bit of a drive away, but if you need a cup of sugar, just call your neighbor. Someone is always willing to bring a trailer and haul something for you. There tends to be a small library with someone half-ancient at the counter. The town workers know when you have a water leak and you slip the utility payments through a slot in the office door. The bank is small and they have treats for your dog when you come in. There is a coffee gathering that goes by various names, not all mentionable in polite society. It's not strange to have antlers on the barbershop walls. And, for good or bad, there is no Chinese food in town. But pizza usually is not far away.

The characters in this book may seem imaginary, but are they? Sometimes the imaginary does not stray far from reality. Look around you and see the uniqueness of the person being walked by their dogs or driving that big pickup truck with the 2x10 treated pine bumper. There are stories and personalities all around us. In fact, you may recognize some of the characters in Winston Corner.

Few secrets exist in such places. Quirks and oddities, skills and hobbies, public self and private reality are known to all. Everybody knows where so-and-so lives and who lived there before. They know your business and they know your history. Those of you who live in a Winston Corner know the dirt of those around, but also the sense of security, the close friendships and the deep caring for one another. You know that when something bad happens, the first thing you'll hear are doors closing and footsteps coming up your drive. You know you're not alone.

Yes, Winston Corner does exist.

It may be your town.

1

Both men jumped in surprise when the wrench fell atop the pump and the noise shattered the darkness. Eyes wide, they crouched and looked nervously around.

Everything depended on secrecy.

"Careful!" Jake hissed.

"Sorry!" Bub hissed back.

They worked quickly but with a practiced pattern a mile or so outside Winston Corner. The whole process was cloaked in darkness, with just the occasional flicker of a flashlight when absolutely necessary. Now the mini mag had been on a few seconds longer than they liked in order to locate the loose wire next to the deep cell marine battery. They could have groped blindly in the dark to reconnect, but the jolt was not pleasurable.

Any unnecessary second of light made them nervous. Both had served time and didn't want to do it again.

"Hurry!" Another hiss from Jake.

"I'm going as fast as I can."

"Don't talk."

"You talked first."

"Shut up."

"You shut up. I'll bean you with this wrench, Jake!"

"Quiet!"

"You be quiet first."

Finally they got the pump running and let it work for ten minutes at a time. Three times they did this, moving the hose each time. Water was essential. The pump had a good muffler, but sound carried easily on calm nights and they both remained silent, listening closely to the night after each session with the pump.

This isolated field was a great location and both men felt relatively safe from discovery. Straightening, one shoved a candy bar in his mouth and reached to stuff the wrapper in his pocket. Realizing his pajama pants had no pocket, he wadded it into a ball, glanced furtively in the darkness to his partner and threw it to the ground. Gathering their tools, they slipped into the night.

They had to get up earlier than usual. Tomorrow was shopping day.

Both wore frayed, dark colored pajama pants and equally dark t-shirts picked up at Goodwill. In fact, Goodwill was their favorite shopping place because the clothes were free. It was all in the method and the timing. Wearing old clothes in at busy times, they picked new clothes off the rack and went into the dressing rooms and changed, hanging their old clothes on the hangers. Then they stayed near the back of the store for a while until the staff was busy and slipped past to the doors. They did the same with underclothes at Wal-Mart, getting out with multiple pairs of boxers on, having smuggled them into the dressing rooms amidst shirts and pants they had no intention of buying. And it was always a delight to get new socks. Sometimes the workers at the stores were obviously suspicious, but restrictive shoplifting and liability laws combined with low wages caused them to turn their heads. In cold weather they were able to get quality jackets by going to funerals and helping themselves when they made excuses and left early.

They called it low overhead.

Tomorrow was a fifty percent off Saturday at Goodwill, and it would be crowded, so the mud and sweat of tonight would be hanging on the rack.

2

Awaking with a start, Gavin knew something was wrong. Seriously wrong.

In the other room, Jean glanced up from her devotions.

Both looked to their watches. 7:40 a.m.

It was unmistakably Cuthbert's truck they were hearing, but something definitely was wrong.

Winston Corner was a quiet town, especially on Saturdays. Sleeping in was a tradition…at least until 9:20. For at exactly 9:20 Cuthbert could be heard approaching town from the north, out where farmland still held sway. Interspersed amongst the fields were a few scattered former townsfolk turned pioneers who decided to plant a house out where there were no snow-plows and they could more freely pursue the American dream, meaning a bigger lawn, a bigger mower, a bigger chainsaw and a bigger weed eater. They were subject to Saturday tradition also, just a few minutes earlier than those in town.

The roar increased and decreased as Cuthbert slowed or accelerated or turned. It served as a sort of slow awakening until the noise built to an earsplitting crescendo where 650 West met Main Street.

Cuthbert, whose given name was Walter, drove a mostly oxi-dized blue 1972 Chevy C-10 stick shift with no muffler. He didn't believe in spending money on something designed to rot out every three years – a bit less on the farm with the constant splashing of livestock leavings. When his first muffler rotted out, people thought he'd put on glass packs. They raised their eyebrows in wonder until it became clear that, no, there was a definite rot factor. Finally there was nothing but rotted pipe

3

crumbling at the headers. Mothers would hear him coming and rush their kids into stores or grimace and cover little ears until the din passed.

Acceleration of any kind created a throbbing factor and the noise increased to exceed known decibel scales, and Cuthbert never wasted time getting to speed.

It wasn't just the muffler. The same exposure had rotted out the floorboards. Gaping holes showed the road flashing underneath the cab. When he pumped the brakes and jammed them to the hilt at a stop sign, the cab would fill with exhaust from the headers and Cuthbert could be seen gasping and fanning. Some children thought he was waving and would smile and wave back. Cuthbert would hurriedly roll down the window, lean out to suck air, then gun the truck to blow the fumes out. Wing windows were turned inwards to blow right on his face.

Gavin hurriedly arose with brow crinkled and slipped his feet into fleece-lined moccasins beside the bed.

3

On a normal Saturday morning, Cuthbert reached Pine and Main at exactly 9:23, and the noise reverberated off the large windows of the old storefronts on both sides of the narrow street. Vibration and sound nearly blasted Willy Bates out of his bed in the apartment over the hardware store. He'd tried using earplugs, wrapping his pillow around his head and playing music over headphones. None of it worked. It was like a badly tuned freight train going right through the living room.

The only thing Willy could do that seemed to help was curse. But it was only a temporary fix and within moments he would be staring at the ceiling.

"I'm sorry, Lord. Please forgive me."

It was usually about Pine and Main when people glanced to their clocks to set them to the correct time, commonly referred to as Cuthbert Time, but as reliable as Greenwich Mean Time or the time on any digital device.

Today was supposed to be the same, but it wasn't.

4

In the midst of her study of the book of Ruth, daydreaming about what it would be like to be married to a rich man like Boaz, Jean was jarred to reality by Cuthbert's early arrival. Now she stood at the window listening intently as Gavin came to within six inches of her left shoulder and said:

"That's odd."

Jean's heart skipped a beat. She jumped, turned and slapped Gavin's chest before grabbing her own.

"My lands! How many times have I got to tell you don't sneak up on me? You about gave me a heart attack."

"I wasn't sneaking. You were listening to Cuthbert and missed me coming. If I'd been a killer you'd be dead right now."

She was ready to jump all over him for that thought, but she turned and looked back to the window. Gavin stared intently and concern accented his words.

"Something's wrong."

Jean nodded.

"7:47. Gavin, what do you think?"

"What I just said. Something's wrong."

His hand went to his hip out of lifelong habit, though a gun no longer nestled there. As a federal agent, the gun on his hip had been as much a fixture as a pair of pliers on the hip of a farmer. And feeling for its presence was as natural as a preacher checking his tie and fly before entering the pulpit. A Glock was department issue, but Gavin preferred the faultless performance of a revolver, and used to carry one off duty. Despite the limit of six bullets, he contended six was enough. And it seemed to fit his hand better. On the range one day, a younger agent, proud of his new department issued Glock, had smirked at Gavin's Smith and Wesson until Gavin let the young man shoot it, loaded with full .357 magnums. The young man was sold on the power and feel of the gun and readily apologized to Gavin.

Now Gavin kept a Smith in the nightstand and another in the cabinet by the back door, where he could easily grab it and clip it on his belt. Gavin wiggled his fingers nervously and dropped his hand as he and his wife stared in the direction where the truck stopped.

They weren't alone.

5

"Dagnabbit and dad-blast-it!" Cuthbert yelled aloud in his truck.

Cuthbert always arrived at Schmeisser's Donuts and Bratwurst promptly at 9:25. Only then could anybody in town get back to sleep. Townsfolk said the only noise more irritating was the sound of fingernails on a chalkboard into a microphone on steroids.

Raising mostly crops, Cuthbert kept a few cows and a double-handful of hogs. Not into it enough to be picky, his hogs wandered freely around the farm. Occasionally one wandered a bit far and Cuthbert would scratch his jaw, grab his prod stick and go looking. It was a wonder they didn't go further more often, for the old farmer barely kept things together and a visitor could see old plywood braced against holes in the barn with cinderblocks. His favorite go-to for fences was the stash of lumber his granddad had milled nearly 100 years ago. Almost filling a large stall in the barn, the white oak planks were dust covered and harder than ever with age. In fact, Cuthbert had to drill them before he could drive a nail. Nails were rare, though, what with his preference for baling wire.

6

One day someone asked him about the holes in the floorboards. He replied, suppressing a grin.

"Them's for safety. If the motor stops the truck will still run. Just stick your feet out like the Flintstones and start running!"

He would laugh at his own joke.

The truth was…he was just blessed tight with a penny. He said it was the only way a farmer could survive.

The truck bed, held on by overstretched and frayed bungee cords, rattled and swayed and barely contained the mess of bailing wire, straw, feed sacks, spilled corn, scoop shovel, buckets with broken handles and other miscellany left in the bed until it formed a sort of bonded and sodden mass. Up next to the cab it was common to see sprouted corn, soybeans and even tomatoes. One year a lucky employee at the farm store hurriedly looked both ways, reached in and plucked a ripe tomato for his lunch. It was a good fist-sized Rutgers sprouted from a discarded Burpee seed packet buried in the corner.

About average height and sort of bowlegged on one side, he wore ripped Carhartt coveralls stained by accumulated filth and, on the bib, evidence of the "farmer blow." Whenever he took off his soiled Co-op cap, hair fell over on one side like a flapping wing. Vain in a sense, Cuthbert grew his hair long on one side and combed it over his bald dome. The effect was that every time he took his cap off, the hair lifted with it and by the end of the day it was in total disarray, with some hanging down to his neck on the grow side.

Cuthbert didn't wear a face shield when using the cutting torch, so his eyeglass lenses were scratched and pitted something awful. He could be seen glancing at flyers on bulletin boards with a sort of rolling head motion, seeking a gap between pits.

Nonetheless, he was like faithful Big Ben in London: trustworthy and always keeping accurate time.

But not today. And today he didn't turn.

Bleary-eyed townsfolk now sat upright in bed, fully awake.

All over town eyebrows touched hairlines. Ears rotated like radar.

The truck stopped shortly and everybody knew exactly where by a sort of unconscious calculation of the town layout and counting the seconds.

The Cop Shop.

7

Terry Jones had just come on duty at the Cop Shop.

Even he accepted the local lingo for the police station, because he was part of the reason.

At five-foot eleven, he was muscular, prone to doing push-ups to kill extra time. If he ate too much, he'd force himself to do fifty extra. His dark brown hair framed his square jaw and when asked what he looked like, people tended to stop a moment, think, and say, "hippie average."

Growing up a few miles north in Beedersville, everybody thought he'd wind up working at the Chrysler plant. Instead, he joined the Air Force and, after his discharge, returned to Beedersville to just sort of get his bearings. Somehow he never left. There were a few dates and what he thought was a serious relationship, but it all fell apart when he realized she had absolutely no ambition but to sit in front of the TV set. At twenty-nine, Terry wanted more.

Before applying for the police job, he worked at a motor-cycle business in Beedersville called The Chop Shop and wore his hair long and sported a tuft of a beard. His job was to make choppers out of normal bikes, and he was a natural. When the owner gave it up, Terry needed a job. One of Winston Corner's local officers moved to Indianapolis for a better paying job and the town was in a bind. Terry trimmed his hair, shaved and applied. The town especially liked that he'd worked for the military police in the service. So they hired him. He started to grow his hair again, but no one ever mentioned the grooming aspect and it just sort of fell to the wayside. It was not super long, just enough to come down to his shirt collar. Kids in

11

town admired his muscle and the confident way he walked. One day he showed up to watch at the skate park in Beedersville and stood outside his car slipping off his police shirt to don an off-duty t-shirt. He grinned inside as he spotted several teens staring at his muscled torso.

In the service, he was stationed at Mountain Home Air Force Base in Idaho. Terry took to hiking and backpacking in his time off. Now, living in the Midwest, he missed the mountains. So he saved his vacation days and went to Idaho every summer to backpack with an old hiking buddy. He called it his "ten days of Heaven."

8

Robert didn't hear a thing.

Virtually deaf in his left ear, he was dozing on his right side, never missing the beat of the dream he was having. In fact he was smiling. If his wife, Darla, could have seen the hula dancers he was seeing, and the way he was drooling in his dream, she would have slugged him and sent him to the backyard to sleep in the doghouse. Instead, he just snored contentedly.

That is, he slept until the dog stuck its nose into his face. For an instant in his dream he smiled as one of the hula dancers leaned over and kissed him, but then he jarred awake as an internal alarm erupted and he stared into the eyes of a dog.

He didn't own a dog!

Then he remembered, as he wiped his arm across his mouth and spit. Darla's father was staying with them for a while and insisted on bringing his Labrador retriever, a totally black beast with the stupid name of Coochee-Coo. His father-in-law called the animal "Cuckoo." Robert made a circle around his ear with his finger and mouthed the dog's name when his father-in-law was not looking. Darla usually slapped him when she was close enough. But it was only half-heartedly, as she was in agreement. The dog was an absolute irritant. Cuckoo padded around the wood floors interminably and created a constant racket with his claws. Twice Robert found scratches where Cuckoo made a quick turn. He'd shake his head and get out the Old English to touch up. But the clickety-clack was irritating when he tried to sleep. Only by laying with his bad ear up did he succeed in going to sleep. Darla didn't like that because it necessitated him facing her and he tended to breathe right in

13

her face with an animated poofing.

Now spluttering and cussing the dog and stumbling in a panic to the bathroom, Robert rinsed his mouth with mouthwash to get the dog taste out and kill the germs. Looking back, he realized his wife was not in bed. It was Saturday and she always slept in until Cuthbert's truck awakened her.

"Robert..." She walked in with a concerned look on her face.

"What's the matter? Your father...?" He hoped maybe his father-in-law had moved out in the night. But that hope couldn't be true because the dog was still here and the man would not leave his dog. He wiped his mouth in remembrance.

"Cuthbert's truck already came to town. And it missed the turn. Stopped at the Cop Shop."

Robert's brow furrowed deeply.

9

When Cuthbert's truck went straight at the turn, Terry looked up, intent.

Arriving early today, he told Wally to go ahead and leave. Then he'd cranked his Bluetooth speaker to enjoy his daily dose of Max Thorogood singing "Bad to the Bone."

Saturday morning was laid back and Terry enjoyed the quiet of the sleepy town weekend. On the average weekday he logged into the Indiana Data Communications System, then opened the National Crime Information Center to check on what was up. But Saturday was different. His tradition was to take a few minutes to eat his oatmeal and savor his coffee while reading a chapter of a western just before clock-in time. Today he had a copy of Louis L'Amour's *Silver Canyon* opened to the good part.

When the truck lurched to a stop outside and bumped the parking block, Terry put his oatmeal down and took a quick slug of coffee as the engine rattled and popped for a few seconds and the door of the truck opened on squeaky hinges and slammed shut. Terry shoved the western into the desk and put a spearmint lifesaver into his mouth and chewed it quickly, barely avoiding a coughing fit as Cuthbert burst though the door.

The look on the man's face brought Terry to his feet.

10

Birdhouse Johnson had chronic insomnia.

It was 2 a.m. when he slipped quietly into his clothes, made a cup of decaf and headed out to the workshop. Passing between the house and workshop, he looked across the yard to where his back fence joined farmland behind. For a moment he thought he saw lights in Cuthbert's woods in the distance. It was just a flicker, as a flashlight or weak headlight flicked on and then off. It seemed he'd seen the same thing a week ago. He stood there a moment and watched, but nothing more was to be seen so he shrugged his shoulders and ducked into the woodshop.

He liked the mornings, and he started by turning on the old CD player on the shelf. He always cranked the volume and sang. Today it was Frank Sinatra.

"And more, much more than this, I did it myyyyyyy wayyyyyyy!" He crooned, waving his arms and pivoting before his big project.

It was a wren hotel, a special order from a contact he'd made on Facebook.

Not adept at anything electronic, six months ago he rolled his eyes and gave in to his daughter's urging to post pictures of his birdhouses online. Facebook intimidated him initially but the surprising response in orders caused Birdhouse to suffer through issues like wireless Internet and tiresome formatting and uploading of photos.

Birdhouse started making bird domiciles years ago, seemingly able to construct them out of materials and knick-knacks others saw as trash. Bent silverware, insulators, old pan lids and a host of other things found their way into his incredible creations. Two years were spent creating a series of fifty state birdhouses that now lined the trim of his garage in order of their statehood. His table was popular at craft fairs and people would stop and marvel at catawampus birdhouses and even some mounted on shovels you pushed into the ground which he privately called "cat buffet's." Birdhouses of all sorts covered the sides of his garage and lined the fences, trees and even the top bar of the swing set.

This wren hotel was his crowning glory. Forty wren homes, made of pine recycled from an old dresser, were all connected by fancy gingerbread trim and about the size of two doors placed side by side.

Now, putting a couple hinges on a clean-out door, Birdhouse was chuckling to himself. His daughter was a teacher over to the local school and told him recently about a prank played on a new teacher. The day had been rainy and a soon to retire teacher walked into the new teacher's room and whispered.

"Just got word," he looked around carefully, "we're gonna have a surprise flash flood drill during fourth period. Be ready."

Then he slipped out, looking back knowingly at the new teacher. The naïve new teacher frantically looked through the procedure manual for a drill that didn't exist. Finally, worried for two hours about her evaluation by the principal, she slipped into the office with her procedure manual and quietly approached the secretary.

"What's the procedure for a flash flood drill? I can't find it."

The secretary laughed and explained. The new teacher turned red.

It was the talk of the teachers' lounge.

Birdhouse laughed aloud, but his laugh was interrupted as he registered Cuthbert's truck. Had he been working that long? Glancing at his watch and noting the early hour, he paused for a moment and looked out the window.

Why would Cuthbert be here so early?

11

Taking off his glasses, Birdhouse grabbed his cold coffee and headed to the house to tell Patty. Stopping outside and dumping the coffee on the grass, he almost took an eye out on a perch of the closest birdhouse. This side was special. He rented these out to others in town. One dollar a month. He chuckled and shook his head. He remembered the day his neighbor wandered over about dusk.

"Hey, Birdhouse."

"What's up, Tim?"

Glancing carefully back at his house, where his wife stood at the kitchen window washing dishes, Tim looked sheepish.

"Got a question. Promise you won't tell anybody."

"O…k. Promise."

"I…er…need a place where I can…well…stash a little spending money. Alice is a bit tight, and seems to sniff out anything I hide. I was wondering if I might…like…use one of the birdhouses you have here on the side of the shop? I'd just plug the hole and use the clean out door."

Birdhouse felt the light bulb brighten to 100 watts in his head. Always keen to make a buck, he instantly saw the possibilities.

"Well, I reckon that would be ok. But I'd have to have a little something to keep it here, as opposed to taking the birdhouse to the fair or selling it on Facebook. Say, a buck a month, two year minimum?"

Tim scratched his head and nodded, holding out his hand to seal the deal.

"Not a word to Alice?"

"A word about what?"

And so it started. Usually after dark or in the gray of early morning, he would see Tim slip over, open the door on his "bank" and make a deposit or withdrawal. The first of the month, Tim pushed a dollar into the special "Manager's" birdhouse with the swivel cover on the hole and the lock on the cleanout. Birdhouse quietly spread the word and before long had multiple "renters." A couple ladies also joined the ranks and even Tim's wife, Alice, had her quiet stash.

That took care of his coffee money. He wondered if the birds were offended with so many birdhouse holes stopped up. The plugs were camouflaged with black and birds would sort of sit there and poke, wondering why they couldn't get in.

Jarring himself back to the present, Birdhouse headed to the kitchen. Patty was already standing there, looking towards town.

"What's happened?" she said, worry lines accenting her eyes.

"Don't know."

12

Cuthbert threw the Cop Shop door open, springing the hinges, and stomped in, rubber boots dropping clumps of still-wet manure mixed with mud and straw across the floor. He looked almost apoplectic. Terry grimaced, despite the look on the old farmer's face. After all, he'd spent a good portion of yesterday afternoon scrubbing the floor. Usually he spent down time reading books on law enforcement, but his shoes were sticking to the filthy floor. Wally had spilled one too many sodas and was never good at cleaning up. Terry bent his back - and knees - to the task. Looking through cabinets, the only thing he'd found was an ancient can of Bar Keepers Friend powder and he set to work with a vengeance.

Now Terry watched mud mixed with hog leavings scatter in all directions.

"Cuthbert! My floor!"

"Blast your floor, long-hair! I got a problem! I'm being over-run by criminals!"

Stomping for emphasis on the last word, chunks popped around, forming a sort of silhouette around the rubber boots. The right boot had a chunk of the toe missing with a once-white-now-green sock sticking out. Terry mused that the boots were obviously just a symbol since they really were ineffective, except for scattering refuse all over his floor.

"What's wrong, Cuthbert?"

The man looked around.

"I gotta sit."

Oh, no, Terry thought. He wants to spread the mess around more. But he was caught. After all, he was a public servant.

Thinking quickly, he reached over and drew a folding metal chair over.

"Here. Now just calm yourself, sit down and take a few deep breaths."

Cuthbert whipped off his hat and looked at the chair. Part of his hair fell over the other side, while some stood up, like some sort of punk Mohawk. Usually stifling a grin at this hairdo, Terry had no inclination to see it humorously today.

"I don't have time to sit! And you ain't got the time to sit, neither. Bout time you got off your lazy hindquarters and did something other than watch TV!" He gestured to the TV in the corner tuned mutely to the Weather Channel.

"Dagnabbit, Cuthbert! How am I supposed to help if you won't tell me what's wrong?"

"Maryjewanna."

"Mary who?"

"Not Mary who! Mary JEWANNA!"

"What?"

Cuthbert stomped, scattering more chunks. His face reddened.

"It's what you seemed to smoke too much of when you was younger – and maybe still, judging by your looks and intelligence, or lack thereof!"

"Marijuana?"

"That's what I been trying to say, if you'd just listen." He flopped onto the metal chair with resignation and stomped his boots from a seated position, causing Terry to lose all hope for his floor.

"What about marijuana?"

"It's in my back field. One of my hogs got loose last night and I trailed it this morning to that woods at the east corner of my place and was shooshing it to get it back to the barn lot when I looked over and saw rows of something I didn't plant. They were all the same and they was footprints up and down."

"You were going to shoosh that hog all that way? Best to bring a trailer."

"My hitch rotted off last week. Gotta find a way to weld it to the frame." Turning red as a beet, he spluttered, "There you go, getting off track! Sorta natural to someone who probably went to that Woodstock thing and smoked the stuff and got all immoral, dancing naked and such. You probably got kids you don't know about. I seen the pictures – all sorts of wallowing in mud and such."

"Woodstock was before my time."

Cuthbert tried and failed to comb his wing over his head, finally patting it down.

"Why are we at Woodstock? I got maryjewanna in my field!"

"You were the one who brought up Woodstock."

"Well, hang it! You keep draggin' me off on a side-path!"

"Take a deep breath, Cuthbert, and tell me about this marijuana."

"I'm tryin' to!" He sat red faced with hair swaying between half-up and half-down and a piece of farm straw and muck clinging to his cheek.

"Cuthbert, how would you even know what marijuana looks like?"

"I seen it in a magazine, and this looks bezactly like the picture."

"How'd it get there?"

"Somebody planted it, dummy! I don't know! That's why I come to you! Blast it!" He stomped his feet for emphasis. More mess.

"Calm down, Cuthbert."

"Well, what are you gonna do about what's growing out there?"

"I'll drive out there in a few minutes and look it over. See what I can figure out."

"Likely not much. Should call the sheriff up north. Probably need to call in the feds. This is big time crime. Beyond your skills."

Terry turned red, but contained himself.

"I'll go take a look."

"I reckon I best get to the coffee shop and leave you to pretend to do your duty. Our tax dollars at work!" Getting up, Cuthbert started to trip and scattered whatever loose chunks were left on his boots clear over to the desk. He pushed through the door roughly and in a moment Terry heard the truck door open and slam again and the bungees wangle.

Dang! Terry reached for the broom.

"One thing for sure," Terry muttered to himself. "Schmeisser's will be crowded this morning."

13

Schmeisser's Donuts and Bratwurst was, indeed, very busy.

Greg wished there were more days like this.

He whistled as he cooked.

It was during the war that German refugee Heinrich Schmeisser came at the behest of the American Friends Service Committee and was embraced by the local Quakers. They called him Heiny at first but people blushed and it was switched to Henny.

Many locals at that time talked of "that Nazi" and refused to associate with Henny. Suspicion ran deep and several cleaned their shotguns and locked their doors at night for the first time. Setting up a small business making and selling bratwurst from a cart, Henny barely made ends meet until a sly and sympathetic local Quaker who ran a now-defunct corner diner served Henny's bratwurst one day as an all-you-can-eat special. He called them sausages to overcome the stigma. Well, all-you-can-eat trumped suspicion that day and eyebrows – and appetites – soared and Henny began to get orders. Taking a gamble, he opened a corner market for his wares and took a suggestion from the kind Quaker and offered free coffee from 6-9 a.m. Once again, locals came grinning for free coffee and found not only an excellent brew, but slowly began to purchase bratwurst, still calling them sausages until they became a staple. His bratwurst continued to gain popularity and Henny slowly became accepted and respected. This allowed him to bring his wife from Pittsburgh to join him, and soon Helga grew rotund and gave birth to Greg.

Doors no longer were locked at night.

Henny and Helga were gone now, resting up in Cornerview Cemetery under a Beech tree planted by the town. Greg and his wife, Janet, maintained a good business and were integral to the town, with Greg attending the evening Optimist Club and Janet helping with club activities.

Schmeisser's was now a local institution and one of only two foundational eating places in town, the other being the Burger Barn, which served burgers and tacos and pizza. Greg served hot dogs, bratwurst, a mean chef salad and miscellaneous other items. Aside from the bratwurst, customers raved over the hot German potato salad and the signature Thursday special, chicken pot pie, which was made, of course, with a hearty dose of bratwurst grease for flavor. Greg knew his trade and did not short on the helpings. Janet was known for her own expertise in making pies and serving generous portions of the same. The morning donuts came from Dave's Donuts up in Beedersville. Most customers finished their meal by sitting back, groaning and belching with satisfaction.

Once, a few years back, during the middle of Thursday dinner as patrons spooned pot pie into their smiling faces, somebody passing through on the interstate wearing spandex, running shoes and a t-shirt that said, "Love your cow, eat vegan," ordered a dinner salad with balsamic vinegar dressing and made a loud comment about obesity in the Midwest. Forks stopped in mid air and the visitor was stared down until he paid his bill and left, eyes following him all the way through the door.

You don't mess with Winston Corner.

14

"Say 'no' to crack."

"Shut up, Jake."

Hitching his pajama pants up in the back, Bub rubbed his eyes and walked sleepily into the convenience store repeatedly hiking his waistband. The elastic was all stretched out and he desperately needed new pajamas.

Normally they would sleep till noon, but this was the first Saturday of the month and the crowds would be heaviest at Goodwill right at opening. It was the best time to switch out clothes, as the harried clerks were bleary-eyed and overwhelmed. So, despite their nocturnal natures, both men arose early and planned to head to McDonald's for breakfast off the dollar menu with an additional 32 oz. Mountain Dew.

Bub had to get his candy bars first.

Jake sat in the truck as Bub went inside. They'd both been paid the day before, so Bub wanted to stock up on his beloved O'Henry bars. Jake didn't understand the pull Bub had to them, but it was too early in the morning to argue. He was amazed at how many people walked in at this time of morning and came out carrying 64 oz. cups of soft drink. Jake also suspected several of those exiting already had stood at the fountain machine and gulped 12 oz. before refilling and putting a lid on. In a two-minute timespan he counted ten 64-ouncers leaving the store, with the buyer usually fumbling to hold some sort of Hostess pastry and a pack or two of cigarettes.

He wondered how many actually paid for the pastry. He preferred to get his for free at the truck stop. The displays there were situated so he could merely grab one off the rack by the door and walk out. Once again, nobody was going to run after you, as they were already short staffed and the cash registers were at the far end from the door. In fact, he had a sudden hankering for a cinnamon bun. Maybe after Goodwill...

Bub slammed the store door open, hitting a young boy in the head who stumbled, spilled his drink and grabbed at his head. Bub didn't even notice, clutching the sack like a newborn baby, eager for his first O'Henry of the day. Saying nothing, but smiling, he got in.

Jake looked over, disgusted, and shifted into gear.

"You spend too much on candy bars."

"You drink too much Mountain Dew."

"Do not."

"Do too."

15

Winston Corner held to simple patterns and was very content with those patterns. Whenever a pattern was disturbed, normally calm people shifted nervously, stared out windows, paced and ate chocolate – or went to Schmeisser's where news broke first.

Today was one of those days and all over Winston Corner people stopped whatever they were doing, ears turned toward they knew not what and waited for something to come of this. A few quickly dressed and walked briskly to Schmeisser's.

Myra Spencer, long time official town historian and librarian, already was awake and getting ready to head to Schmeisser's. She would not be the first to arrive, but she would look proper when she did.

Whenever a question of local history came up, everybody went to Myra. She knew all the history and was quick to fill in gaps with interesting details. Those listening to her historical treatises wondered where she got all of the details and whispered now and then that what Myra didn't know for sure, she made up.

Myra self-published a book on the town several years back and optimistically ordered a hundred copies, seeing it as reasonable that every household and business would want a copy on hand. Several were piled in the town building that served as utilities office, maintenance office and chamber of commerce. In actuality, Myra sold twenty-five books, which equaled the number of those who were totally intimidated by her minus those who successfully hid behind closed doors when she came up the walk to sell copies.

Winston Corner was a town with a rich heritage.

16

Like most small towns in the Midwest, Winston Corner was birthed at a crossroad where farmers stopped their wagons to talk and then began to do a bit of trading. Questionable but accepted documentation claimed 1848 as the beginning. It was the first of generations of farmers markets and became the habit of Saturday mornings.

Myra claimed the first business was a door set on empty barrels where an opportunistic farmer's wife named Isabel Winston decided to serve lunch. One farmer gave her a quarter and it soon became expected to leave money for the lunch she prepared.

The foundation of a community began. Town names being freely bestowed in those days, and Isabel being for some reason attuned to posterity and also rather stout and intimidating, the name Winston Corner stuck.

According to Myra's uncontested research, another farmer, handy with tools and woodworking, set up a weekend shop across from Isabel, who was now in a tent due to not wanting rain to interfere with profit. Just a week later, a tinker with a wagon pulled up, saw the gathering, and made a handsome sum. Finding the settled life preferable to travel, he squatted on some nearby farmland belonging to Isabel's husband, later purchasing the ground under threat from Isabel. He erected a small structure, lining it with items of household use, and left his son in charge as he traveled to bring in supplies.

The tinker had a dalliance of sorts with Isabel, or so her husband thought. His threats resulted in the nighttime departure of the newcomer. Isabel walked across the road the next day, scanned the still-filled shelves of the building and instantly asserted her claim. She was now the owner of two businesses. Hiring a local farm wife to run the eatery, Isabel took to measuring any passerby for potential profit.

A blacksmith traveling with dreamy eyes to the storied Great Plains stopped one day and ate at Isabel's. Tasting the first real food he'd had in weeks, he succumbed to the persuasion of Isabel and planted himself on the fourth corner. With a loan from Isabel, he erected a smithy and rapidly became busy. That made Isabel the owner of the first mortgage of Winston Corner. It also launched her newest venture as the self-authorized banker in the area. She built a tiny office next to the eatery and sent back East for a safe. Truth be told, however, she preferred to tuck the money in her blouse, rationalizing any thief would have a more difficult time carrying her off than a defenseless safe. Besides, by that time she weighed a trifle more than the safe.

17

Isabel's husband, being smaller than her and rather meek, took to fixing his own simple meals back at the farmhouse. He kept his grumbling to himself for obvious reasons. One day, disgusted at another day of porridge and side meat, he saddled his plow horse and rode to Winston Corner. Sitting at the counter, he ordered eggs and bread and coffee. Feeling he had some sort of proprietary rights to the meal, he started to walk out without paying. Isabel happened to be in the back that morning making her supply list. Seeing her husband leaving without putting coins on the counter, she yelled at him. Shocked and not prone to argue with her, he grudgingly reached into his pocket and placed money on the counter. Her glare created another rule: three times a week he came to town and always paid for his meal.

Isabel built a modest home behind the store, leaving her husband alone on the farm. The carpenter who helped her had an entrepreneurial spirit and brought in a mill, buying up – on credit from Isabel – area woodlands and providing lumber to area farms and new businesses.

Over time, Isabel grew old and gray, and took to sitting frequently on the porch of the store as a sort of figurehead for the town. She still held sway behind the scenes, giving approval or disapproval of any new venture in the area. Isabel allowed no bawdy houses, though a few women were allowed as servers in a small saloon. Most left when Isabel discovered they were making extra income through side work. Except for her rumored dalliances, Isabel was determined to keep morality firm.

Like many small towns in that day, a strong Quaker influence entered the fray through a millinery and haberdashery, bringing with it astute business sense and strong work ethic. Isabel approved, as she was favorable to the moral strength of the newcomers. She also was quite agreeable to their allowing of leadership roles to women. The only problem was the Quakers were frugal and did not borrow. So, sensing another opportunity and tending more to sitting now, Isabel sold the bank to a couple of Quaker men and sat even more.

Isabel had no heirs, likely due in part to her living in town while her husband remained on the farm, so when she died the several businesses fell to different hands. The only person enriched by Isabel was the undertaker, who just happened to be the first to find her dead in her front room and it was speculated for years as to the amount of money he found on her person. He claimed she was penniless, but most nodded knowingly. Especially when he bought a brand new buggy and a fine horse and moved back East with a smile and a wave.

More people settled over the ensuing years and businesses prospered. Buying groceries, residents paid the store, which paid the workers, which paid the diner, which paid for wood for heat and so on and so forth and all settled into a comfortable coexistence where money sort of circulated and kept everybody afloat.

The town looked after its own, watching for interlopers and forsaking profit to keep big chain stores out. They knew their lifeblood required supporting the locals and not paying their money to out of town companies. It didn't take rocket science to know the big stores used the guise of jobs and variety and whatever else they touted to drive small business and local economy downhill. This made all dependent on the bigger companies for low wage jobs and goods while distant entities reaped the profits and used Winston Corner's hard-earned dollars to build bigger mansions. The younger set was prone to drive for cheaper groceries and other items, not factoring in the cost of gas and the effects on others. They just weren't insightful enough to see into the future. There were many who chose to live in Winston Corner while commuting to outlying places to work.

Winston Corner stayed much the same, with life steady and generally pleasurable. The local Optimist Club met every Thursday evening in the backroom of Schmeisser's. There were also two churches still standing – Quaker and Methodist.

Ten miles north was Beedersville, the county seat. It was where people went to shop and see their doctors. Buckner Community Hospital was at the north edge of Beedersville. Along the state highway cutting through Beedersville was a line of various restaurants and other businesses. To the west of Beedersville, about twenty miles, was Galetown. It was a decent size town, but the locals there went north for shopping, with a few heading to Beedersville. With clear geographical separation, each town, as others, retained its distinction and particular flavor.

18

Terry stared.

Marijuana. Sure enough.

Ten rows, each about twenty feet long, right at the edge of Cuthbert's back cornfield, abutting a woods. The plants were well taken care of and growing fast. Boot tracks came in from the dirt road about a quarter mile away. Whoever was doing this was making an attempt to hide the trail by taking four or five different routes in.

It had been a long time since he'd seen pot plants growing. Times were so different now. There was all this legislation going on and pot was being legalized in different states and derivative products like cannabidiol, commonly called CBD, were available. Did he really want to spend his time dealing with this? By the time it went to court the law might be changed. He didn't agree with it, but it was a reality. And a trespassing charge wouldn't result in much.

Glancing to the ground, Terry stooped and picked up what appeared to be a candy wrapper. Looking up, he happened to catch a shine in the nearby woods. Probably a hundred yards away, it was a small woods consisting of mostly maple and shagbark hickory and choked underneath by wild honeysuckle. It was just one of those small remnants of what the farmland used to look like before it was cleared for cultivation. Back then, firewood was basically a crop and landowners kept woodlots to heat their homes and cook their food. Over the years, many switched to propane or gas, but the woods remained.

Walking to the woods, Terry contemplated the recent trend to turn fencerows into cropland. Looking across the landscape, he remembered just three years ago there were more fencerows filled with wildlife. Then, machinery came in and toppled the trees, destroying a complete ecosystem. Even more bothersome to him was that it was done in the winter, when the small animals were hibernating. He wondered how many were killed. It seemed there was a total focus on profits over the long term care of the land. It used to be that farmers cherished and cared for the land, but that was changing. Some no longer looked to future generations. Still, there were farmers around who left their woodlots, some giving hunting rights and others using them only for the annual pursuit of mushrooms. Terry knew one farmer who just liked to walk the woods, sit on a fallen tree and experience the peace.

This little woods of Cuthbert's could serve no purpose in bringing equipment out to cultivate. Profit would be negligible if any. But to wildlife it was a sanctuary.

Entering the edge of the wood, Terry saw no reflection, but there was a well-worn path. Something made his hair stand up. This was really remote, and here he was investigating. Maybe he should call the sheriff. But he could see dew on the grass, so it hadn't been traveled since at least the middle of the night.

Loosening his Glock, he momentarily wondered what he would do if he came across someone – or something. He'd known how to use a gun since he was a kid, but never had used it in the line of duty. Even in the military police he'd never had occasion to pull it.

Suddenly he stopped.

19

Gavin and Jean had no kids. It just never happened and they never explored why. It just was what it was and they were happy. They had nieces and nephews and focused on them. They delighted in adding to needy young people's college accounts and being there to help with laptop computers and textbooks.

They weren't rich, but they were comfortable.

Jean's siblings could be noted by several pushpins on a map. She was on the phone a lot with them and there were occasional visits, but none was closer than a 10-hour drive. Contact was occasional and enjoyable, but the busyness of everybody's careers had prevented a lot of visits. Gavin, on the other hand, was like the young man a hundred years ago who set off on the wagon train. He left his family behind and never looked back. Never close, his parents were only superficial in their connection with the four kids. His dad had worked hard to support them, but seemed to consider that his main contribution. His mother was very self-centered, controlling and friendless, and it carried over to her relationship with her kids. Gavin struggled himself with friendships, tending to be secretive. Jean had learned over the years to draw him out, but even with her there was a barrier and she accepted it as it was. It was part of his childhood and part of his career and she realized it was a waste of time to try to change her husband into the image she desired. So she learned to rejoice in his good qualities and not worry about the ways she wanted him to be.

His career required several moves and Jean developed friends around the country and retained those friends when they moved. But when retirement loomed, it just seemed that Winston Corner had a bit more stability in her heart than any other place. Gavin had no objections. His goal was to be away from any place where he'd been in action.

Still, investigation was in his blood.

And he was good at it.

He had to restrain his curiosity now.

20

In front of Terry was an electric pump, with a deep-cell marine battery alongside. Close by was a rough coil of old hose. From the back of the pump was another hose, trailing off the back towards the creek. So there was the water supply. The reflection he'd seen must have been the sun catching the switch plate at just the right angle. Probably wouldn't happen again in a hundred years, standing in just the right spot at the right time and facing the right direction.

Back at the Cop Shop, he pondered the situation. His right hand held the candy bar wrapper found in the field. O'Henry. Not a common candy bar. He didn't think they were sold anywhere in town.

The problem was the field and woods were not really in his jurisdiction, being that far out of town. The best thing to do would be to turn it over to the sheriff up at Beedersville. But they were understaffed and working with too few deputies to cover a county this size. Besides, he was chomping at the bit to do something more important than issuing parking tickets and warnings for California stops. He didn't know why they were called California stops, this rolling through stop signs at 5 mph. But that's all they did around here, and if he ticketed for that, he'd be beheaded like King Charles by Cromwell's forces. So most the time he just let it go. All he'd gotten in the past two weeks were two loose dogs and a complaint of a dump truck kicking a stone through Emaline Poovy's windshield. Emaline was known to drive right on people's bumpers and he didn't doubt the truck driver might've goosed it to try and throw something at her. Max Mason threw a milkshake out once,

38

plastering Emaline's hood and eliciting a complaint. But she didn't hug his bumper anymore.

It was great being right in town. Though not making as much as he might in a larger town or over in Indy, a cruiser to drive home was a real perk. He lived simply and saved his money for his annual trip to Idaho. Last time he heard of Wally having a night call was a long time ago. Dispatch was no longer local, having been moved to a countywide system based in Beedersville.

So Terry really wanted to take this new crime on. Tapping his fingers on the desk, he looked at the evidence. There was a small but well-kept stand of marijuana and a candy bar wrapper. And footsteps to the road. He shook his head.

Not a lot to go on.

Cuthbert was probably babbling his mouth off all over town, letting everybody know the patch was found. If whoever it was came from around here, they might not be back. But they had to have been here sometime to find the right spot, and they had to live close enough to make trips over, though how often was unknown. How often did a pot patch have to be trimmed and watered? And for how long so that it would flourish?

He reached for the keyboard and clicked on the search bar.

Not likely to be anyone from Winston Corner. Beedersville, possibly.

21

Up at the grocery in Beedersville that evening, Kim turned her cart around the corner and scanned down the vegetable aisle to locate cauliflower. Her eyes landed on Terry Jones, who appeared to be examining the kale at the far end. Off duty, his t-shirt accented his muscular build.

Wow! If a woman was attracted to a physique, his was definitely eye grabbing. Kim forced her eyes to look at the vegetables.

Glancing up a minute later, she noted he was still a distance away and headed towards checkout. Strangely disappointed, she stared while reaching upward for a produce bag. Her fingers flexed at the air almost a foot from the roll of bags.

"Young lady?"

Kim looked to see an elderly woman smiling.

"Yes?"

The woman grinned, glancing toward checkout where Terry was turning a corner.

"The bags are a bit further to the left."

Kim grinned.

"I guess I was a bit distracted."

"Good reason to be. If I was forty years younger…"

22

Slinking to the barbershop Sunday afternoon, Max was brooding. A black curtain of barely restrained despondency hung across his thoughts. It took extra effort to turn the key and enter the shop. He felt like he carried the weight of the world on his shoulders.

Would business go downhill? He already felt the world was following Merle Haggard's lyrics and "Rolling downhill like a snowball headed for hell." And now this.

But he had to do it.

Agonizing for weeks, Max sat on the porch one night with his head in his hands, almost in despair. Glancing to the glass-topped wicker table, he saw his Bible.

Flopping it open, his eyes landed on 1 Timothy 5:18 "Do not muzzle an ox while it is treading out the grain" and "The worker deserves his wages."

Taking that as affirmation from above, the next day he marched into the printer in Beedersville and ordered the new price board. Still riddled with self-doubt, he wasn't sure if this would impact his business. He'd already lost a lot of the younger crowd. Some were shaving their heads now and others were buying clippers and giving themselves buzzes.

Still, he hadn't raised prices for years. His costs kept rising and his profit margin kept shrinking. Butch Wax was up to eight-fifty now if he ordered through Amazon. He could order it cheaper through a barber supply, but postage ate it up and it wound up being the same.

Shaky hands took the old price board down and hung the new one.

Well, at least he knew what the topic of conversation would be for the next two weeks.

Haircuts, twelve dollars.

23

Gavin finally heard all the news Monday morning during his habitual visit to Schmeisser's.

Since moving here sixteen months ago, he tried his best to build new friendships, but still felt like an outsider. Jean used to come to Winston Corner to see her grandparents, and a few of the old fellas remembered her, but he was never just "Gavin." It was always something like "Jean's Gavin." Or he was greeted with the token nod accompanied by "Mr. Crockett."

When he worked for the Feds he went by "Crockett" or by his first name. When the locals added the preface of "Mr." it felt very impersonal. He talked to Jean about it, and she shrugged it off and merely said to give it time. Well, for Pete's sake, it'd been sixteen months! He knew he was sort of standoffish, but that was the federal agent in him. He'd learned to play things close to the vest. Saved a lot of struggle with some of the things he'd seen. It was self-preservation to stuff it down inside. So maybe it was partly his fault, but he was what he was.

Initially, Gavin found the slow pace tedious, compared to Philadelphia. Retirement was slowdown enough, much less moving to a small Midwest town. At first he took the Jeep out a lot and just coursed the grid of country roads, looking for who knows what but somehow feeling a sense of purpose in looking for something, even though he had no idea what it might be. After a fashion he mellowed and spent a lot of time reading. But he needed more. He was only fifty-four years old. He'd heard about people retiring and having little reason to get up in the morning. Reading the papers and special Fed email newsletters appeased him for a few moments each day, but still left an empty spot.

The locals rolled their eyes as he walked in and glanced around, always sitting where he could see the door. If no seats facing the door were available, he would sit nervously somewhere else, glancing up all the time until a seat vacated and he would move and visibly relax. It was a habit of his career. Over time, the locals grudgingly left a seat open in the back, facing the door. It was better to let "Mr. Crockett" sit where he wanted than to have all of them suffer his interminable craning of his neck to see the door. It wasn't so much his turning, but their instinctive turning also to see what he might be looking at, that caused them to vacate a seat. Bart Pederson had fused vertebrae in his neck and each time Gavin craned, Bart would have to laboriously twist and squirm to turn his whole body to see whatever the devil it was Mr. Crockett was seeing. Bart finally prevailed on the others to leave a seat open, "for Mr. Crockett to see the blasted door." Interestingly enough, this craning to see the door was not something Gavin started until he came to Winston Corner. Perhaps it was the hope that he might see something requiring his attention.

24

Walking in the door of Schmeisser's on Monday, Gavin returned the cursory nods and one irritating "Mr. Crockett" from the Liar's Table before settling into his usual booth with the morning paper. It wasn't much of a paper, but it gave him a bit of mental exercise with the Sudoku and crossword. It was the simple pleasures that gave joy to the morning. One morning he pulled the concerned look and Bart twisted to see and then twisted back and stared at Gavin, who just sat nursing his coffee and working the crossword. Bart whispered under his breath.

"Blast it, Mr. Crockett!"

It was sort of a game, and Gavin always won, because Bart couldn't resist looking.

Kim brought his coffee without instruction. He caught the looks and headshakes from the others when she plopped down the creamer. Sweetener he brought himself, with three or four packets tucked in his shirt pocket. Schmeisser's carried only an off-brand sweetener with the odd name of Genuine Joe. The use of cream and sweetener by any human male elicited questions of manhood by the regulars.

"Thanks, Kim."

"You're welcome, Mr. Crockett." He looked at her as she walked away. You'd think by now she could call him by his first name. A couple of the early crowd gave him disgusted glances. He knew what was coming.

Pratt, usually the first one here, started the routine.

"Ain't right to drink a milkshake for breakfast, Dinky."

"I know, Pratt, but they's some people can't handle coffee the

45

way God made it. They put poison in it."

"Hey, Mr. Crockett!" Pratt held his cup up. "Here's a man's drink. Black and strong."

They all hooted. Gavin smiled and nodded and capped off the moment with a concerned glance out the door. Bart twisted and muttered and glanced at Gavin with a disgusted look.

Odd place, this business of Schmeisser's. Donuts and Brat-wurst. Who'd ever think of that combination? No sauerkraut was served. It was notorious for infusing its taste and smell on the other foods. Still, there was a steady crowd. The Liar's Table showed up at 5:30 every morning. Greg didn't officially open till 6 o'clock, but always put a pot on when he got there at 5 o'clock. It was understood it was ok to come early if you helped yourself to your own cup and left him alone till the clock pointed straight up. Don't even say a polite "good morning." He'd look down his nose at you and kill you with a stare. This was his time to wrap his mind about the day, pull brat-wurst from the freezer and get everything ready for breakfast and some of the basics for lunch. That and hum along to his Internet radio on the Bluetooth speaker his daughter gave him a couple years back for Christmas. At exactly 6 o'clock he came to the serving counter and lightly tapped the bell to signify he was officially open. Kim arrived on the dot at 6:05, in time to deliver the first orders. She wasn't needed to take orders first thing.

Once the bell rang, there was a chorus of voices. Greg knew all the voices and didn't even have to look up.

"Usual, boss man!"

"Same here, Greg."

"Just a donut for me – the kind with the nuts."

"I'll have the bratwurst omelet. Wheat toast today. Marjorie says my butt's getting too big!"

"The bratwurst ain't helping your butt none."

"That's why I ordered the wheat toast. Compensating."

"From the looks of things, you need to do a lot of compensating! 'Bout to need two chairs to hold it all."

"Who're you to talk, blubber gut?"

"Hey! I've lost five pounds."

"Probably all from your brain. Atrophy of the head."

Hoots all around.

Renner looked to the slip of sky to be seen across the street. "Looks like rain."

Pratt looked to his cup.

"Yup, but it smells like coffee."

"Weak this morning. Greg's trying to cut corners. Might as well serve tea."

"Ain't never been able to handle tea. Looks and tastes like puddle water. Can't see no reason to drink it. Now coffee, black and strong, that's a man's drink." Renner glanced to Gavin.

Gavin glanced to the kitchen. It was a wonder the little Bluetooth speaker even worked anymore. Hanging by a length of swing set chain from the wall behind Greg, it was beat up from falling. Constant cleaning of the grill had worn the color off.

Routine dictated that Greg look Gavin's way. Gavin nodded and gave a subtle thumb up to Greg's raised eyebrows. It was their way of communicating that Gavin wanted his usual: three eggs over medium, bratwurst links and wheat toast. It was an unspoken understanding that there was no bacon served at Schmeisser's. Anyone needing bacon had to go to Beedersville or snag an imitation bacon, egg and cheese biscuit at the Quick Stop. Here there was only bratwurst in regular bun size or in a smaller form they called links.

Greg was the one person here who really seemed to extend friendship to Gavin. Despite his morning surliness, he really was a kind soul. He'd driven by the Sunday Gavin and Jean moved in and actually stopped to help wrestle the furniture from the U-Haul to the house.

Sipping his coffee, Gavin listened to conversation from the Liar's Table with a practiced method of seeming not to be even aware. He called it his Fed Face. If people caught you looking at them, it frequently stopped the conversation. When he'd been on stakeouts in the past, he sometimes sat right next to those he was observing, pretending to be busy, often with a writing pad, doodling and actually writing a combination of nonsense and grocery list, looking up occasionally as if for inspiration. Today, he just sat and stared at his cup. And listened.

What an interesting group of people.

25

The Liar's Table.

It was the same all across America and in countries around the world. They existed in big cities and in small towns. Some gathered in diners, some in coffee shops, some at truck stops and some on benches in a town square. Composed of retirees and others with flexible schedules, the groups passed local gossip and information and solved all the world's problems. The problem was, nobody beyond the circle of coffee cups heard or heeded their advice.

The Liar's Table served a community purpose. Almost quicker than cell phones or texting, and certainly more reliable, this network ensured any news or gossip was transmitted to a broad cross section of the area. Full names of the network in Winston Corner were not used, and they went by Renner, Dinky, Dobbs, Pratt and Bart, with a few others not quite as regular. Pratt was a retired plumber, Renner'd had a fuel oil business, and the others had spent careers in the factory.

"Ol' Cuthbert was hotter than a pistol."

"Said he found a whole field of that there funny weed growin' in his back-forty."

"I heard it was just a small patch."

"Nope. Got it from Bill it was almost fifty acres. Biggest field ever found in the state. All laid out in rows nice as can be."

"Bill who?"

"Fella works at the parts counter up at the Dodge dealer."

"Well, he once told Williamson at the factory that he needed a new alternator and fuel injector and such and all it needed was a sensor. I wouldn't take what he said as gospel."

"What's this got to do with gospel? We're talking about a doggone cargo ship full of the stuff."

"I hear tell they burn those fields in some states. When they come in with the agents, people hurry and test the wind so they can get their beer and pizza and go downwind. Doesn't take long and they're hopping around and acting like crazed idiots. It's legalized pot smoking and cheap!"

Renner shook his head and spoke up.

"Hey, Dinky! What's the morning joke?"

Dinky Wyant spent his days perusing magazines and anywhere he could find a joke. A few years ago he'd told a couple on back-to-back days and it sort of became a ritual. Some were repeated several times, so he felt an obligation to find new material.

"One day a man went to an auction. While there, he bid on an exotic parrot. He really wanted this bird, so he got caught up in the bidding. He kept on bidding, but kept getting outbid, so he bid higher and higher and higher. Finally, after he bid way more than he intended, he won the bid. The price was high but the exotic bird was finally his! As he was paying for the parrot, he said to the auctioneer, 'I sure hope this parrot can talk. I'd hate to have paid this much for it, only to find out that he can't talk!' 'Don't worry,' said the Auctioneer, 'He can talk. Who do you think kept bidding against you?'"

The group laughed.

"That was ok, Dinky, but not very high caliber on the laugh scale."

"Can't tell a winner every day. Sometimes it has to do with the quality of the listeners." He stared right at Renner.

"Yeah, right!"

"I hear Terry drove off after Cuthbert stormed from his office."

"I don't worry so much about those people that smoke that there Mary Jane. Long as they do it at home and don't drive through my yard, I'm ok."

"I dunno. I seen a feller once at my son's college and he was higher than a kite. Something wrong with going around with your eyes all red and grinning from ear to ear and being all silly-like."

"Judgment is impaired they say."

Dinky couldn't leave that alone.

"Truth be told they's a bunch of you all with impaired judgment sitting here every day. Why else would anybody be sitting here drinking this nasty coffee and eating over-priced bratwurst and sin-sized donuts?" His voice lowered and a furtive glance was cast to the kitchen.

"I heard that!"

Greg emerged from the kitchen with a dripping egg whisk. Shaking the whisk, the men watched egg splattering around as he mini-lectured and walked right to the table.

"If you all don't appreciate my coffee, then you can just go ahead and drive ten miles up the road and drink some of that stuff made from concentrate and filled with whatever they put in it to get it to stay liquid. I hear the stuff will stay good on a shelf for twenty-five years with all the preservatives in it. Give you cancer. Rats are dying in the labs when they give them that stuff. And the donuts they serve are shipped from some little place in China that makes little kids work for nothing. Takes a week to ship the things and they last on the shelves forever. You go ahead and eat that stuff if you want!"

The last swing of the whisk got most of them with egg. Greg muttered as he stomped to the kitchen.

"Must be a bad day." Renner looked around, spotting Gavin. Lowering his voice to a whisper, the others leaned in as he spoke. "Being a retired Fed, he probably knows all about weed and such."

Gavin heard everything, despite the man's whisper.

26

Indeed he did know about such things. Too much, in fact. The last ten years of his career had been with narcotics, and he knew a lot more than they would ever know. He'd also seen things they never wanted to see. But, changing laws were making people almost yawn when pot was brought up as a crime anymore. Gavin knew legalization was on a sort of roll. Even though he had softened to the issue, he knew it wasn't - and never would be - a harmless crop. Wherever there was a market for it, there would be crime. Even the development of CBD oil products would not stop the crime. The legalizing of pot hung upon the growing base of research showing the uses of the non-high part of the plant. Glaucoma sufferers had benefitted for years, but had at first to smoke it to get the CBD benefits. Other conditions also were eliciting results from CBD. Still, the majority of those wanting pot, Gavin felt, would never be those looking for some medicinal value, but those wanting the high, the mellow, the effect of smoking and the THC, or Tetrahydrocannabinol, component. When someone, lost to reality and inhibition, left the confines of their house, there was a problem. The oil came from the hemp part, and hemp producers bred the plants for more hemp and less leaves and buds, while THC producers and smokers bred for more leaves and buds and cared not for the hemp. Now the hemp would be touted to legalize the growth. Who was going to determine when a plant was grown for which end of the market? CBD oil would become a major pharmaceutical over time, but the other parts of the plant would always be a byproduct and draw crime. There was no way the companies would throw away the prime buds which elicited the best product for smoking, as well as the less potent leaves. So the watch list for the feds would expand from the CBD production facilities and on down the chain to the "waste" disposal process. The whole process would elicit crime, or temptation to crime, from start to finish. Not to mention a whole new hierarchy of government regulations and employees.

And it wasn't just pot.

Gavin knew some of the main syndicates laced their pot and even derivative products with other drugs to "enhance" the effects. Crystal meth was a big one, and it resulted in some unpredictable effects. What that really meant was an increased death rate. Others would mix with Fentanyl. The mixing of many suppliers was neither scientific nor sanitary. All they cared about was money and, though they didn't deliberately intend to kill their customers, they didn't always make sure the laced drugs were spread evenly. On top of that, further down the supply chain others did their own lacing, even if aware that other drugs had been added already. The potential mortality rate increased as each link of the supply chain brought the product closer to the user. It was all about money. And it was Harrison Tyler's game. A deadly game.

He looked up as Kim filled his coffee.

"Thanks, Kim."

"Welcome, Mr. Crockett."

27

"I heard this morning that Wally's gone off on a leave. Guess his mom is real bad over to Kansas. Took a nasty fall and broke her hip. Wally's the only child, so he's headed over. Terry's gonna be holding the fort and will be on call at night."

"Well, I just hope Terry can get to the bottom of this. But I look to him to try and cut some for himself. He looks the type."

"Aw, Terry's ok. Just a throwback to the 60's somehow – at least in his heart. He ain't that old. And you gotta admit he's got the muscle none of us never had."

"I used to be pretty rugged myself, back in the day."

"Yep, you did have good muscle – table muscle!"

Guffaws.

"Maybe Terry just wants to save money on haircuts. Lot to that, what with it costing twelve dollars for a haircut now."

"Twelve dollars!"

"Yep, Max put the new prices up yesterday. I was out walking and ran into him walking home. Said he hadn't raised prices for five years."

"Yeah, but jumping from nine dollars to twelve dollars? It just ain't right to pass by ten. That's gouging. He's gonna be rolling in it! Probably needs to renew his magazine subscriptions."

"Might be best to go to Emaline's. She's got a following now amongst the men."

"If you can put up with her continuous jabbering."

Emaline Poovy's beauty salon was on Cedar, across the back alley from Gibson's Hardware. Emaline thought much of herself and wasn't afraid to share how wonderful she was. She was proud of her new slogan painted across the window of her shop. It said, in big, bold letters, "Come to Poovy's for an Impoovment." Below was painted in small letters, "Ain't nothing we can't fix." She'd painted it herself and ran out of space and had to put the last four letters squeezed underneath like cornered ants.

"I ain't going to Emaline. She charges twenty dollars."

"Twenty bucks! Doggone! I ain't looking for style, just a quick haircut."

"Ok, let's look at this. Only takes ten minutes to do a haircut. At twenty per haircut, and a slow day with only four waiting, that's still eighty smackers an hour!"

"We're trapped! Get robbed or grow long hair. Wife would go ape if'n I let it touch my ears. I guess we got to go to Beedersville and join the lineup."

There was quiet for a few moments as the group absorbed reality. Then the topic shifted.

"Pot ain't frowned on like it used to be. Now they're using it for medicine. Says it helps with some pain things when nothing else will work. Like that glaucoma stuff."

"I got that. They test my eyes every month. Maybe I ought to grow my own medicine."

Laughter filled the room.

28

Walking home later, curiosity caused Gavin to take the long way and swing over to Cedar. Reaching the Quick Mart, he sat on the bench looking to the edge of town. By sitting on the extreme left end, he could see Cuthbert's woods in the distance. The conversation and information was questionable, but still the fact remained there was a field with illegal marijuana. If there was one there, how many others were around?

Shading his eyes from the morning sun, he looked to the tufted treetops at the south end of Cuthbert's land in the distance. According to the word at Schmeisser's, it was over by those woods where the pot was growing. Why there? The obvious reason was seclusion. But many times there was more to such things than the obvious.

What about water? In a dry spell the plants could shrivel and reduce profit. There was a stream cutting by the far edge of the woods. He remembered seeing it when driving over that way. So whoever was caring for the crop was taking care to have water available if it turned dry.

Experience told him there would be more patches around. Gavin scanned outwards from Cuthbert's woods. In places the view was obstructed by the alignment of trees and barns and such. Still, he had been out many times just exploring for the sake of doing something and he could fill in some of the gaps. As a federal agent, he'd been well trained by senior agents to note details and commit them to memory. Building a case required care for it to stand up in court. There had even been times when noting details likely saved his life. He found it natural to drive around and take notice of things others would never see.

Jean made him get out of the house. There were times she was worried about him and thought he needed another job. So he got out, drove around in his 2015 Jeep Rubicon, exploring for miles. The Midwest never ceased to amaze him with its grid of roads every quarter mile. There were times in his career where he'd been sent to places like Washington state, where one main road led to each of the four corners of the compass, with a topographical pattern of logging roads in the back country. Long hikes often preceded access for stakeouts.

Jamison's Creek. That was the creek running through the area and it curved not far from Cuthbert's woods. He could picture it as it wound further to the north and east, running by several patches of woods that happened to also run close to the remote edges of cultivated fields.

Something in his gut told him there was more here than what seemed obvious.

Gavin tended to shake his head when others looked at him and spoke of the statistics, or of decisions being "data driven." There was a place for stats and data with normal people, but criminals, whom Gavin considered to be abnormal, paid no attention to such things. He had been highly successful in his career by trusting his instincts of people and their habits and what might go on in their minds. He would piece together little bits of "data" but then set it aside and ask, "If I was in their shoes, what would I do?" Over the years he learned to trust his "gut feeling," which was really a combination of filtered data, human psychology and instinct.

Yes, indeed, there was more here than met the eye. He was sure of it.

29

A honey-do list was a tradition among retired men. Gavin realized his never ended. When he was working and building a case, a checklist was either in his mind or written in a file and he could gauge progress by the checkmarks and the thickening file. Since retirement, he kept a list on his little section of the kitchen counter.

Actually, it was Jean's list. Jean would add to it and he would check off items as they were completed. When the paper was full of checkmarks, he at first smiled with satisfaction, but over time he realized that a completed list meant absolutely nothing. The next morning he would find a new or re-written list and the process would start anew.

Truth be told, though, he sort of thrived on a task.

It was Thursday morning and Jean was in Beedersville to meet girlfriends. He was fixing the bathroom door hinges. With the screws always working out where the hinge was screwed into the jamb, Gavin speculated there must have been teenagers in the house before they bought it. Teens had a tendency to slam doors and he really couldn't figure out any other reason for this problem. After all these months of alternately tightening screws every two weeks, the project appeared on his list. Jean sometimes left things off the honey-do list, giving him the benefit of the doubt that he would take care of obvious issues, but this had gone on too long. This morning he came home from Schmeisser's and collected the tools for the task – longer screws and a couple toothpicks and his Craftsman cordless drill. The screws didn't match, but who cared?

Gavin collected odd screws and washers in old paint cans,

just like his father. Over the years he rarely needed to buy any. Jean sometimes rolled her eyes when he picked them up in parking lots and other places and put them in his pocket to deposit in the can later. It was common to have three or four screws and washers sitting on the corner of the counter until he took the few seconds needed to take them to the garage. An old sheet cake pan leaned against the leg of the workbench, in which he would pour out a few screws at a time and run through until he found what he needed. In recent years he'd taken to throwing out any with standard heads. There was no reason to fight with a standard screw when Phillips was so much easier. And decking screws were, to Gavin, a special gift from God.

Working through the hinge screws one at a time, he took them out and replaced them with longer ones. In a couple of the holes, the longer screw wasn't enough and he broke off a piece of toothpick, inserting it into the hole first to add bite for the screw.

There was a knock on the screen door as he tightened the last screw. The weather was mild for spring and he'd decided to air out the house. He put the Craftsman down and trotted to the door. Rounding the corner he smiled wide.

"Brian Phillips!"

"Hey, Gavin!"

Brian was a fellow agent and always brought a smile to his days in the office. The younger man was always cheerful and the negative and gory exposures of their profession seemed never to dampen Brian's outlook. Brian stood now in coat and tie and, Gavin knew, a Glock in a shoulder holster. Probably still carrying the Walther in an ankle holster.

But Brian lived in Philly! As Fed Agents they were exposed to a lot of traveling, and Gavin sensed something in this sudden and unexpected appearance.

"You are the absolute last person I expected to see at my door! Come on in, Brian!"

"Don't mind if I do."

Gavin looked at Brian with a question in his brow. Brian registered this but waited.

"Ok, Brian, I know you didn't just drop by to see an old friend. Transfer or here on a case?"

Brian grinned and shook his head in affirmation.

"Honestly, Gavin, I have been working on a case and wanted your input, and thought no better way than to just drop by and see how retirement is treating you."

"Well, a cup of coffee always lubes the tubes. Come on in and rest your weary backside." Gavin gestured to the living room as he went to get the coffee. Returning, he handed one cup to his friend with a smile.

"Still one cream, one Splenda?"

"You got it! Thanks, Gavin." Brian took a sip and looked at his friend. "You're looking good, though I think I detect a little thickening of the middle."

Gavin patted his stomach.

"I've put on a few pounds. I'm not pounding the pavement and eating salads." When he was actively working, Gavin usually ate small salads at lunch to keep trim. It also made it less strenuous to pass the annual physical. "Ok, Brian…spill it. We can catch up later. Tell me you've nailed Harrison Tyler."

Gavin Crockett could not forget losing that case. It was three years ago. He still felt dejected about it.

Harrison Tyler had been guilty. He knew that in his heart. The man was crooked as a corkscrew, with his tentacles going every which way. Gavin even suspected there were people in high places in his pocket. At the trial, it was looking hopeful until a star witness turned tables on him. Instead of being firm in his testimony, he vacillated and gave the defense the opening they needed. No conviction. Despite protection, somehow Tyler had gotten to the witness with a threat. Worst of it was, Harrison had openly and brazenly come up to Gavin in the lobby of the courtroom to shake his hand. Gavin refused and Harrison grinned, looked around and whispered viciously in his face. "Yes, I was guilty. You were right. But I have the best lawyer and the right people in my pocket. You'll never get handcuffs on me, Crockett."

Patting Gavin belittlingly on the shoulder, he walked off, still grinning.

Of all the cases he'd brought to court, it was the one Gavin carried in his heart. If he could have nailed Harrison Tyler, he would have had peace of mind. Gavin knew Tyler would move all his operations – overnight – to new locations. It would take a whole new investigation to start the gathering of evidence again. With retirement on the horizon, Gavin's new supervisor had nixed the pursuit, wanting Tyler to get more entrenched and confident and the trails to be more pointed. Gavin knew there was some logic to this, as Tyler would be extra vigilant so soon after the trial.

Brian looked at Gavin for a moment before speaking.

"I wish I was telling you that, but it is about Harrison Tyler."

Gavin tilted his head.

"A thorn in my flesh."

"Yeah, I know how you feel and how you tried to get him. It was the only case you were never able to tie up, wasn't it?"

"Yes, it was, and Harrison laughed in my face over it. Sort of a black spot in my career. I would be lying if I didn't tell you I sometimes lay awake running it through my mind and wonder what more I could have done." He reached behind his back to the leather handcuff holder. Brian noticed.

"Still keep those there? Can't let it go? Pete sakes, Gavin. You're retired. You had the highest conviction rate of anybody."

"I know, but it still irks me that Harrison got off without a charge. I keep these here to remind me that justice is not always served. When I hear Harrison Tyler is behind bars, I'll take them off. I know it's strange, Brian. It's just my thing."

"I know, and that's why I'm here. I want you to go over what you remember of your experiences with Harrison. He's elusive, and rarely goes from his ivory tower into the trenches. But we have indicators that he is venturing out, building his tentacles again. I want to nail him. I want him out of circulation – for good."

Gavin nodded.

"Brian? There's something you're not telling me."

His friend looked at him squarely. Gavin's eyes widened.

"Here? Brian, are you telling me he's here?"

"We're not sure exactly, Gavin, but some of the data coming in indicates an expansion into the Midwest."

Gavin stood and walked across the room, then turned to his long time friend.

"Tell me more, Brian."

Two hours later, Brian looked at his watch and smiled.

"I need to get back to Indy. Got a flight out at five."

"It's been great catching up, my friend. I wish Jean was here today. She'll be sorry she missed you."

"Well, give her my best. She actually might not like me dredging up past memories."

"On the contrary, I think she would welcome me feeling useful again."

Brian noted a momentary sadness cross Gavin's face. He nodded.

"I'll be in touch, Gavin. Thanks for the insights."

The two men shook hands warmly. Gavin clapped a hand to Brian's shoulder.

"Feel free. You've got my number. Or just holler and I can meet you somewhere."

Watching his friend drive down the street a minute later, Gavin stood at the door, thoughtful.

Harrison Tyler. To see him behind bars would be a blessing to the world. But it would really be more than that. It would be a belated feather in his cap.

30

Hubert had a reputation as perhaps the grumpiest person alive. The story was well known of his reaction to machinery breaking down last year at the mill in Beedersville, where he had worked all his adult years. He ran the duplicating machine. Apparently his foreman broke the news to him.

Hubert was irritated.

"It could be worse" the foreman suggested.

Hubert Griffin grunted and sulked. He didn't believe it for a moment.

After all, what could be worse than it taking a week to fix the machinery? He hated inactivity. Some of the others relished the time to sit and draw wages and play cards or pretend they were busy doing other things. Not Hubert. He lived to run the machinery. He thrived on a purpose.

Perpetually scowling, Hubert's nickname at the mill was Grumpy. When other workers wondered amongst themselves if he would ever be happy, the response was always the same.

"When pigs fly."

Anybody meeting Hubert and having just a few minutes of interaction would opine, "Boy, he's a grumpy sort." Jokes never got through to him. While the rest of the break room erupted with cackles, he would sit with his scowl and maybe offer a grunt of disapproval. And if something went wrong or caused a delay, he grunted and sulked.

Hubert thought it was the end of the world when the unexpected happened, like a breakdown on the line. The foreman, a good-natured man, would look at Hubert and shake his head and respond cheerfully.

"It could be worse."

Hubert would grunt and sulk and mumble.

Routine was his anchor. He counted on an eight-hour work-day, followed by a quiet dinner and reading the paper. Then he would fall asleep in his chair, later to arise and go to bed.

He disliked any disruption of routine.

Traveling was out of the question.

He was really stewed the day the union representative told them they needed to forego a raise in order to keep the contract with the yard. Though others were a bit upset, none were like Hubert, who grunted excessively, shaking his head in despair. The foreman looked at him.

"It could be worse. They could be shutting us down."

Hubert just grunted.

There came a day when he left work at the end of his shift and returned to his "castle," as he called it. His home was his peace and his mood sometimes lightened a single iota when he walked into the door.

Eula Mae, his wife of thirty years, always greeted him with a smile and a kiss. Sometimes she gave him a longer kiss and his shoulders might be seen to raise another eighth of an inch, but never more. She was buxom, strong and cheerful.

Eula Mae had somehow adapted to his ways and merely smiled at his shrugs and chattered cheerfully as he scowled and grunted.

It happened on a Wednesday.

And during the meatloaf.

Hubert dearly loved his wife's meatloaf. To him, it was the dearest thing to Heaven and caused his scowl lines to lighten perceptibly as he plowed his way through at least two large helpings, accompanied by mashed potatoes and green beans. A meat and potatoes man, his wife knew not to get fancy.

It was just as he scooped a large bite to his mouth that Eula Mae spoke.

"Aunt Mabel in New York City is doing poorly."

He grunted, chewed twice and swallowed. It was not uncommon for her to visit her aunt.

"I need to go visit. This weekend."

Another grunt and a heaping fork of meatloaf and potatoes went into his mouth and out came the empty fork.

"You're going with me."

When asked later, even Eula Mae admitted she faced widowhood as Hubert choked, spewing barely-chewed meatloaf and potatoes across the table and into her face. Twisting off his chair, he fell to the floor and began to move his lips soundlessly, eyes wide. The whole effect was similar to a fish tossed onto the beach, staring upward, unblinking with puckered and pulsating lips. Eula Mae didn't know what to do and recalled something about the Heimlich maneuver she'd seen Robin Williams do on "Mrs. Doubtfire."

Quickly moving to his side, she was about to kneel down when he gave a spasmodic heave, kicking and skewing the table leg and knocking over both milk glasses. As the milk cascaded over both of them and onto the floor, Eula Mae slipped in the milk, tore muscles in both inner thighs doing an almost complete splits and tumbled across her husband. It had the same effect as the Heimlich and Hubert coughed, ejecting the blockage into Eula Mae's left ear.

For just a half second both of them lay gasping. Hubert, recovering from the choking but unable to get any air because of the weight of his wife, suddenly began to panic and kick, painting the floor and rug with milk and other things. Eula Mae, not prone to sudden movement by nature, had exceeded her quota for the day but still managed now to push herself up, using her husband's stomach for support. Hubert panicked again, and in his quest for survival, shoved upward on Eula Mae, blindly grasping at whatever came to hand, which happened at this point to be her ears.

Eula Mae, in her mad scrambling to get loose of the hands gripping her ears mercilessly, reached across the table corner as it slanted downward precariously. Giving a mighty heave, the table gave way, meatloaf and mashed potatoes and green beans plopped and poured over them both. Eula Mae lost her grip and fell back across her husband, eliciting a panicked gasp.

Eula Mae always served green beans extra hot because the love of her life liked them that way, and now did not get any pleasure from the hot liquid plastering her upper thigh and back end where her skirt was pushed up almost to her waist. Still, it had a positive effect, as she jumped as never before, almost reaching her feet before slipping on the mashed potatoes and doing another set of splits and landing this time sitting on her husband's head. Hubert panicked as never before. When she landed, his mouth had been wide open in a life-seeking gasp and now his jaws clamped in panic upon Eula Mae's backside, eliciting a desperate scream and a mighty heave. Rising up and doing a vibrant squiggle dance, she succeeded in scrambling to a dry spot and stood, sprawl-legged, burned, bruised and shaking, leaning upon the now three-legged table. As she quivered there, pain wracking her entire body, she had a moment of despair.

Hubert lay upon the floor, eyes closed and trying to recover some sense of life, gratefully drawing air into his lungs when the table, incapable of supporting her weight on a good day, tilted and teetered, bringing the corner crashing down on his stomach.

Followed once again by Eula Mae.

Hubert called in the next morning and took the rest of the week off and went to New York City with Eula Mae.

It was a long time before she fixed meatloaf again.

A couple weeks later when his machine broke down, mouths dropped as Hubert stepped back, put his hands to his hips and spoke with unusual calmness.

"It could be worse."

Coworkers looked at the sky for flying pigs.

31

Later that week Jean suddenly put her book down and stared at the ceiling for a moment. It hit her that something was different about Gavin. For the first time in months he seemed preoccupied. Most wives would not like that in a husband, but for Jean it was a Godsend. Gavin exhibited only fleeting pleasure or purpose since his retirement and she missed his former self when he was preoccupied with a case. Never mind that it used to bother her when she would try to talk to him and it took several comments to get a response as he sat musing, sifting evidence in his mind. Now she relished his seeming sense of purpose with this issue of Cuthbert.

He sat on the couch, deep in thought.

Gavin was a top agent throughout his career. He enjoyed the quiet gathering of evidence, putting it together to slowly draw the net around a guilty party.

Gavin looked closely at what he knew so far. Cuthbert had a patch of marijuana on his farm. Terry was out of his jurisdiction. There were several reports of strange lights at night out in the fields. Probably a flashlight or brief flicker of headlight. Not much to go on, but this was where his trained speculation came into play.

With the field cultivated, it would indicate there was a vehicle, likely a pickup to blend in to farm country. Somebody was determined to have a good crop. Brian's visit capped it off that there might be more to this than meets the eye.

Meth? Some other mix? Questions filled his mind.

Now all this put together led to one thought: Gavin Crockett, retired, had no jurisdiction or authority and was sticking

6 7

his nose into something that could get big. The best thing to do was let the local authorities handle it. Terry'd probably refer it to the overworked sheriff up north who had other priorities. What Gavin should do is pull up Netflix and watch some old movie having nothing to do with real life.

"Die Hard," "James Bond" or something Stallone. That's what he should do.

But…he needed to talk to Terry.

Jean watched him over her reading glasses as he cleaned his already spotless Smith & Wesson. She was happy for him, humming with pleasure at his inattention.

32

"I don't know, Wilma. Business is down like crazy. Maybe I shouldn't have raised the prices."

"You had to, Max. Everything's gone up around us, but never your prices. You've got to keep up."

"I know, but I've lost customers. And it's more than that. I'm missing all the latest news. Like this thing with the pot."

"They'll be back. Men are creatures of habit and it's more than the haircut."

"What do you mean, Wilma?"

"They come for the friendship and the jabbering you men do when you're sitting around. Besides, we all know that Winston Corner cares for it's own. Your customers will come back. Give it a haircut or two."

"I hope you're right."

"I've been right ever since I picked you as my man, Max."

She gave him a peck on the forehead.

Max smiled, remembering driving through on his way to Cincinnati all those years ago. A cocky young fella at the time, he stopped at the truck stop up the road to get gas and, looking over to the pump across the way, he spotted this cute little thing filling up next to him. Beginning to act like he was hot stuff, he opened the hood and immediately jagged his finger on a bolt and cursed as blood started to run. Then the hood came down and hit him on the head. Looking over to the young lady, he saw her smiling. Their eyes met and Wilma offered a Band-Aid. Two hours later they finished their small fountain drinks inside and Max was no longer headed to Cincinnati. Instead, he began a barbering class in Indy. Six months later they were married and Max opened the barbershop. They kept a small brick home with a small lawn to mow. He loved low maintenance. Wilma worked in the school cafeteria up at Beedersville.

"Yep, you did get a prime one, Wilma."

33

"Stupid jerk! Punk!"

Relaxed and sauntering down the street with nary a thought other than how to configure his trap under the sink to accommodate the new garbage disposal, Hubert missed the approaching wheels. Just about to make the turn into the doorway of Schmeisser's, he jumped as Bobby Hernly zipped between him and the building.

Hubert Griffin grabbed his back and yelled again at the twelve-year-old riding the skateboard.

"Doggone bloomin' idiot!" Hubert hollered as the boy zipped ahead, doing one of those moves sliding along the curb that only skateboarders can and want to do.

Hubert shook his fist at the lad. Leaning against the entry, he missed the looks of surprise inside as he stumbled and slammed against the window like a June bug on a windshield. A couple guys sloshed their cups and Pratt spit his coffee across the table. Dinky cursed and scrambled as he took the brunt of the spray across his glasses and shirt. He grabbed a handful of napkins and swabbed at himself. Greg, turning an egg, looked up in time to see Dinky grab a double handful, about emptying the napkin holder.

"Hey! Those napkins cost a pretty penny!"

Just moments earlier all had been peaceful in Hubert's life. It was on one of those rare days off that Eula Mae pressed Hubert to take care of things around the house. This time it was plumbing – the bane of a homeowner's existence. Many things could be put off to another day, but plumbing tended to be urgent. Of course, his biological clock went off at 5:30 a.m.

and he lay there awake, until he decided to make a rare visit to Schmeisser's to catch the latest garbage, smut and gossip from the Liar's Table before the hardware store opened at 8:00.

"Dad gum it!"

Opening the door, he strode in. The Liar's Table was there. Bart Pederson was wide-eyed. He'd seen the dance.

"What in blue blazes just happened, Hubert?"

"That Hernly boy 'bout give me a heart attack out there! We need to have one of them there ordinances passed banning them four-wheeled killers from the streets. Ain't natural to ride one anyhow. It's gettin' so's a body can't even walk the sidewalks in safety anymore!"

Hubert did not like the equilibrium of his life disturbed.

Instead of joining the others, he stood by the door, leaning his elbow on the glass counter by the cash register, brushing aside the toothpick dispenser, a little aluminum thingy with a turn knob. Kim came over with a cup and the pot.

"You ok, Hubert?"

"Gimme a minute. I just seen my life flash before my eyes. 'Bout died."

"Ok." Kim rolled her eyes as she looked back at the Liar's Table.

Hubert took a few seconds to get himself together before he slipped into the end seat at the Liar's Table. He glanced up at Dinky, seeing the mess on his shirtfront.

"What happened to you?"

34

Bobby Hernly did a grind along the curb and a kick flip at the alley. Smooth as silk, he knew he was good. He didn't mean to scare Mr. Griffin like he did. It was a last-second challenge he couldn't resist, so he cut between Hubert and the doorway like a surfer cutting through a half-pipe. Only this time Hubert was the pipe as he twisted and arms flew and Bobby slipped right under the man's left armpit.

Twelve years old, his unruly tow-headed hair straggled out from his cap. A t-shirt, in his favorite color of blue, was rough around the edges, but clean. Scuffed and worn, his sneakers were about at their end.

Bobby was rough on clothes, but even when they were worn, his mom kept them clean.

Mature for his age – based on necessity at times – he was a boy caught in the usual complexity of boyhood transitioning to adolescence. Coupled with life on the edge of financial disaster as he and his single mother had to trust each other and God to survive.

Bobby lived for his skateboard. It was a DGK board with custom wheels. He longed for a Busenitz board, but knew it was out of the question. Money was tight and his mom did what she could. He was not blind to her sacrifices, so he took good care of his board.

He loved his mom dearly.

Cora Hernly worked as a clerk at Red's Pharmacy over on Cedar. Widowed three years ago, Cora worked hard to provide for herself and Bobby. Knowing her son's love of the skateboard, she'd taken on extra work for a while at the Quick Mart

to get him the DGK. Then she dropped the extra job, preferring the time with her son, eating meals together and helping
him with homework.

When she saw Bobby do some of the moves he did on the
DGK, she made time to take him over to the skate park at
Beedersville. It was hard for her to watch at first, fearing for
his life and limb, but she grew accustomed to it and loved to
see his enthusiasm and skill. Bobby entered some competitions
and did well. Last month she had surprised him with a Triple
Eight helmet and pads.

But there was no money to do more.

Bobby was on a mission this morning. With only an hour
before he needed to leave for school, he moved quickly.

35

Late last night, Bobby was hurrying home from Dan Pratt's. It was after dark and he carried his board under his arm. Not wanting to worry his mom, he called just before leaving and hurried down the street.

He and Dan were best friends, though they had nothing in common. Dan loved to sit and eat potato chips and play video games and watch murder mysteries, while Bobby liked skateboards and detested potato chips. But Dan also watched skateboarding videos on YouTube and gave Bobby ideas. He was sort of an armchair coach.

Looking at a video of the recent Vans Park Series World Championships, they were enthralled with world champion Oskar Rozenberg Hallberg's final skate. Mouths open and staring, Bobby suddenly glanced at the clock on the screen and broke the reverie.

"Oh, man! I got to go. Mom will be worried." Pulling out his cell phone, he dialed and told her he was on his way.

Now he walked and was about to turn on Main when he caught a movement out of the corner of his eye. Something had turned behind the abandoned gas station. Or was it just his imagination. It was just a different shadow of sorts that flicked across the darkness. He looked twice.

Strange. And no sound. The rest of the way home, he kept looking back and wondering if something was following.

So now here he was the next morning, having about nailed Hubert Griffin on his way to do a skate-by of the old station.

Giving an extra burst of speed, he approached the station and noted it was still all boarded up, the plywood over the door and windows gray and peeling. From all appearances, it was totally abandoned. Braking, Bobby kicked the board up and grabbed it.

The building was old, probably boarded up since before he was born. Maybe even since his mom was a teenager. It was the old-style gas station with a single bay and an overhang over the island where pumps once stood. Walking around the side, he noted the restroom doors securely locked, hasps and Master Locks clearly intact.

Looking back towards town, Bobby was a bit spooked to go around the back. He'd be totally out of sight of anybody. His hair stood up as he peeked around the corner.

Nobody. But something had been here. There were small tire tracks in the pea gravel and dirt. Creeping further, he stopped and stared.

There was a new padlock on the door.

On the ground was a candy wrapper. Bending over, he peered at it and read aloud,

"O'Henry. Never heard of that one."

36

"Buckner County Sheriff. This is Sheriff Burris."

Terry made the call first thing that morning. He'd fought with it, but to follow the best course of action he sat and punched in the number for the Buckner County Sheriff. He'd met Sheriff Burris last year at a training day. Elbows on the desk, he straightened when the phone was answered at the other end.

"Sheriff, this is Terry Jones of the Winston Corner Police. We met last year at the firearms training."

"Yes, Terry! I remember. Longhaired fella. You were the newcomer and you showed my men up on the course. "

Terry's shooting skills were excellent, and he outshot several deputies.

"I hope I didn't get them too mad."

"Not at all, Terry. I got so tickled. Being humbled was good for their souls!" he chuckled. "But I know you didn't call about that, so let's cut to the chase. What's up?"

"I guess I'm doing my duty, Sheriff. I've got a decent-sized patch of pot growing near town in a field. It's really in your jurisdiction."

"Terry, you sound disappointed to tell me this."

"Well, Sheriff…"

"Call me Dave. And, by the way, I hear tell you're short a man down there. Man off on leave. Give a call if you need a hand."

"Ok…Dave. Just being blunt, I'd really like to look into this, but I don't want to step on your toes."

"Ok, Terry, let me take a guess and you tell me if I'm right.

77

Life is a bit hum-drum down there, what with the same boring routine every day. Suddenly there's this situation and you find yourself eager to solve something bigger, something that will sort of cement your reputation?"

"Well…"

"Am I right?"

"Yes."

Terry heard another chuckle.

"Terry, I haven't always been a sheriff. I paid my early dues in a small dot in the road in Missouri. Spent a lot of time cleaning the restroom out of boredom. Even cleaned baseboards! Got right down on my hands and knees and scrubbed the tops of them with a toothbrush. Kept thinking to myself, 'is this all there is?' Fetched cats out of trees now and then, served a few summons and generally irritated people with trying to feel important."

"I think you hit the nail on the head, Dave."

"Thought so. Ok, so here's the scoop. We are swamped and very understaffed. We have to pick our battles. In all honesty, we've got our hands tied with patrol and some major investigations up here. And I ain't too caught up in jurisdictions. If you've got the time to check on this field, I willingly grant this to you. You just got to promise me one thing."

"What's that?"

"Don't do any take-downs without letting me know. Keep me in the loop. I've got confidence in you, but I've got more experienced manpower. Be careful. You might want to join us up here sometime and you have to be healthy to do that."

Terry was smiling now.

"Thanks, Sheriff, will do."

"Oh, and Terry?"

"Yes?"

"That toothbrush I used? It belonged to the guy on night shift. Used it every morning after he dozed all night. I never told him, just put it back where I found it." Terry heard the guffaws.

Hours later he walked the field again in the darkness. Ears tuned to the slighted sound, he wondered if there would be any activity that night.

37

Getting out of his chair Thursday evening, Gavin donned a dark shirt over his Wranglers and slipped into worn cammo boots. Jean looked up from her Sudoku, noting the slight bulge of Gavin's Smith clipped to his belt next to his mini Mag flashlight. Both were hidden under his shirt tail. She smiled inside and spoke as if to a child going to play.

"Where you headed, Sweetheart?"

"Just gonna do some checking."

"I'll bet it has to do with Cuthbert's truck and the plants."

"I'm just curious. Wanta go prowl a bit."

"Stay safe and be back by bedtime."

Offering her forehead for a kiss, Gavin obliged and gave her a preoccupied peck before grabbing his Radar cap, snugged it to his ears and headed to the door. He was arrested by a deep sound of concern in Jean's voice as she spoke again.

"Gavin?"

"Yes, Dear?"

"Did you feed the cat?"

"Yes, I did."

"Thanks, I was worried. Poor thing acts about starved."

Gavin walked out the door, musing distractedly about the cat, Jack, who was as far from starvation as any living creature could be. At the last vet visit he weighed in at twenty pounds and it resulted in an embarrassing lecture on proper feeding. They'd started the cat on one of those fancy and overly expensive dry foods, but still the cat stayed fat. Jack didn't walk, he waddled, and flabby rolls they referred to as his "floppers" swayed back and forth. Jack lived to eat and their attempts to cut back on his food usually met with excessive begging, and either Jean or Gavin would sneak him Whisker Lickin's soft snacks through the day. Each knew the other was doing it, but they kept it up out of pity for the poor starving thing and the cat flourished. Recently, Jack had faltered in jumping to the chair. Both knew the cat needed to be starved for a while, but he was just so cute and meowed so plaintively they couldn't resist. Letting the cat wallow in obesity was better than the incessant begging that started two hours before feeding time.

Speaking of weight, he would have "floppers" himself if he didn't watch out! Jean's cooking didn't help! Her idea of portions was beyond what Weight Watchers would deem appropriate. Take tonight for instance. She had fixed ribs with baked beans, bread and coleslaw. But land sakes the pile of ribs she made! It was a heaping platter and rather than put just a few out and leave the rest for the fridge, she piled the whole platter full. He ate several, and now here he was, getting ready to trek about in the dark already winded and bloated because of the stupid ribs. Not to mention the slaw, beans and two slices of bread. Of course, it all came down to the truth – nobody ever forced a bite into his mouth. It had always been voluntary. Normally in his career, when he was going to be out a lot, he ate little, preferring the clarity of mind and speed on his feet that leanness gave. And besides, he'd have to do dozens of extra push-ups to minimize the damage of tonight's dinner. Better yet, instead of driving, he'd just walk to Cuthbert's.

Shaking his head to get focused again, Gavin strode through the streets, staying as much in the shadows as possible as he worked his way across town.

38

Emaline Poovy was working extra late, having finished her after-hours perm for Lola Peck. Usually she was open late only on Tuesdays, but had made an exception for Lola, whose nephew was getting married outside Indianapolis on Saturday. Besides, Lola always tipped well, something not common in Winston Corner where people kept their dollar bills close to their backsides or stashed deeply in their purses where green never saw the light of day. A week ago, Annabelle O'Reilly was in the chair for a tint and Emaline couldn't help but look down and see a big wad of green tucked in the outside pouch of Annabelle's purse. Seeing all that cash tucked so securely, Emaline kept looking and trying to guess what denomination the bills might be. One thing she knew for sure was that Annabelle was tight with her cash! A sixty-dollar perm would net Emaline a piddly tip. It was the way of Winston Corner. And she had to smile and say "thank you" as if she was blessed with the pot of gold from the end of the rainbow! Holding her tongue was difficult.

Pondering such important issues as she unpacked her hair care inventory from the boxes delivered today, Emaline happened to glance up through the back door window and paused for just a moment.

What was that?

For just a second she thought she saw someone in the shadows. Peering between the racks, she saw it again just as the figure crossed under the dim security light over the back of Gibson's Hardware. It was dim because Gibson was known to be tight and used a 40-watt bulb in his security light. She

82

peered more intently, shading her eyes to cut the glare of her shop lights overhead.

It was Jean's Gavin!

What was he doing out in this area? And keeping to the shadows like some criminal.

She'd heard the rumors about Cuthbert's place, but never suspected anybody local might be involved. Now here she was witnessing a retired federal officer waltzing off to a life of hidden crime.

"Well, I'll be dinged," she thought to herself as she slipped out the back door.

39

Gavin slowly worked his way to Cuthbert's property. When he reached the field, he stopped to catch his breath. About to move again, instinct told him to look back towards town. His hair bristled with warning, and he stood for some time and saw nothing. Finally, shaking his head, he glanced back one more time and moved into the field.

40

Emaline Poovy wondered at herself. Slipping from building to building, she remembered seeing on TV how the cops ran at a squat across open spaces and she tried to mimic this. Problem was she had received a new pair of glittery high heels in the mail and put them on back at the shop to look them over. Without changing, she worked on the unpacking of the boxes, sort of stumbling now and then. Neglecting to change before she followed Gavin, she was crossing the last road when she stumbled, broke off a heel and tumbled into the side ditch. She lay there on her back trying to roll to her stomach in the narrow dip, but could only make short little hoppy-twist motions for several minutes before succeeding in getting turned and her knees drawn underneath. It was this subtle sound that Gavin heard, and Emaline's difficulty in turning kept her out of sight.

Finally getting to her knees, Emaline looked ahead and spotted Gavin as he faded into the darkness. She about cried out when she noticed she was all muddy and her blouse torn. Grasping her front embarrassingly, she looked around and quickly rose to her feet. One shoe was without a heel and the other had a broken strap.

Doggone! Mission incomplete. Taking both shoes off, but unable to recover the missing heel, Emaline headed back to the shop.

Jean's Gavin! A criminal? She'd just have to dig a bit.

41

Gavin found himself at the edge of a cornfield and turned north toward the farthest end. Walking only a hundred feet before he sensed a change and, reaching to his left, found his hand brushing the marijuana plants. The distinctive five-point leaf clusters were lined in what appeared to be straight rows, but the night was dark and how long the rows were was unknown. Grasping for his mini Mag and intending to turn it rapidly on and off near the ground for just an instant, he froze as another flashlight beam suddenly appeared ahead and around the corner of the field. Slipping to the ground, he hugged the dirt as the beam flicked over his position, but farther up on the plants.

Hearing footsteps approaching, Gavin's training came into play. Lifting his body slowly and slightly, his hand slipped to his revolver and brought it upwards. Tensing, eyes wide and seeking, he shifted to the side. Just as suddenly, the footsteps went the other way and faded into the night.

42

Terry walked the rows. First time he'd been here in a week. Probably ten rows of about ten plants each. A small patch, but there may be several more patches, which would add up.

At one point he thought he sensed movement, but after shining the light and then walking that way in the dark, he saw nothing more. Likely a raccoon or possum.

Slowly working his way around the patch to the road on the other side of the woods, he got in his car and drove without lights for a distance, squinting ahead. As he neared town he turned the lights on.

43

Gavin lay still for some time, all senses alert. He could not see the face behind the flashlight before it shut off. He really wanted to move, because his shirt was bunched over his stomach and he felt something crawling on his back. But he waited as he heard the subtle footsteps recede in the distance. Finally, sensing nothing, he holstered his revolver.

Enough for tonight, he thought. That was close. Too close.

44

Emaline stood by the shop window with the lights off for forty-five minutes, until she spotted Gavin working his way back through the shadows across the street. She shook her head in the dim light.

Yes, the bad element sure could fool you.

45

Max and Wilma were still in shock.

The Telfa pads and tape on Max's knees and elbows attested to the day's main event.

Sometimes survival itself was enough to bring satisfaction. It wasn't easy to process. Instead, they sat quietly, holding hands.

Max had that exact satisfaction already this day.

It was Monday, a traditional day off for barbers.

Always an early riser, Max sat on the back porch at first light that morning clad only in his sleeping shorts and slippers, drinking coffee and squinting in the half-light at the usual bad news in the paper. He had been after Wilma to hire somebody to enclose the porch into a sunroom, due to seasons when mosquitoes were prevalent. With West Nile virus gaining in the Midwest, Wilma was spending more and more on insect spray just to sit on the porch. Combine that with the way she slathered it on both of them and the cost of hot water for showers to wash it off before bed, Max felt in about five years they could break even on the cost of an enclosed sunroom. But she had vetoed the project, saying the expense was frivolous.

It was a great morning and he was relaxed and carefree.

All was right with the world.

The possum was almost to the porch before Max jumped and spilled coffee on his lap. Standing suddenly, straddle-legged and clutching the paper, he backed into the corner as the critter sauntered just-as-you-please up the steps and stood on the porch looking at Max with that nasty toothed look only possums can give.

Then it snarled.

Max paled and glanced around. The beast blocked all escape.

Max always wondered at the purpose of the possum. It almost seemed as if God had sort of messed up or just thrown together a few spare parts when he created the beast. They were ugly, looking like they had the mange, waddled awkwardly, smiled and hissed, ate dead stuff, looked both threatening and pitiful and yet even a child could beat them in a race. Yet, here Max stood in the corner of the porch with his rear pressed to the bricks like his life depended on it. He could sense his ampleness taking on the impression of the serrated bricks as he scrunched to get away. This particular version of the scavenger was about the biggest he had ever seen, probably weighing in at fifteen pounds. It was a monster!

The possum, seeming to instinctively know he had the advantage over this strange new human, lumbered ever closer to where Max stood. Twisting its head sideways, it bared its teeth and hissed. Having heard repeatedly about rabies in animals, Max was really scared. He reached out his hand and felt the plastic-webbed chair and, pulling it over, all but jumped onto it. Standing there, one hand on the brick wall, he felt the plastic webbing stretching beyond factory intentions. One web snapped, and he rolled his left foot sideways to keep from falling through.

It all went to pieces in the next few seconds.

A blur went by his peripheral vision as Fifi, their Jack Russell terrier, swooped to the rescue yet accomplished just the opposite.

Plowing into the invader, Fifi effectively hit a wall, for possums by their build and low center of gravity, were like running into a sack of oats. It gave but didn't budge as Fifi dropped in her tracks. Stunned for just a moment, the canine guardian of the home stood and snarled at the ugly apparition and attacked from the possum's vulnerable rear. Turning to face the dog, the surprised possum bared its teeth, backing defensively into the corner under the chair where Max stood precariously. Max clung to the brick wall behind with his fingertips, trying to avoid putting weight on the chair. His eyes became big as soup bowls with absolute fear while the battle raged right below him. Max paled to a bright white and made indecipherable sounds, some of which desperately beseeched God for deliverance.

The scene was instinctual if viewed by a biologist. First there was a man instinctively grappling to avoid a mouthful of nasty teeth, a possum, also backed by instinct and assuming a defensive position, and finally, a dog instinctively defending hearth and home of its beloved master.

Fifi had caused Max and Wilma consternation in the past as she attacked and killed various varmints with her quick eye and blazing speed. With a duty to defend Max and Wilma from all comers, large or small, her skills brought wariness. It was never wise to take a toy from Fifi when she brought it to you. There were good odds it was what remained of some sort of invader she had dispatched with vim and vigor. It seemed her secondary goal in life was to drag a trophy kill around the house, leaving blood and other viscera all over. More than once Wilma swore the dog would have to go, but then the lipid eyes and the contented loving looks Fifi gave when snuggled on their laps at night performed wonders and turned their hearts every time.

Wilma heard the ruckus and went to the kitchen window, which overlooked the unfolding scene like a million-dollar suite at a hockey game.

Taking it all in, Wilma reacted instinctively also – clasping her hand over her mouth and crying out to God.

Fifi and the invader faced each other. Unafraid, Fifi made several feints, managing to bloody the possum and causing it to scrunch further under the chair.

Another section of chair web snapped under the weight above.

Max started to panic.

Fifi sensed her owner's fear and shifted into overdrive with a bloodlust. She and the possum began to connect over and over, each with their purpose. The possum jerked defensively back and forth in a sort of slow motion, more than once bumping into Max's left foot.

Never one to enjoy dancing, Max began to waddle a slow dance as he tried to keep his weight off the weakened chair, succeeding in getting his feet placed over the metal frame of the seat. Wilma watched open-mouthed. The only saving grace for Max was the creature's intentness on immediate threat.

The chair frame started to bend. Max grabbed it with his toes and began to gasp.

Barking attracted the neighbor, who glanced out of his screen door to see what was going on.

Fifi, making a crazed lunge, succeeded in jumping upon and seriously biting the posterior of the possum. The jump now placed her in the corner, and the possum turned, facing the snarling and nipping canine. Head flying around, jaws snipping at the air and canine adrenaline all created a scene of utter despair to Max. A man falling into a pitched battle between a canine and a monster possum did not portend any sort of rosy outcome. Max emitted a guttural cry.

Awareness suddenly seemed to dawn on the possum and it backed laboriously away and down the steps. Fifi moved up, feinting and biting at the invader's only half effective rear-guard action as it retreated off the porch, onto the grass and into the Forsythia bushes. A horrible sound erupted from the bushes as they disappeared from sight.

At that moment, the chair broke on one side and Max fell, half straddling the remains of the chair and the rest of him outstretched on the porch.

Wilma rushed outside and knelt by her husband.

"Are you ok?" She looked down.

Max caught his breath and grasped Wilma's hand.

"I think I'm ok."

Moments later both shifted their eyes at the sound of Fifi. She proudly emerged from the Forsythias, dragging the dead possum by its tail with labored backward movement. Pausing in the yard, she turned and looked proudly to her owners.

It was just an hour later that Wilma, of her own volition,

called Harvey, the local handyman, to come look at building a sunroom.

It seemed like a valid expense now.

They sat that evening on the front porch, smeared with bug spray and facing town. Still plenty of light, but all was quiet in Winston Corner.

A vehicle approached.

Max and Wilma did what all small town folks do – they strained to see who was driving.

It was not a car they recognized.

46

Cooter was at it again.

A man prone to short-lived obsessions, Lisa had gotten used to rolling her eyes now and then. One of the necessary mantras of her marriage was "For better or for worse." For a couple years Cooter collected old hand-pushed garden cultivators, and there were still a half dozen perched in various spots with an old flowerpot and some mulch. Then he got into LEGOs, of all things, and built creations that sat in the back room collecting dust. Then it was "Sergeant Rock" comic books. At least those didn't take up much space.

Living in the middle of a 230-acre farm, it was pretty isolated. Their lane was 150 yards long. When you're isolated like that you can develop some isolated habits. It's usually guys – women maintain their sophistication longer than men and spend a lot of time worrying about what others might think if that once every 100 years visit should happen.

Cooter took to not using indoor plumbing any more than necessary. He seemed to take a rather undue pleasure in his freedom. Lisa tried to urge restraint, telling him he was killing the grass. She pointed out the dead circles off the porch. Cooter got irritated, saying something about scientific method. He took to watching the grass and actually found Lisa was right.

Pride would not allow him to tell her she was right, though. He just quietly moved his attacks closer to the barn where he found some weeds lived and some did not.

Lisa knew other wives had this same issue. Living in the country sort of brought something out in boys. In actuality, Lisa was jealous that she could not do the same. Why was it

God created men so they had the option, but women had to incessantly look for a restroom? With public restrooms often questionable, she'd shake her head at Cooter when he just walked into the woods or behind a shed.

Then it happened. A new obsession came unexpectedly.

Digging through an old box that came from his mom's attic after she passed, stored for years in the back room, Cooter's life was forever changed. Looking through letters and old photos, he opened a manila envelope and his mouth dropped open. In his hand was a black and white photo of an Indian woman, long braids draping down her deerskin dress. Beads adorned the front. The face was unmistakable in its Native American features and conveyed a stern pride and determination. But what startled Cooter most of all was the pencil writing along the border. In his mother's distinct handwriting, it said, "Great Grandmother Dancing Fawn Wilson."

Digging further in the box, he found a few more photos that included the woman. Her face conveyed the same look and he could almost picture her moving about amongst teepees and chewing deerskin to make it soft for sewing.

He sat and stared into the distance, his mind adrift.

Cooter became obsessed with his Indian heritage, scanning all the genealogy websites. Finding nothing, he began to add his own information. Researching the tribes, he knew his family came from what is now Oklahoma. Digging further, he believed her features were Apache, and that there was a tribe of the Plains Apache in that area.

Apache! He came from Apache heritage!

47

Lisa was at first pleased with his attention to this family tree business, noting how he spent less time outdoors and the plumbing issue faded because he was inside all the time. She became curious as he spent hour after hour online. He would go into the back room and she'd pop in once in a while and find her husband staring dreamily at old photos of Apache Indians and even at old John Wayne movie posters of such films as "Hondo" and "Fort Apache". He printed off pictures of Geronimo, Victorio and Mangus Colorado and taped them to the computer table.

One day she saw him standing outside and when he turned around he had this look she'd never seen before. He marched into the back room to the computer and later emerged silent.

A few days later a package arrived. Cooter signed for it and went with determination to the bedroom and shut the door. He emerged a few minutes later and Lisa clapped her hand to her mouth in surprise. Cooter was wearing – only – an Indian breechcloth. He didn't look at her, but marched outside and strutted along the porch.

That evening, Lisa carefully asked about this new purchase. Cooter said he was finding his Apache heritage. Pausing, she was gentle when she spoke.

"Sweetheart..."

"Dancing Wolf."

Lisa stared. Gentleness faded.

"Dancing Wolf?"

"My new Indian name. I registered it online."

Lisa stared long. Cooter – Dancing Wolf – stared back.

"Is there something wrong with our life, Cooter – I mean, Dancing Wolf?"

"There's nothing wrong."

"I see." She stared until he got nervous.

"There is something special about knowing I have wild Apache in my blood."

"'Wild' Apache? Why does it have to be 'wild' Apache?"

"They're always wild."

Lisa stared again, then just looked back to her book.

"For better or for worse," she said to herself. She said it then and a few more times over the days ahead.

48

Cooter took to wearing the breechcloth outdoors to do his chores. Wearing it proudly, he'd go out to start the car, empty the trash, move the sprinkler, or a host of other simple tasks. Seeing Lisa in the window shaking her head, he would strut even prouder.

The fact that Cooter a.k.a Dancing Wolf was not exactly slim and trim did not help the situation.

Getting bolder, one day Cooter stood his ground shortly after breakfast as the UPS truck drove in. The driver, a big man with a round, fleshy face and huge eyes stared in disbelief. Cooter stood there as the man got down with a package and carefully approached Cooter without breaking eye contact. Acting nonchalant, the driver wordlessly held the clipboard for a signature, handed the package to the apparition in front of him and walked back to the truck. Quickly reversing, the man drove off at a greater clip than when he arrived.

Lisa was getting exasperated until she finally and hesitantly confided in a friend who said, "Why are you making this into your problem. Just sit tight. He'll get over it."

Lisa first considered counseling when Cooter disappeared into the back room once more and came out with that look again. A week later another package arrived.

Deerskin leggings – with beads all up and down.

Cooter would go to work dressed normal, but immediately upon arriving home, change into his "wild"Apache clothing. His whole demeanor would change as he walked proudly.

Lisa was at her wits end. The only positive was her husband had started to eat better and actually was dropping pounds.

And he was running around the fields. Granted, he was jumping and hooting also, but there was a definite physical change. Rufus the dog, thrilled at his owner's newfound energy, bounded along happily, yipping with delight.

Rumors floated around town of Cooter's new obsession, but Buster, his neighbor to the south, saw it firsthand one evening. He recounted the next day at Schmeisser's how he drove up the Wilson lane just after dusk and found Cooter walking around in his breechcloth, with a still ample spare tire flopping above. It was not the most pleasant sight.

Buster, in the tradition of manhood, rolled down the window and acted as if nothing was unusual in seeing a full-grown man wearing an Indian breechcloth in the driveway.

"Cooter, just wondering if I can hunt your woods tonight."

"Yeah, go ahead."

Buster shut the window and glanced to the dash to slip it into reverse. He heard a knocking on the glass and turned, rolling down the window. Cooter stood there with a strange look. But he didn't say anything. Buster looked at his neighbor's eyes and saw a strange glint.

"You ok, Cooter?"

A pause. Then Cooter straightened his face a bit and spoke. "Buster, you can call me Dancing Wolf."

"O…kay."

Rolling up the window, he turned the truck around and headed out of the drive. Still shocked, all he could think was, "How do I explain this to my wife?"

He chose not to.

49

Max's Barbershop was a fun place to be – usually. Customers jokingly referred to themselves as "victims" and Max would holler, "Next victim!"

Of course, there was a small kernel of truth to the comment. When Max really got into a conversation, he would start to gesticulate and tended to pull at the end of a scissor stroke, causing the "victim" to wince. Of course, barbershop etiquette required them to act as if nothing was wrong. Working through the bottom little bit of his trifocals, the look on his face often was akin to someone suddenly glancing at the sun, with that puckered, squint-eyed look.

On a normal day, Max'd breeze through haircuts and hear the latest in those little ten-minute sound bites barbers got as they changed from customer to customer and topic to topic. He knew some secrets he would have to take to his grave. Sometimes he wondered about the money he would make if he opened a counseling office. Once, years back, he read about a man who opened up his own business as a "listener." That's all he did – listen. And made like twenty-five dollars an hour to sit and listen.

The regulars, who had rather quickly filtered back from their protest visits to Emaline and a shop up at Beedersville after Max raised prices, noticed the difference this morning.

Max was obviously preoccupied, and the first couple of "victims" stiffened a mite when he took the straight razor to the backs of their necks. They knew from the TV shows that just a slight horizontal motion would splay them open. Sweat broke out on more than one brow. Renner actually opened his wallet and made sure his insurance card was there.

Being guys, they didn't pry.

About 9 o'clock, it came out. Max paused in the midst of a haircut, waved his comb to the window, and spoke.

"You guys seen a strange car around town?"

Renner replied, "You mean besides Cuthbert's?"

"Yeah. A little tiny job. Looks to be smaller than a VW Bug. Quiet."

"Nope. Seen one up to Beedersville, though, once't. I think it was one of them electric numbers. Don't understand why somebody wants a car that you can't plan a long trip without knowing where the outlets are. Only make extension cords so long!"

Max gestured with the scissors.

"Thought I saw one in town last night. Too dark to tell, but it seemed strange. And driving slow."

"Don't know of anybody in town that owns one."

"Not that I know of, either. And like I said it was driving too slow. Like it was casing the place."

50

It took a lot of thinking and praying.

Lisa learned early on she was not going to control her husband. In fact, she realized any time she tried to tell him what to do he just went right on and did whatever it was. She knew she couldn't make him into her image, but just needed to accept him for all he was.

It sorely tried her at times. But she knew he loved her and she found the more she let him be himself, in a strange sort of way they grew closer. He'd never responded to the negative comments anyhow, except to glance at her with distaste. Still, she got irritated at times.

And at least he was wearing the leggings now over the breechcloth. Of course, with the weather a mite cooler in the evenings, he was prone to wear a threadbare Carhartt t-shirt and the whole outfit looked a bit comical.

She glanced at him now as he slipped out of the house in leggings and breechcloth, Carhartt shirt and unlaced work boots. Glancing at the clock, she knew: 10 o'clock. Time to get the mail. He always got the mail late at night.

Cooter took up the challenges of his heritage, and tonight he strode proudly for the first three hundred feet down the lane. Then beginning to feel his Indian roots, he found himself crouching as to sneak up on a wagon train. With nothing but bean fields to the left and right, his fantasy was the only reality.

Two hundred feet to go.

Rumors were rampant about Cooter's ways, and even the most modest townsperson found themselves glancing up the lane as they passed 300N, with occasional sightings of a white

Indian apparition in the distance. Some older folk would look disgusted, but then crane their necks to try and see more.

One hundred feet.

Making a last pause to see if the cavalry was coming, and seeing all was clear, Cooter strode with confidence. He reached the mailbox – a big farm box, and stood reaching into the back to get the mail when he heard it go by. A shadow passed. He jumped, looking around to see a small, quiet car, with no lights. It was shaped like one of the old humped and rounded Play-school cars with the perpetually smiling wooden peg people.

Turning at the sound, Cooter thought he saw a wide-eyed face pressed against the glass. It wasn't a smile. Caught flat-footed, he shook his head in wonder.

Why hadn't he heard it coming?

51

"This preacher fella goes into a nursing home to visit people from his church. As he goes through the lobby, he sees this lady in a wheelchair by the fake fireplace and she's whining and grasping one side of her head. 'Oh, my ear! My ear! Oh, it hurts so bad!' This fella's in a rush, so he just goes ahead and sees his people, then heads to go out. As he passes the front room again, the lady is still there. 'Oh, my ear! It hurts so bad!' The preacher, he decides he needs to help and he goes up to the lady. 'Ma'am, what's the matter?' 'Oh, my ear! It hurts so bad!' The preacher looks in her ear and then gets this look on his face and bends to look again. 'Ma'am, you have a suppository in your ear!' She looks at him and then a look of wonder crosses her face. 'Well,' she says, 'I guess I know what happened to my hearing aid.'"

The Liar's Table lost it completely. Even Kim had to stop pouring coffee for a minute as she laughed.

Gavin smiled from the back booth. That really was a good joke. He'd tell it to Jean later.

"Where'd you find that one, Dinky?" Renner sipped his decaf.

"My son heard it out in Seattle and called to tell me last night."

Bart took out a napkin.

"Hey, I got to fix a leaky faucet in the bathroom. It's been twenty years since I had to do that. What am I gonna need?"

Renner held up a finger.

"First thing, don't forget to turn off the water under the sink. I made that mistake when we first got married. Standing there taking the faucet apart and the whole thing suddenly blew like a Mercury missile."

Pratt nodded and grinned, then added, "Need two wrenches, one of them water pump pliers. Probably just that little spring thingy and the plastic cap down under the valve. Try that before you replace the valves. You can buy them packages with replacement valves that supposedly fit all of the same brands, but they really don't. The stops are wrong."

"What brand faucet is it?"

"Delta."

"Two handles?"

"Yep."

"Gibson's will have the little package with a set of two sizes of springs. You gotta get both. Need needle nose pliers to deal with the spring."

"Sometimes it's a bit hard to seat the valve again, but just push it down and then the nut will snug it as you tighten."

Dinky couldn't pass it up.

"More exciting if you leave the water on."

"Really funny."

"Hey!" Pratt was staring out the front window.

"Hey, what?"

"Here comes Poovy. What on earth?"

Bart turned his whole body to look.

52

Emaline was on a mission.

She rarely ate breakfast at Schmeisser's, preferring to grab a bagel and cream cheese at home.

For two days she stewed over what she'd seen out there in the field. Always keen on gossip, she had an ear for mystery. Though usually wearing embroidered jeans and a sequined t-shirt, in her mind she was wearing a Sherlock Holmes tweed hat and could've had a pipe hanging from her lips.

First shift was still at Schmeisser's as she came in the door, bell jangling. She noticed them staring as she walked in. Glancing around, she noted Dinky pretending to be absorbed in the Wall Street Journal and the others gazing at her.

Just as she suspected, Jean's Gavin sat in the corner. Finding a seat that took in the sweep of the room, Emaline sat down to watch. She'd seen this done on TV and knew she was just supposed to sit and wait and the bad guy would make a stupid move. It always happened on those cop shows.

"Well! Emaline Poovy, of all people." It was Kim, carrying a mug in one hand and the orange decaf pot in the other. "Don't often see you here this early."

"Morning, Kim. Just wanting a change today." She glanced at the whiteboard by the kitchen window. "Give me the special."

"How do you want your eggs?"

"Over medium, and wheat toast."

"Coming right up. Decaf?"

"Please."

Striding to the kitchen, Kim stopped beside Greg where he

was reaching for a link, stuffing it into his mouth and working it in with his lips.

"Emaline Poovy just came in, Greg. Did Vesuvius erupt?"

"Vassoo what?"

"Never mind. Something must be up."

Emaline stared at Gavin before she shook herself and looked around.

"What you staring at, Emmy?" Dinky looked from her to Gavin. He pointed at Gavin with a finger and a questioning look. He pursed his lips. The others looked up from their conversations. They hadn't noticed her staring, but entered into the topic with glee.

"She ain't staring at you, Dinky."

"Yeah, ain't a whole lot to look at."

"I'm better looking that any of you."

"I'd say your wife was fishing in the dark when she caught you. Didn't get a good look till daylight and by then it was too late to throw you back!"

Hoots all around, Dinky included.

"Hey, Emmy?"

"My name is Emaline to you."

"Ok, Miss hoity-toity Poovy." Dinky rose and bowed dramatically. "I hear tell somebody's seeing lights out in Cuthbert's field. You got your ear to the pavement. You know anything?"

Emaline glanced at Gavin, who continued to look at his coffee cup. Did his head turn just slightly?

"Nope."

"Well, I heard Cooter Wilson's seeing things, too."

"He's got worse problems than seeing things!"

Others laughed.

"No, seriously," Dinky said. "Weird things."

"What kind of things?"

"Like a car going by that makes no sound."

"When was this?"

"Two nights back. He was out to get the mail." The men all looked around at each other and laughed. "Surprised whatever it was stayed on the road, what with the glimpse they must've gotten!"

Emaline looked over at Gavin. His head was turned just a mite further, and he raised it further and caught Emaline's eye, holding for just a moment before turning back to his coffee.

Gavin's mind was working. Car that makes no noise? That would be an electric car. A Smart Car? It would make it easy to sneak around the back roads at night and nobody'd notice. It also meant this was a determined outfit. Any two-bit drug ring would be using two-bit vehicles. Smart Cars required a cash outlay and would not be used for only one patch. It was too much of an outlay.

53

Hubert drove to Beedersville Thursday afternoon. He needed a different kind of dimmer switch for the dining room, and the local store didn't have one. On the way home, he stopped at the Frosty Cone to get a shake and drove to the park to find a quiet spot to suck it down. Eula Mae was cutting them both back on desserts. It happened now and then and lasted about two weeks. So he needed to eat the shake carefully, avoid telltale drips down his shirt and then dispose of the evidence before he got home.

Passing a bunch of kids, he looked to the side and was stunned by what he saw.

The sign said, "Beedersville Skatepark." Holy smokes, Hubert thought. Now they're even catering to a bunch of idiots who run people over on the sidewalk. There must be thirty kids here, all of them riding – or whatever you called it – dangerously.

He parked and watched. Wasn't there anything better for these kids to do than zip up and down curves and through tunnels? In his day they ran around the woods and rode bikes.

Hey! Hubert squinted as one young man did a loop-to-loop around the tunnel and emerged into the sunlight. He was wearing a blue shirt.

It was the Hernly boy!

Hubert wanted to go out and confront the murdering twit, but found himself instead watching as Bobby made swoops and jumps and did that sliding thing along the railing.

His heart lurched as he watched two skateboarders nearly collide, each swerving at the last minute and jumping through the air. Without realizing it, Hubert was swiveling his hips and turning his shoulders as he watched Bobby. He found himself talking aloud.

"Watch out! There's another one coming!" He winced as Bobby took a fall, but merely rolled and came up moving.

"Daggone! Kind of a stupid thing to do, but he's really good at doing stupid things."

Hubert sat mesmerized, forgetting his shake until the whip cream started to drip down. He sucked at it and got it down below the rim and then sat staring again.

"There's another stupid stunt. Way to go! Wow!"

Hubert didn't quite smile, but it was close, the way his mouth twitched at the one corner.

54

Jake and Bub sat staring at the wall. It had been a long, hard night. For some unknown reason, Bub decided to go up a few streets in Winston Corner and look at houses. He liked to look in windows with inside lights on and see what you couldn't see in the daytime. Jake had warned him that it was unneeded exposure, and they saw more than one porch-sitter glaring at them. Then they went to work. After spending a few hours tending to the marijuana, they'd begun the next step of the process. It was dangerous and Jake watched Bub carefully as they put the ingredients together for the meth. By the end of the night they both had headaches and Bub stumbled once with a moment of dizziness. When they were done, they both were wiped out. Heading home to get to bed, the call came.

"Jake, go to the warehouse and help unload the stuff. Right away."

"Boss, we're tired."

A pause at the other end.

"Are you refusing?" The tone was unmistakable, and Jake gulped.

"No, we're on our way."

"I thought so."

Dead air.

"We ain't going to bed yet, Bub."

When they were approached months ago to help with this outfit, Jake knew to keep his mouth shut. When drugs were involved, he knew that ignorance was the best for safety. It meant not asking questions and just doing as you were told. Little bits and pieces filled in some gaps, but he kept it to himself. The money was good and like clockwork, so this looked like a good gig. Now, though, the job was getting overwhelming. Initially it was just the pot plants, but then expanded into meth production and now into this new thing.

Several boxes arrived the other night and he and Jake were given specific directions to the old house where a van was parked and spent an hour unloading boxes of who knows what. The driver was nowhere in sight. It was not hard work, but tonight they just wanted to get to bed. They left and knew the van would also be gone by morning.

"Don't ask, don't tell" was a good motto for what they did. Another one was to do as they were told. The tone of the voice on the other end of the line was pretty clear on that.

55

Hubert Griffin walked into the library. Myra Spencer, serving as official librarian and defacto town historian, ordered many books for Hubert through interlibrary loan. Looking up from her desk, she greeted him.

"Evening, Hubert."

He nodded. "Myra."

"Your books haven't come in yet. Probably be tomorrow."

"I need something else."

"What's that?"

"I need to use a computer."

Myra's jaw dropped.

"You ever use one?"

"Never."

"Why now?"

"Something I want to check on. Can you show me how?"

"Oh…kay."

After instruction and a few "dang its" and calling Myra a few times from her desk, he finally learned how to put words in what Myra called the search bar and then hit that return button. Then he would waggle the round plastic thing she called a mouse and click on an entry. Myra had to warn him, "Hubert, you don't pound on it like it was a big hairy spider, you just tap it like so."

Not used to tapping on anything, he was pretty hard on the mouse, not tapping but pressing down with the large hands of a man used to hard work. Myra could hear it from the desk and found herself wincing. Especially the double-clicks. They didn't have a big budget for electronics.

A couple weeks later, Hubert wandered into the library. He'd been in a few times, always to work on the computer. Myra merely waved him on. One time her curiosity took over and she strolled over and looked up the history after he left.

"Hm…that's interesting," she said to herself as she glanced to the window and watched his truck go down the street.

56

Dinky didn't even wait to sit before having to spread the news.

"I hear tell somebody stole a birdhouse off Johnson's garage."

Bart took a sip of coffee and grimaced.

"Dang, Kim! This is all-fired hot."

"You'd gripe if it was cold, too."

"Well, dagnabbit, I'm going to pull a Crockett – pass me the cream."

Gavin smiled as Bart continued with the news.

"I heard the same thing, Dinky. Some kid named Kovacs. But Johnson caught wind and went right to the kid's house. Parents 'bout whooped the kid to perdition right in front of Johnson. He stopped them and said he wanted the kid to do community service in his shop. So now he's been teaching the kid to make birdhouses."

"A good whooping does a boy good."

"You should know, Renner."

"That the Kovacs over on Linden?"

"Yep, used to be the old Eilar place."

"Eilar! Remember him? Bald as can be. Saw him in a turtle-neck sweater one day and he looked like a roll-on deodorant!"

Chuckles all around. Gavin spluttered. Dinky noticed and pointed.

"I got a fan over yonder. The man appreciates good humor."

"Ain't laughing at the joke. He's laughing at you."

Dinky threw his napkin at Bart.

"I got to get my hair cut today. I don't know, though. Twelve bucks. Remember when it used to be two bucks?"

"Yep, we talk of those as the good old days. Had to use the privy, too."

"The good old days had their issues, that's for sure."

Dinky smirked mischievously.

"You know what they call a high-priced barber shop?"

"Oh, boy. Here it comes – the bad joke of the day. I don't know - what do they call a high-priced barber shop?"

"A clip joint."

No laughs.

Dinky looked around.

"Can't win 'em all. Read that one in a fishing magazine."

"Suppose Max would be offended if we made a big paper sign and put it on the shop door?" Renner held his hands wide. "Clip joint – in foot tall letters."

"I wouldn't want to be first in line after he saw it. Keeps that straight edge stropped and you wouldn't know it if he wanted to do you in."

Bart looked at Kim.

"Kim? What is this cream stuff? Somebody let me borrow some reading glasses."

Kim wandered over.

"It's Irish Cream flavor."

"It's got booze in it?"

"No, Bart, it's just flavor. Sugar and flavoring."

"Huh. Actually tastes kind of good."

Dinky leaned back and guffawed.

"Kim! We're losing a man!"

Bart glanced around.

"Dinky, you just haven't got the guts to try it!"

"Yeah, right."

"No, I'm serious. I don't think you got the guts to try it."

"Gimme a couple of those. If you're gonna have fake booze in your coffee, Bart, you ought to do it right. A real man uses two dollops!"

57

It was a Wednesday afternoon when Hubert wandered into Red's to get his script refilled and found himself at the window with Cora Hernly. She handed him his blood pressure meds with the information sheet stapled to the bag.

Hubert wondered about the waste. They gave that information sheet each time. How many actually read it? Maybe the medicine could be cheaper if they saved a few trees!

"Is that all you need, Mr. Griffin?" She always avoided chit-chat with him because it got her down.

"Yes."

Hubert was turning away when he paused. Cora looked up again.

"Is everything ok, Mr. Griffin?"

He stared at her for a moment.

"Mr. Griffin?"

Hubert rubbed his chin, and then spoke.

"Was over to Beedersville yesterday. Seen your boy at that skate park thing with all the dips and swoops and such."

"I see."

"Kids were doing all sorts of stupid stuff."

"I see." Here we go, she thought.

"Your son was a lot better at stupid stuff than any of the other kids there."

"Um…I guess I should say 'thank you?'"

"Well, there was a lot of kids doing stupid stuff and falling and such, but he didn't fall near as much as the others. Fact is he only fell once that I saw."

Cora was shocked to hear an actual compliment…if that

was what it was.

"How long did you watch?"

"About an hour."

Cora stared for a few seconds.

"Bobby is really good at skateboarding, Mr. Griffin. After his father died, the first time I saw him smile was when he rode his skateboard down the library railing. I was shocked, but I realized something. My son has talent." She choked and wiped a tear. "It's hard sometimes, but I do what I can to support him. It takes some hard choices at times, but I want to encourage him. He wants to be a champion, and I want to help him get there."

Hubert was silent for a moment, staring. He had no idea Bobby had no father.

"They got competitions for that stupid stuff."

"Yes, they do."

Hubert turned to walk away again, then turned back.

"Expensive to do that stuff?"

"It can be. And to really get into it takes more than I can afford right now. So many of the big competitions are in places like Florida and California. Maybe next year."

"How old is Bobby now?"

"Twelve. Sometimes he seems fifteen and sometimes seven. It's been hard on him, and the skateboard has been a good thing."

58

Lisa shook her head. It was about to the point that the UPS man needed to be put on the Christmas list.

This time it was moccasins.

Not just any moccasins. They were high topped and beaded. Cooter – Dancing Wolf – put them on and sort of shuffle-walked to the barn, imagining himself carefully feeling for rocks and branches as he snuck up on an unsuspecting cavalry-man.

Lisa rolled her eyes.

Cooter was getting more daring. Instead of just seeing him in their nearby fields, there were times he was gone for hours. He was venturing farther and farther. At the grocery store the other evening, she overheard Jean Ann Henry at the produce aisle talking to Marge Morrow about sighting an Indian skulking through the woods back of their place. When Lisa rounded the aisle and came into sight, Jean Ann looked up and gestured to Marge and they both glanced over and then started talking about the difference between head lettuce and Romaine hearts.

Doggone, Cooter.

Then there came a day when the UPS man drove in and Cooter did not open the package, but hefted it, smiled knowingly and took it to the barn.

She did not even want to ask.

59

Bobby was at the Beedersville Park again a couple weeks later when, after a good run, he kicked up his board and glanced at the parking lot, noting the truck sitting there again.

He wondered. Same truck pulls in twice a week, shortly after he starts skating. He never saw anybody get out of it. His mom dropped him off every Wednesday after school and left him for a couple hours while she ran errands.

Walking to the drinking fountain near the sidewalk, Bobby looked again at the truck, catching a face in the glare of the shadows.

Hubert Griffin!

60

Harvey had been there all day, working on the new sunroom. The place was a mess, but Max was excited. Ever since the possum incident he'd not been able to relax on the porch anyhow, and they were pleased that Harvey had a gap in his schedule that allowed him to get started right away.

Max had seen no sign of the strange car since that one sighting.

Business was better than ever. He'd gained some customers from Beedersville. Apparently the barber there raised his prices to thirteen dollars, and some saw it as bad luck. Others said he was starting to drink a bit and had gotten a bit careless.

Max felt good.

61

"Ok, now hold that firmly against the guide. The blade will come straight down. Never have your thumb or any part of your body too close to the blade. Ain't a birdhouse anywhere worth that. It's all about safety."

"Like this?"

"Perfect."

Pulling the trigger, Seth Kovacs pulled the saw down and cut the board.

Birdhouse liked having the young man in the shop. Ever since convincing the boy's parents to let him "serve time" in the woodshop, Seth had taken naturally to the skills. At first he was surly and a bit resentful, but when he saw the wren house completed, something clicked. Now he was coming in most every day.

"Go ahead and put the hole in that piece, Seth. I'll get another board."

Seth strode with confidence to the drill press and began to change the drill bit.

"Birdhouse? What did you do with the key?"

Birdhouse scrambled into his bib overalls pocket.

"Oops. Here it is."

"I thought you taught me that the key stays with the machinery?"

"My bad. Do as I say, not as I do."

"Supposed to practice what you preach, Birdhouse."

They both laughed.

As Birdhouse went to grab another board, he heard Seth whistling as he changed the bit. It was "Moonlight Bay", and

Birdhouse sang it all the time. He loved Bing Crosby, for no other reason than his own father used to have the radio tuned to the old crooners. Sinatra, Rosemary Clooney, Tony Bennett, Nat King Cole and so many others. They were good old songs. And now, here was Seth learning them.

Birdhouse smiled. Lots of good learning in the woodshop.

62

Hubert walked into Red's. Nobody was there but Cora and Red. Red looked up.

"Morning, Hubert."

Hubert nodded, then walked up to Cora. He thought she looked pale.

"What can I help you with, Mr. Griffin?"

"There's one in Indianapolis."

"One what in Indianapolis?"

"Skateboard competition."

Cora squinted at Hubert.

"How do you know that?"

"Found it on the Internet. It's in a couple months. Carmel Clay somewhere or other. Must be one of them skate parks."

"Bobby mentioned it."

"So he should go."

"He's saving for a new board and wheels."

"So if he had a new board he could do all that stupid stuff even better?"

Cora nodded and smiled.

"Bobby's board is pretty beat up. It's all he does. Boards do wear out and the sidewalks are extra rough on boards."

"Where do you get those things?"

"Not sure. Bobby knows all that. Knows exactly what he wants."

"I see. You take care."

"Thanks, Mr. Griffin."

63

Gavin was awkwardly working to clean the dryer vent when his phone rang. Squatting behind the pulled-out washer, he barely managed to pull the phone out of the leather holder on his right hip. Glancing at the screen, he recognized the number.

"Hey, Brian!"

"Hey, Gavin. How's the honey-do list going?"

Gavin chuckled.

"I'm sitting scrunched behind the dryer like a circus contortionist."

"Let me guess…cleaning the dryer vent?"

"You got it. What's up?"

"I wish I could say we nailed Tyler, but…"

"But what?"

"Got some evidence that our old nemesis is expanding into new territory."

"Tell me more."

"Found a finger into meth production. Fake pharms and specifically bringing in Fentanyl from Mexico. Found a load recently listed as motion sickness tablets but was Fentanyl."

"Really. Somehow that doesn't surprise me. The low life will make a buck or a million wherever he can."

"Meth source is in Indy, Gavin."

Gavin held his breath for a moment.

"Into the Midwest. Must be getting hot back there."

"I think he's wanting fresh territory and knows we're keeping tabs on him here."

"Pot has been his empire, Brian. Any hint at why he's expanding?"

"My guess is pure profit. There are indicators he's lacing pot with the meth, maybe the Fentanyl also. More addiction, more profit."

Some producers were lacing pot with other chemicals. And some were not too picky. Sometimes it was LSD, other times meth, cocaine, even embalming fluid and laundry detergent. Now Fentanyl. It was all about profit, and often sold to others who in turn sold to the lower levels of society. Upper class users were too picky and any bad reactions to smoking pot were scrutinized closely and supply chains were more easily picked up. At the lower levels there was very little repercussion or investigation of deaths. It was just considered an overdose and files remained dormant.

"More deadly."

"The only life that matters to Tyler is his own. Lot of profit rolls in when he hooks a new one. That allows Tyler to live in the lap of luxury. Got a lead a day or so ago that he's even got his own men buying stolen goods, so there's profit at another level."

"I'd love to see him in line at San Quentin wearing wrinkled scrubs with his own personal number."

"I know, Gavin. That's why I'm calling."

"Explain."

"Ok, so I'm stepping across a line and this is between you and me."

"Understood." They had always trusted each other implicitly.

"I'm not asking you to look around, my friend. Just saying if you happen across something I wouldn't mind getting some info. You know what I'm looking for. You know this man. And being that close to Indy...well, who knows."

"Well, that is certainly interesting."

"What's interesting?"

"Stuff going on around here, Brian." He proceeded to outline what he found in the fields nearby.

"All that has just cropped up?" Brian chuckled. "No pun

intended."

"Yes."

"Gavin, if there's a connection, there likely will be some sort of meth production or mixing operation nearby. Either a larger kitchen or a series of smaller operations all tied together. Or, it may just be that he's bringing meth in from Mexico."

"Is it getting that much cheaper to import meth than cook it?"

"Pretty much. And less oversight. Big cooking labs changed to shake and bake and now mass import."

"Oh, yes." Shake and bake was the method of putting ingredients for meth in a two-liter bottle and shaking it to combine. Some referred to them as portable labs. In the beginning of major meth production, one of the giveaways was people purchasing large quantities of pseudoephedrine pills. When laws were enacted to restrict the purchase to a few pills, the shake and bake method became popular to create small batches with a legally purchased quantity of the cold medicine in a regular two-liter bottle. Some just put the bottle into their back seats and let them jiggle. If the old, bigger cooking labs turned sour or caught on fire, the "cooks" could just run away. If not very careful with the two-liter method, some sorry sucker was usually holding the bottle when it exploded. Police were specially trained to handle these mobile labs as they could be incredibly dangerous.

Brian paused. "You're retired, Gavin. Play this close to the vest. Just keep me informed."

"Will do, friend."

After he hung up the phone, Gavin thought a few minutes and smiled. He was well aware that Brian knew he would do whatever he could to put Harrison Tyler behind bars.

64

Two days later Bobby saw the truck again in Winston Corner. Hubert was just sitting in the truck, this time a half block down from the town office, when Bobby made his usual stunts along the street. The curbs were clean there and the railings solid. The people in the town office tolerated his boarding. Some, in fact, came to the glass doors to watch. He tried mostly to be there after four when they were closed.

To get to the best driveway chute in town - by the volunteer fire station - he had to go right by Hubert's truck.

The window rolled down.

"Hey! Kid!"

Bobby stopped, kicked up his board, snatched it in mid air and stood across the sidewalk. He spoke hesitantly.

"Hello, Mr. Griffin."

"I saw you over at Beedersville at that skate park."

"I saw you there, too."

"You're really good at all those stupid things you do on that skateboard."

Bobby stared. Hubert took off his hat, slapped it on the steering wheel and spoke again.

"What's a good brand of them boards?"

Bobby was rather shocked at the turn of the conversation.

"Busenitz."

Hubert just stared. "Boo...what?"

"Busenitz."

"I see." Hubert paused and rubbed his chin. "Meet me at the library tomorrow after school."

"What for?"

Hubert started his truck and shifted into drive.

"See you then…Bobby."

Bobby stood for several moments, thinking of what just happened. Shaking his head, he put his board down and pushed off, looking over his shoulder in wonder. Why was he to go to the library?

65

"So, the Busenitz board and you also need what?"

"Spitfire Formula Four 55mm wheels."

Hubert and Bobby sat at the computer in the library. Myra Spencer was frozen speechless when she saw Hubert Griffin, of all people, walk in with Bobby Hernly. Casting Myra a glance that stopped her words, Hubert led the way to the computer, where he gestured for Bobby to sit in the wood chair he'd pulled up beside the computer.

"What's this all about, Mr. Griffin?"

"How do you spell that skateboard name you said yesterday?"

"Why?"

"Just tell me."

"Busenitz."

"How do you spell that?"

"B...u...s...e...the 'n' is over there."

"This dumb thing makes no sense!" He put his hands in his lap. Then he got up. "Here. You sit in the driver's seat. I'll copilot. Take us to one of them places that sells that board."

Bobby typed.

Hubert looked at it. Some site called "Zumiez." Were these all foreign jobbies? Whatever happened to good old American names like Wilson and Spalding?

"There it is."

"There's eight of them there."

"This one." Bobby put his finger on the screen.

Myra, watching while trying to pretend she wasn't, suddenly had to chirp.

"You can point without touching the screen. I have to clean all those smudges off."

"Sorry, Miss Myra."

Hubert gave Myra a hard stare. She glared back at him.

"I have a lot to do here, Hubert. Got no time to clean screens after people been picking their noses and playing with their gum and then feel they need to rub their fingers on my computer screens."

"Neither one of us been picking our noses, Myra."

"Well, you still don't need to touch. You can point without touching, can't you? Watch this." She dramatically stuck her hand out and turned to point her finger at her nose. "See? I can point to my nose without touching it."

Hubert turned back to the screen.

66

Late that afternoon, Bobby watched his Mom's face as he told her the story. They were cleaning up from dinner. Cora Hernly was absolutely shocked.

"And he bought you the board and wheels you wanted?"

"He did, Mom! And even some skateboard shoes!"

"For real? Hubert Griffin? Of all people."

"He's really nice, Mom, when you get to know him."

Cora sat down, tired.

"You ok, Mom?"

"Yes, just a bit worn out from work, I think. Hey, what say we go get some pot pie? It's two-for-one night at Schmeisser's"

"Awesome!" He paused. "Hey, Mom?"

"What?"

"I've been saving for that board. Got near fifty dollars. Now Mr. Griffin bought me the board. What say I buy tonight?"

Cora smiled.

"That would be very special! Thank you. Just give me a few minutes to rest."

Bobby ran to his closet and pulled out his money jar. He let his mom sleep for an hour. She looked pale.

Must've been a real rough day, he thought.

67

Birdhouse spent many hours working quietly in his shop on the anniversary present.

Patty would be surprised. It was something she'd been secretly wanting for many years. It was in the early days of their marriage when she mentioned it with a sort of dreamy look.

Switzerland.

Of course, it wasn't possible in those early days of struggle. Married just a year when their first child, Amy, was born, they followed about every year and a half with another child. There was Amy, then Mike, Jr., Alice and Mandy in rapid succession. It left no freedom for many years, as they were determined for Patty to be at home and give the kids the best start.

Not being any good at book learning, he spent his entire career at the cement plant until he retired a couple years ago. Though never rolling in dough, they always had enough. Once a year they would fly to Seattle to see Mandy. Thank goodness the others were within a days drive.

Saving secretly through the years, it had taken him a full ten years to reach this point and he wanted to do it up special. So this past week he spent extra hours in the shop creating his surprise. It was a ruby red double-decker birdhouse with brass hinges on the clean out doors. He'd cut mini shingles for the roof out of a few spares from the house. Using a jigsaw, he'd made intricate gingerbread along the roofline. It was a fine piece of work and he knew she'd be pleased. Especially with the tickets she would find inside.

Patty was at Bible Study Fellowship that evening in Gale-town when he carefully wrapped the birdhouse on the kitchen table, then stashed it for later. Today was thirty-seven years and they agreed they would wait till she returned from Bible study to celebrate. She was children's director and wanted to make sure all went well.

There was a special reason for him to do this now. Patty's sister, Debbie, had died unexpectedly a few months ago and they both reeled in shock and the realization that there were no guarantees. Shortly after that, Patty had a hysterectomy and struggled to get her energy back. She just wasn't the same and carried a depression over her sister. She and Debbie were best friends and had called each other weekly, crying or laughing for hours depending on the issue of the day.

He was waiting when she drove in. Holding the door for her, he gave her a kiss.

Now they sat on the couch, wrapping paper on the floor.

"Oh, Mike! This is the most beautiful birdhouse you've ever built. Thank you."

"It's a special birdhouse, Sweetie. You might say there's a lot of love inside."

"I'm sure there is, Mike. You are the best builder of birdhouses in the region." She paused and took a breath. "Now, I have a gift for you."

"But, dear…"

"No, you just wait. I'll be right back. It's in my purse." She arose and went to the kitchen.

Glancing at the birdhouse, he wrinkled his brow.

"Here it is." She handed him an envelope.

Opening it slowly, he unfolded a piece of paper.

"Oh, Honey. This is incredible!"

"I knew you'd like it."

"A certificate for this fall's workshop with Tom Burke in Delaware. Sweetie, how on earth? He's the most famous birdhouse maker in America. I never dreamed I'd meet him, much less attend a workshop."

Patty beamed as Mike leaned over and gave her a tender kiss.

"Thank you."

"You're very welcome, Michael."

"Now, you need to do something, Patty."

"What?"

"The birdhouse needs to be cleaned out."

"Cleaned out?"

"Yes, there's something inside that needs to be cleaned out." He set the birdhouse on her lap. "Start with the bottom door."

Patty gave him a questioning look as she gently undid the latch and opened the door.

"There's an envelope in here!" She drew out the rolled envelope and glanced at her husband as she opened it. Her eyes grew wide. Pulling out paper bills, she slowly counted out. "Michael, there's a thousand dollars here."

Mike Johnson was choked up and had to pause. She waited, wondering. He was not a man to express emotion. Finally he spoke softly, "It goes with what you'll find in the top cleanout door."

Patty opened the latch, peered in and pulled out another envelope. Opening the flap, she drew out papers. Staring at them for a full twenty seconds, tears ran down her face. When she spoke, it was almost a croak.

"Switzerland."

Patty leaned into her husband's shoulder and hugged him.

68

Lisa rolled her eyes again.

Dancing Wolf, a.k.a Cooter, was sequestered in the computer room again.

She knew what that meant. It meant another package would soon arrive.

Five days later her wondering was answered. Her husband was home when the UPS driver arrived again to face this pseudo Indian apparition. Then her husband disappeared into the bedroom. Lisa waited and when the bedroom door opened she turned and stared blankly.

Dancing Wolf stood in breechcloth, leggings and a fancy beaded deerskin tunic. It didn't fit the best, riding a bit on his spare tire.

Sighing, Lisa went to the kitchen.

Early the next morning she dug in her purse and pulled out a card given to her by a coworker. It had been there for a month. Today she called.

"Good morning. This is Haven Heights Family Counseling. We are currently with a client or out of the office. Please leave a message and we'll get back with you."

Lisa held the phone to her shoulder and waited for the beep. When it came, she did nothing. Finally, she hung up the phone and just stared out the kitchen window. Looking down, her knuckles were white where she was gripping the edge of the sink. Suddenly, inspiration hit her.

She'd call Harvey.

69

Harvey was a fixture in town as a handyman. Nobody knew his last name. Some knew he lived west of town a ways. His beat up truck was always parked there of an evening and there were bits and pieces of this and that stacked around. Many times he had just what was needed to do a job, and he never charged for the stuff he brought from home. After all, it was just leftovers. But he was the go-to person for any repair and for some construction projects. Whenever a faucet leaked or a doghouse needed to be built or a shed or small room added, it was just natural for people to look the situation over and nod and say, "Guess I'll give Harvey a call."

Harvey's rates were reasonable, and his business card was hanging in many of the houses and buildings in town, usually right alongside the calendar and the dentist appointment reminders. Many were just stuck haphazardly under the metal frame of bulletin boards. But all were easily accessible. The card was simple and read:

**I can fix it
765-4Harvey**

A quiet man for the most part, Harvey was privy to much of the local gossip. Whenever he was on a job, homeowners and shopkeepers seemed compelled to talk to him.

Harvey enjoyed his job.

It was hard to listen to those who droned on and on about nothing, seeming only to need to hear themselves talk. Others opened up to him about everything from their dreams to marital issues. Sometimes he felt they really could have dealt with the project themselves, but they wanted to have a listening ear.

Just listening.

That was the problem. Nobody had time to sit and listen anymore. Most didn't even want a solution. They just needed to be heard. Sometimes he ventured in and asked a question.

Today he was starting at Wilson's place. A small plumbing job. Wilsons didn't call that often, Cooter being a handy sort. Harvey figured this was a counseling session. After that he'd head to Max and Wilma's, where he was enclosing the back porch into a sort of sunroom.

He was right about Wilsons.

Lisa met him at the door and led him to the kitchen where she pointed to the sink.

"It's not draining right, Harvey."

Kneeling and opening the cabinet doors, he craned his neck under to look and a small smile came to his face. He didn't let Lisa see it. It was obvious somebody had unscrewed the couplings of the pipes.

Yep, this was a counseling session. It was but a moment until Lisa spoke.

"Cooter doesn't seem to have time to fix this."

"Busy, huh?"

"Genealogy."

Harvey kept under the sink, pretending to be checking and working. He let her talk a minute, then excused himself to get some tools. He returned with an orange five-gallon Porter Paints bucket with miscellaneous tools. It took seconds to align the pipes and put some Teflon tape on the threads and recouple the pipes.

Lisa talked on and on about something with Cooter and Indian heritage and buckskins and beads and such. Harvey tinkered under the sink for a few minutes more, then sat back on his knees and looked up at Lisa.

"Does he beat you?"

She looked surprised.

"No."

"Does he go to work?"

"Yes."

"I hear of a fella collects perfume bottles. Don't understand why. Hundreds of them in the house. Stinks, what with all them flavors mixed in the air. Bothered his wife at first, but then she realized it kept him busy. And he enjoyed it. If she'd told him not to, what would he be doing? It could be worse. Look for the good in it."

Lisa stared at Harvey. She realized Cooter used to wander around in the evenings looking for stuff to do, filled with nervous energy. It usually resulted in an incessant pattering around that annoyed her. The new heritage obsession kept him busy, running around outside, getting air, and – honestly – he was looking pretty good after running and jumping off much of his spare tire.

"Thanks, Harvey." She paused and looked to the sink. "I'm sure glad you could come on such short notice. How much do I owe you?"

70

"This couple drives down a country road for several miles, not saying a word. Just had an argument and neither of them was gonna give ground on their position. Stubborn. As they passed a barnyard they looked over and saw mules, goats, and pigs. Wife points and asks sarcastically, 'Relatives of yours?' 'Yep,' the husband says, 'in-laws.'"

Dinky laughed uproariously at his own joke. Pratt tried to hold it in, but finally burst out, and then choked. Across the table Renner was shaking. Dobbs chuckled. In the kitchen, Greg was heard to suck air and bellow.

Dinky was pleased with himself. He looked to the kitchen and saw Greg shaking his head and mumbling, "in-laws."

Pratt looked to Greg and hollered, "Hey, Greg? You serving in-laws today?"

"Yup. Yours!"

Laughter erupted again around the table.

Pratt gestured to where Gavin sat in the corner, shaking and grinning.

"Even Mr. Crockett liked that one!"

Once again it was 'Mr. Crockett.' When would he ever fit in? He smiled, looked to his coffee, and continued his thoughts.

"Hey, Kim?"

"Yes, Bart?"

"You got any of those French Vanilla creamers in the back? None left here."

"Sure do. Be right back."

Kim smiled and went to the back. Ever since Bart dared Dinky to try the Irish cream, she could hardly keep them sup-

141

plied. Gone were the old comments about black coffee and manhood. Dinky still liked the Irish cream, while Bart preferred French Vanilla. Greg was a bit miffed that it was at least a nickel per creamer cup, especially since he caught Dinky throwing back one Irish cream cup like a shot of the real stuff. Some of the holdouts were starting to look more closely at the little cups. They had Irish cream, French Vanilla, and hazelnut in addition to the plain. Dinky was actually starting to experiment with mixing them.

Greg was talking about raising the price of a cup of coffee, but feared a rebellion.

Kim told Greg that Dinky had asked her the other day where you go to get that Splenda stuff that Crockett used.

Kim loved this group, despite it all. It was like a sociology class. There were all these studies on societies and culture, but she felt a lot of people were missing some of these grass roots changes like less people drinking black coffee and adding creamers and sweeteners and turning to things like decaf skinny vanilla lattes. Coffee shops were everywhere and coffee had become like liquid candy bars. Most people didn't look at the calorie count and see that so many of the coffees were seriously the calories of a meal.

Dropping half a dozen creamers on the Liar's Table, she made the rounds.

"Warm up, Mr. Crockett?"

"Yes, please, Kim. And thanks."

He watched as Kim smoothly went about her duties. One evening, running into Greg at the hardware store, Gavin asked about Kim. Greg said she had an associate degree in accounting and had done some traveling years earlier, but just liked the quiet of the small town and being a part of a simpler life. She was taking online classes in business.

Interesting. Gavin jarred back to the present as Renner spoke.

"I must be seeing things. Was coming in from Beedersville last night and thought for sure I seen a flicker of light off across a field at 400 South. Just a quick flicker, then it was no more."

"Fireflies are thick this year. Probably a clump of them all together."

"No. Fireflies are sort of yellow light. This was definitely a burst of white, like them LED lights. Maybe one of them there tactical flashlights."

"Probably just more of that mary-juana. Best stay away."

"Before you know it, we'll have one of them medical growers setting up shop. People will be lining up for jobs. Quality control will be popular."

"Nope. Pot's still illegal here."

"Won't be for long. Federal is illegal, but the states are starting to set up their own laws. Then all them that was criminals won't have to hide any more. They'll strut and pass out their cash and drive fancy cars and sit and laugh at us. We'll see 'em drive by smoking them funny cigarettes and the cops won't be able to pull them over or anything. They'll swerve and knock over dogs and such and kill people, then smile their way home 'cause they'll be all red-eyed and off in la-la land. Probably start to sell the stuff right here at Greg's. Greg probably will put it in a display case with the pies! It'll put a whole new twist to the menu and Thursdays will crowd up something fierce for his pot pie!"

Hoots all around.

"Ain't going to happen here!" Greg yelled from the kitchen, followed by an irritated, "Doggonit!"

"What happened, Greg?" Kim asked.

"Cabinet door just fell off."

"Have to get Harvey in here, boss man. Got several things falling apart."

"I can do it."

"Sure you could. But you won't. That's why it's dangerous to walk in there. You got no time to fix it, nor the tools."

"Best keep your trap shut, Kim. I can find other help."

Kim grinned and winked to the Liar's Table.

"Not in this town, you can't. Have to go awful far to find

someone hard up enough to work for the piddly-squat you pay and put up with your stubbornness."

Liar's Table listened with delight. They loved the way Kim gave it back to Greg. She had worked there for several years and was Greg's right hand. He would no more give her the heave-ho than he would volunteer for combat duty. They picked on each other regularly, but each knew the value their team-work brought to the shop. Greg loved her like she was his own daughter. Really quite an attractive woman, now a year shy of thirty, she never failed to draw the admiring, platonic looks of the men at the Liar's Table. Her long, curly dark hair was always in a bun at work, and despite exposure to the bratwurst, she maintained a lean, slender figure.

"Ten years now, Kim, and you still can't cook bratwurst like I do."

"That's right. I cook them better!" She glanced at the room. "That right, guys?"

A chorus of 'amens.'

Kim laughed, tilted coffee into Dinky's mug, and looked back to see Greg shaking his head, a slight grin on his face.

What many didn't know was how Greg had slowly entrusted more of the bookwork to Kim and she was more involved than ever. He also was paying for her schooling. Still, her love was to be amidst the customers. They were a family to her.

"Hey, Kim?"

"What, Dinky?"

"Know why the brunette couldn't dial 911?"

"No."

"She couldn't find the 11!"

The fellas all looked to Kim, but didn't laugh.

"I feel a spilled coffee pot coming up, Dinky!" She held the pot over his head.

Gavin listened partly to the banter as his mind shifted to the field at Cuthbert's. Now there was another field. He needed to go out again. There had to be some evidence there. Best go out in daylight, see what he might see.

71

Leaving Schmeisser's, he walked back to the house, grabbed the keys and was about to leave when Jean came around the corner.

"Where you headed, dear?"

"Just going to go take a drive."

Jean knew him well. Well enough to know he had to do what he had to do. Gavin's sudden interest in this mystery was enough to bring a smile to her face. She looked to him now.

"Careful, Gavin. I wouldn't want to waste dinner."

It was what she'd said to him for many years back in the city. It was their light-hearted way of avoiding talking about the danger of his job. That's how they handled it – avoiding the conversation. And she respected his quietude. She knew he was best when working on some sort of project in his head.

Gavin smiled, kissed Jean, and left.

He loved his wife. Putting up with him for all these years, she would be surprised when he pulled the tickets out for the cruise. She had always wanted to go on one, but it never really tickled his fancy. He did not relish the idea of sitting on a boat, eating godless amounts from twenty-four hour buffets and sucking on bottomless drinks while watching an endless blue backdrop go by. He figured there were never enough chairs to fit everybody on the deck and he did not find pleasure in the thought of rushing to grab chairs in the shade as four hundred other people did the same thing. Still, he did love his wife and finally caved in and reluctantly bought tickets off Expedia. He'd gotten the bigger cabin, because he'd been told more than once that online pictures made the rooms look gigantic whereas in reality they were tiny. No chairs in the small cabins either. It was sit on the bed – or the commode - or stand. Still, it was on Jean's bucket list and it was about time he just sucked it up and went.

Gavin sat his car near the crossroads of 17 and 400. It was just a wild hunch, but he'd followed hunches before. According to Renner, there was another field of marijuana somewhere out here. Driving around, he saw several secluded areas, but he was looking for something special. Most men cultivating would not be the high-end of the food chain. They were the ones most likely to be thrown to the wolves if push came to shove. Therefore, they were likely peons of sorts, needing to be pushed or threatened to get the job done. They also might be careless. And lazy. Any possible crops would be located so that a car or small truck could be parked in a way that the walk was at least manageable. So he drove around just to see what might come up that fit that pattern.

It took him just twenty minutes to spot the tire tracks.

In front of him was a small track through the roadside grass and into a grove of Maple mixed with already dead Ash and scrub brush. The tracks in the grass were very narrow and not too heavy and turned in from the north. They were tracks of a very small car. Probably the Smart car being mentioned in town. Hardly the mark of a local farmer, who usually preferred trucks. Nor was it deer season. Nope, this was deliberate and unusual.

Gavin paused. He could not use the same track or they would see his when they returned, since his wheelbase was wider. Taking a chance, he drove a hundred yards further to the south and carefully pulled into the long grass at the side of the road. Getting out and looking around, he wandered into the woods.

72

Cora struggled to get out of bed. She was so blessed tired. Too many hours and not enough rest, she figured. Still, she had gone to bed at 8 o'clock last night. Ten hours. Should feel better than she did. Then again, maybe it was a touch of that virus running around town.

Bobby was gone. He often went out early to ride his old skateboard. He'd mentioned to her he was going to do that.

She thought of going to Doc Morton, but she knew he'd tell her it was a virus and she just had to hang in there. So many people wanted antibiotics even though the medicine didn't touch a virus.

She'd pick up some Nyquil or something to bring home tonight.

Dragging through her morning routine, Cora stopped to rest several times. At one point she thought of calling in sick, but she needed the money and had a strong sense of responsibility to Red, who had been busy lately. Annette, a long time employee, recently retired and moved to Oklahoma, and it left just Red and Cora holding the fort. Cora knew how hard it was on Red to do everything when she was gone.

Usually walking to work, Cora took the car today.

73

Terry knew he was still learning, and he had read much about the laws of evidence collection.

That's what he was doing today.

It was his day off. Getting up early, he'd moved his squad car and pulled out his old '02 Chrysler 300 M and cruised up to Beedersville.

He was on the trail of the elusive O'Henry candy bar.

It wasn't a common candy bar. If someone stood in a convenience store and surveyed candy bars to buy, Hershey's and others would go long before an O'Henry. Whoever bought an O'Henry candy bar was specifically looking for one. And if a store carried this candy bar, there had to be enough sales to make it worthwhile.

Another thought occurred to him late last night. Anybody tending fields in the area would not want to travel far. So there was a good chance the culprits were at least nearby.

Driving around Beedersville, he wandered into several gas stations and convenience stores. None of them carried O'Henry bars. With a couple more to check, he looked at his watch and his heart lurched.

Dang! He'd almost forgotten. He was supposed to have lunch with Kim. The waitress from the diner had finally agreed to a date of sorts and they were meeting at the Burger Barn. He'd have to hotfoot it to make it in time.

Nearing Cuthbert's, Terry knew he could cut a minute off his time by heading down the back roads. He could crank it to 60 in spots. About to take the last major turn, he slowed and happened to glance to his right.

Someone was there! He had glanced at just the right moment to see the back end of a car in the woods. It was a good mile away.

Sliding to a stop behind a cornfield, he got out of the car and opened the trunk, where he kept his spotting scope for deer hunting. Heading around the cornfield and reaching a small stand of Sycamores, he uncapped the scope, leaned against the tree and looked to the woods in the distance.

Just the slightest touch of a vehicle could be seen. Moving the scope slowly towards the field, he suddenly lowered the scope, wiped his eyes and then looked again.

"Dang," he said to himself.

Glancing to his watch, he frowned.

"Dang."

74

He pulled into the Burger Barn a few minutes late. Kim was already seated and watched him get out, hiking his pants and checking his fly as he approached. Pausing at the door, he ran his hands through his hair as he stared at his reflection in the glass.

Kim shook her head and smiled.

Why, she thought, do men always have that routine? She'd seen it many times.

Men.

Still, Terry was a kind man. Long single, never married. The older crowd said he'd been a bit wild in years past and was still a bit of a rebel with the rough edges rounded. She'd not been blind to his glances and not surprised when he asked if she'd do lunch. Dates were few and far between in her life. It wasn't because she wasn't attractive. In fact, she'd been approached many times, but there just weren't many men that even interested her. She'd seen several of her friends married and divorced, and didn't want that, so she'd just sort of built her own life. She was content to be alone – most of the time. But then there were those other times. Terry had asked her out as she sat taking a break after the first shift crowd left. A weak moment. He'd been awkward, in a way that actually made her smile to herself.

Ah, well. At least it could be interesting and a bit of a distraction.

Terry walked in and glanced around, spotting Kim in the booth.

It was at the annual Winston Way Days celebration a couple years back that Terry first saw Kim. He was still working at the cycle shop. Schmeisser's had a booth at the festival and the bratwurst was selling like hotcakes. A loyal community, most of the locals looked longingly at Mike's Mackerel Trailer, but then turned back to Schmeisser's and pulled out their wallets. Of course, it helped that every chance he got, Greg would stand behind the grill and survey the crowd. Making eye contact with as many as he could, nodding and smiling and calling out names, he knew what he was doing.

"Bratwurst, Bill?" Bill would look longingly to the Mackerel Trailer, then turn to Greg's booth. Loyalty and shame trumped desire. Greg worked it all day long.

The first year he opened the booth he spent his time focusing on the grill, but profit was not great. The next year he began a looking around and hollering routine and saw his profit rise sixty-five percent. Guilt. Guilt raised profits.

Kim was at the counter that day. Terry heard about Winston Way Days over the years, but never came to it. He still didn't remember why he suddenly drove down from Beedersville that particular Saturday. He was walking around, looking at the flea market stuff and the different church booths and the volunteer fire department raffles and such and was standing holding a vintage Beatles album when he heard a voice.

"Hey, hotshot! You look like it's time for lunch!"

Looking over, Terry saw this incredibly cute brunette smiling at him. He stared for a moment. Wow! Nice figure and bright, cheerful eyes. She wore a new t-shirt with "Schmeisser's" across the front.

He didn't remember what he ate that day, just that he made little glances all afternoon toward the booth.

Now, here it was two years later and he'd finally asked her out.

Smiling, he slid into the other side of the booth.

75

"This is for the skate park, not to wear out on the curbs and sidewalks. You got to use your old board for stupid stuff like that."

"Ok." Bobby grinned at their standing joke.

Hubert handed Bobby the box.

He'd stopped by Hernly's and now he and Bobby sat on the porch. Bobby was pulling at the packing tape but succeeded only in stretching it. The new shoes had already arrived and Bobby wore them now.

"Ain't you got a pocket knife?"

"No."

"Any self-respecting boy needs a pocket knife, for Pete's sake. Here, use mine."

Hubert leaned to one side and reached into his pocket, pulling out a good-sized folding Buck knife. Pulling open the small blade, he handed it backwards to Bobby.

"How's come you pulled the small blade out?"

"Something I learned from my dad. People don't know how to treat a blade, so you pull out the one you want them to use. Then you keep the other blade nice and sharp for yourself. What happened to your dad, anyhow?"

"He was killed at the foundry."

"Oh. Sorry." Hubert was embarrassed.

"That's ok."

"Where are your grandma and grandpa?"

"Don't have any. Mom and Dad were both orphans."

"I see." But he really didn't see. "You got any brothers or sisters?"

"No. Mom says it was rough when she had me and I was their special blessing."

Hubert paused.

"Best open the box."

Bobby ran the knife along the edges awkwardly, but managed to slice all the important tape. He handed the knife back. Hubert jerked back as the blade headed his way. He wanted to yell, but didn't. He carefully took the knife and folded the blade.

"Always hand it back with the blade pointed to yourself. Don't want to poke a hand. In fact, it's best to fold the blade back in before you hand it back."

"Ok."

Lifting the box flaps, Bobby peered into the box. Hubert was peering, too. Bobby chuckled.

"Hey, Mr. Griffin. Gotta let me get the box open."

"Oh, sorry." He leaned back. "Well, hurry up."

Bobby pulled the wrapped board out and carefully slid the bubble wrap off. It was beautiful!

"Jiminy Cricket, Bobby, look at that paint job."

It was purple of various shades, all faded together around the slanted "Busenitz" down the middle.

"And look at the wheels, Mr. Griffin."

"Boy, they are fancy. Them's the Spitfires?"

"Yep."

Hubert pointed to the board. "You gotta break this in, or can you just start riding?"

"You just hop on and go."

"Where's your mom? She still at work?"

"She came home early today. Said she wasn't feeling well."

At that moment the door opened. Cora Hernly, hair a bit disheveled, came out, glancing to the two and then to the board.

"It came! Oh, Bobby, it is beautiful! Mr. Griffin, this is a fine gift. Thank you so much."

"Welcome. Wondering if we might drive to Beedersville and

try it out? Hate to see it sit another day."

"I think you should."

"Can you come along, Mom? If you're feeling better."

"I am feeling more rested. Mr. Griffin? Won't your wife wonder where you are?"

"Eula Mae's visiting her sister for a few days. I'm batching it. So let's get going."

76

Cora and Hubert stood by the fence at Beedersville Skate Park watching as Bobby, grinning from ear to ear, took his new board up and hailed some of his friends. Several all but drooled as he showed off the new Busenitz. Then he perched it on the edge of the half-pipe and stepped onto the board as it dropped.

Cora Hernly turned to Hubert and smiled.

"Mr. Griffin? I want you to know this means an awful lot to me."

"Oh, it's nothing, Mrs. Hernly." Hubert felt awkward and pushed at his white hair.

"There's so many things I want to do for my son, but there's only so much money in the jar."

"It's hard, raising a young one by your lonesome. Sorry about your husband."

"Thanks. It's been hard, but we're ok."

"And you can call me Hubert."

"Ok…Hubert. And please call me Cora."

Bobby swooped near, causing them both to lurch. He hollered as he circled and swooped again and jumped off the board, kicking it up where he grabbed it out of the air.

"What do you think now, Mr. Griffin? I'm doing that 'stupid stuff' better than ever on my new board!" He grinned and ran up the ramp again.

Hubert grinned.

Cora smiled. But she was so tired.

77

Two weeks later, Gavin sat in Schmeisser's and saw Terry walk in. Glancing at his watch, he knew Terry had another forty-five minutes before he started duty. Terry usually took a walk around town before heading in to relieve Wally Carter at the Cop Shop.

Why was he here?

Terry glanced at Kim. She smiled.

Gavin smiled to himself. Something is budding in the romance area.

Even the Liar's Table was caught off-guard.

"Hey, Terry? You got a wild hair? Ain't never seen you at breakfast here before."

"Just thought I'd try it." Gavin glanced over to catch Terry glancing again to Kim.

Dinky cleared his throat, then looked around to make sure everybody knew it was time.

"An elderly man in Phoenix calls his son in New York and says, real firm like, 'I hate to ruin your day, but I have to tell you that your mother and I are divorcing; forty-five years of misery is enough.' 'Pop, what are you talking about?' the son screams. 'We can't stand the sight of each other any longer,' the old man says. 'We're sick of each other, and I'm sick of talking about this, so you call your sister in Chicago and tell her,' and he hangs up. Frantic, the son calls his sister, who explodes on the phone. 'They are NOT getting divorced,' she shouts, 'I'll take care of this.' She calls Phoenix immediately, and screams at the old man, 'You are NOT getting divorced. Don't do a single thing until I get there. I'm calling my brother back, and we'll both be there tomorrow. Until then, don't do a thing, DO YOU HEAR ME?' and hangs up. The old man hangs up his phone too, and turns to his wife. 'Okay,' he says, 'they're coming for Thanksgiving. Now what do we tell them for Christmas?'"

Kim, carrying a mug of leaded, spilled the entire mug as she hooted. Greg had to sit on a stool in back. The others grabbed their stomachs and laughed.

Then Greg fell off his stool. The clatter of the stool brought more laughter.

Gavin couldn't drink his coffee for laughing. Dinky looked over.

"Like that one, Crockett?" He'd dropped the "Mr."

"That was one of the best I've ever heard, Dinky. And I've heard a lot through the years."

Dinky smiled. He always smiled when someone appreciated a joke.

It took a few minutes to get the place back to normal. Kim took a few moments to wipe coffee off the floor.

Greg could be heard in the back, "Coming for Thanksgiving," followed by little hoots.

Dinky sat proud.

78

It wasn't common for Emaline to come to Schmeisser's before lunchtime, and the guys just stared as she walked in and sat at a small table near the window but commanding a view of the room.

Looking to each other with questioning eyes, it was Pratt who threw down the challenge. He couldn't help it. The sign in her front window provided the bait.

"Hey, Emaline! You impoooved anybody's looks lately?" He looked pleased with himself.

First shift laughed, looking to Emaline for a solid comeback.

She caught their stare, glared and responded.

"Pratt, if my dog was as ugly as you, I'd shave his butt and make him walk backwards."

Gray heads at the Liar's Table guffawed. Except for Pratt, who knew he'd taken a major hit.

Renner pointed a finger at Pratt.

"Oooh! Pratt. She got you solid."

Emaline wasn't finished.

"Pratt, you better go home and study on that a bit. You gotta understand it before you know what to say. And while you're at it, your weed beds could use some attention."

Pratt leaned back in his chair and grinned. He and Emaline Poovy had been going at it for years. It's just what they did. Remark and retort, remark and retort. They had been neighbors for years. Pratt was not too particular with his yard, and Emaline was about as particular as anyone could be. Emaline's style did not match up with anybody and Pratt would just look at her yard and roll his eyes at her odd ideas, like the three reflector balls on the little stands next to her mosaic bird-bath. Even twenty years ago he called her yard the "Old Ladies Emporium." It wasn't that they disliked each other; they just sort of had a neutral friendship. Emaline was now fifty-four, never married, and used to doing her own thing. Pratt, at sixty-six, looked younger than his age and was relatively fit. Widowed five years ago, this past year he found himself standing in the kitchen window watching Emaline work her flowerbeds. Rolling his eyes at her picky nature, at one point she bent over to pull a weed and he quit rolling his eyes. In fact, he actually gave a little gulp. He spent quite some time going to different windows trying to get different angles when she worked in the garden. For the first time, he awakened to her appearance.

He stared for a moment at her now, noting her colors might not be the most flattering, but still, the fit was quite kind. The jeans certainly flattered her.

"Emaline, I concede the score of this round to you. I will, indeed, have to study on this a mite."

Emaline glanced over at her neighbor. In ways she felt bad that they always had to make sarcastic comments, but that was just the nature of their relationship. His concession of the round was the closest thing to a compliment that she was likely to get from him.

She still remembered him coming in with his wife when she was crippled with the cancer taking over her body. He would gently help her through the door on her walker, moving chairs to make it easier for her to get to a table. In fact, as was the way in Winston Corner, others would take their plates and drinks and shift tables to allow Ruby Pratt a table nearer the door. He was really a tender man.

Kim came up with a diet Pepsi.

"Caffeine cold. What's on your heart for breakfast, Emaline?"

"Couple scrambled eggs and bratwurst, please, Kim."

"Coming right up. Greg's got some special spicy bratwurst. Wanta try them?"

159

"That a new thing?"

"He's got a wild hair and been experimenting with his grand-dad's recipe."

"Huh. Well...I'll try one regular and one spicy."

Glancing to the corner table, she noted Gavin sitting with a napkin and a pen. She watched as he tore the corner of the napkin trying to get the pen to write, finally looking around and scribbling on the corner of the menu until the ink flowed.

Emaline was on self-imposed surveillance. She'd been watching Gavin as much as she could between appointments at her shop. Nosiness was something she was good at. Sitting late the other night on the back steps of the Post Office, where it was real dark, she watched the main intersection of town and saw Gavin drive by. Unable to follow, she watched and even stepped out into the street to watch as he headed north out of town.

Now she sat, wondering what evil plans he was making on the napkin. Probably plans for a new underground greenhouse and how to plant a hundred thousand pot plants with artificial light and automatic watering with infra-red drying racks to get it to market quick! She wondered if Jean had any idea of her husband's nefarious plans. Probably had her fooled. Or... maybe Jean was in on it. She worked in Indianapolis, but maybe that was just a front. Or maybe she was working on delivery and distribution of those hundred thousand dried plants. How many of those joints would that make? A million? Good Lord, they must be rolling in money! Wouldn't guess it. Probably going to suddenly disappear to their estate in South America, with servants and bodyguards and leather interior sports cars.

Emaline's imagination was known to be powerful, especially with her creations and the fancy styles she pushed on people. Still, she had influence and a steady clientele. Her "impoovments" might be strange, but more than one had resulted in new excitements in households that hadn't seen lightning for years. Her creations tended to start and just roll on into the distance.

In fact she was so intent upon a hundred thousand pot plants she almost missed Pratt stop briefly by the table on his way out and say something hard for him, but much on his heart. He almost croaked as he spoke.

"Have a good day, Emaline."

Intent on pot plants, she glanced at him and just stared blankly.

Pratt walked out.

"Didn't even see me!" He frowned.

But she had.

79

Taking a day off, Cooter met the UPS man in full Apache gear, and held his palm up in greeting. He'd seen it on TV and said it was the Indian way of saying "hello."

The UPS driver stared blankly, chewing gum.

Cooter took the box to the barn.

Lisa stood in the kitchen.

"Dear God," she prayed, "give me strength. I don't know how there can be any good come from this, but I just have to trust. How should I deal with a husband who has become an Indian and seems to be going off the deep end?"

A couple mornings earlier, after Cooter left for work, she stepped into his shop and about fainted. Along the middle of the room lay a dozen or so poles, about eighteen feet long. Piled on the workbench was a folded bundle of canvas.

A tepee?

Lisa was stunned, and found herself quoting a scripture.

"'No temptation has overtaken you except what is common to mankind. And God is faithful; he will not let you be tempted beyond what you can bear. But when you are tempted, he will also provide a way out so that you can endure it.' Dear God, I am tempted to do a lot of things right now, but I will trust and hold my tongue."

80

It was in the afternoon that Pratt looked out the window and spotted Emaline walking through her yard. She was watering flowers and carefully working the hose around the beds. He watched as she had to go back to move the hose frequently so it wouldn't snag or drag over flowers.

Finally, he set his jaw decisively and, grabbing his cap, went out the back door.

Approaching the back of his yard, pretending to just look at the old peach tree at the back of his lot, he kept the corner of his eye trained on Emaline.

Emaline suddenly noticed his presence and caught his eye.

Pratt acted surprised.

"Oh, hello, Emaline."

"Hello."

"Um..."

"Um, what?"

"Um...can I help you move the hose around?"

Emaline stared for a moment, fighting her natural suspicions and inclinations for a snide response. Looking suspiciously at her neighbor for just a moment, she made her decision.

"That would be helpful, Ben. Could you. Please?"

81

The air felt like rain.

Gavin was in the field again, having walked out from town. It was near 11 p.m. and dark as pitch as clouds covered the sky. Sitting about fifty yards away behind some thorn bushes, he'd had the foresight to bring a small tarp to kneel on.

When he'd found the other field a few days back, he decided to watch more closely.

Listening carefully at the coffee shop over the past couple weeks, he found there was a pattern to the spotting of lights. From that pattern, it was likely someone would be here either tonight or tomorrow. Also, through careful exploration, he'd found a half-dozen other fields.

Jean was a gem. Once again, she did not complain as he donned his dark clothes and strapped on the revolver.

"Gavin, the cat food is in the packet on the counter. Please feed Jack before you leave."

"Didn't he eat already?"

"That was just a treat. He was just needing a little tidbit to carry him over."

"Carry him over to what? If we keep feeding him, we'll have to carry him over to the couch, over to the litter box and even over to his food bowl."

"I think he's actually losing weight."

"Where? His floppers are still dragging the floor."

He fed Jack, who waddled over as excitedly as a twenty pound cat could waddle.

Here in the darkness, Gavin knelt, shifting quietly now and then. He kept his eyes moving back and forth, knowing movement often was seen more out of the peripheral vision at night.

Patience was a virtue on surveillance. He'd known investigators who left surveillance positions out of boredom and missed criminals by just a few minutes. Sometimes the criminals did their own surveillance before returning to a scene.

Movement!

Zeroing his eyes into a roving pattern at an area of darkness, he saw it again. But it was a mere sense of something, the darkness was so deep. Sprinkles began to fall.

Someone – or something - was out there!

Waiting, he saw no more, but sat tight. He didn't want to walk into something. There were no lights or activity of any kind. After another half hour, Gavin slowly arose and began to work his way towards the area. Reaching the edge of the field, he paused and turned around the south edge, stepping as lightly as he could.

Snap!

It was not him! Someone was very close! He reached for his revolver.

At that moment, the clouds parted slightly and moonlight revealed them both.

Gavin and Terry both faced each other. Gavin had his revolver out, while Terry was reaching for his Glock.

"Dang! Don't shoot, Crockett!"

"I'm not going to shoot!" Gavin lowered his gun. "Terry, what are you doing out here?"

"I need to ask you the same question! Is this your crop?"

"No! And this is out of your jurisdiction."

"Not hardly. But you're retired."

"I'm trying to figure all this out."

"So'm I."

Both stood in the darkness, adrenaline still shooting through their bodies.

"Dang, Crockett. Like to scared me out of my shoes."

"You shouldn't be out here wandering around."

"Well, I'm the one with the badge."

Gavin paused, then chuckled.

"But the one thing we know is that both of us want to figure this out. Have you seen anything?"

"Not tonight."

"Any clues?"

"Maybe. Say, you got experience with this stuff, don't you?"

"Yes, you?"

"Not really, just smoked a bit of the stuff years ago." Standing in the silence, Terry told Gavin of the conversation with the sheriff.

"Terry, I've got a feeling about this. May be a tie in to a big outfit."

"Why are you even concerned? You're retired."

"Maybe that's the problem. Fixing door hinges is a bit drab after doing investigations all my career."

"Fixing hinges is safer."

"It is that. But this has got my mind working and my blood flowing again."

Terry nodded knowingly.

"Boredom is not good for anybody."

"That's for sure." Gavin looked to Terry. "You said you maybe had some clues."

"Yup. There's a pump in the woods yonder. Hose to the creek. And I found a candy bar wrapper."

"Candy bar?"

"Yes. O'Henry." Terry paused. "Not common. I been looking for places that sell it. Nothing yet."

"Well, there's nobody out here tonight. Not likely to be now."

A subtle noise in the distant brush caused them to turn.

"See anything?" Terry whispered.

Gavin paused, then replied, "No."

82

"You ok, Cora?"

She noticed Red glancing her way a lot through the morn-ing.

"Yes, I think I've got a touch of that virus going around."

"You need to go home?"

"I'll be fine. I might take a bit of a nap at lunch."

Red's was exceptionally busy. It happened once in a while, and Cora worked to help her boss get the prescriptions out. He had always been kind to her. When she was widowed, he allowed her to take some time off and even paid her a bit extra. After a fashion, he spoke to her about sending her to school. She still considered it, but with Bobby…

"This one's for Hubert." Red handed her a bag to put in the pick-up bin.

"Usual, it looks like. Flomax and Metoprolol." She paused a moment. "Isn't this an increase in the Flomax?"

"Yep. You women are lucky you don't have a prostate."

"Yes, of course. We are so lucky to have the monthly issues for forty years followed by a bout of menopause. Yes, I'd call that real luck!"

Both chuckled.

"You got me on that one, Cora." He stood at the counter counting out the next script, just called in from Doc Morton. Phenergan for Molly Bates. It was amazing how much a phar-macist had to keep his mouth shut. He knew so much about so many people by the medicines they took. He laughed to himself. The places he'd seen Viagra go! And he couldn't draw too much conclusion, because one of the Viagra derivatives was also good for the prostate. Over the years he'd caught a few mistakes and seen drugs prescribed that were dangerous when prescribed with others. Usually this was due to different doctors. In the days of mostly general practitioners he'd not seen as many issues. Of course, the development of new drugs had ballooned and it was harder to keep track of it all. Ten years ago he began setting aside Thursday evenings to catch up on med updates. It was overwhelming. In fact, he had a whole stack of flyers to read already and a slew of email notifications.

"Red, I'm going to step to the back a minute."

Red nodded as he counted. Always in fives. His whole world centered around counting in groups of five. He even counted the bites on his plate in fives and cut his steak in fives! As he finished and tipped the pills into a bottle, he heard an odd sound and turned.

Cora!

She was collapsed against a shelf, and sagged limply to the floor as he stood, eyes wide.

A few minutes later locals heard the siren. Ears craned, they pegged it to downtown. Eyebrows rose.

83

"Bobby Hernly, please come to the office immediately."

He raised his head from the test and saw all faces turned to him.

It happened all the time, whenever the call came for anybody to go to the office. Everybody sort of assumed someone was in trouble. And there was always a sudden feeling of guilt, like the one called had actually done something wrong. His heart always took a spin when he heard his name.

Why would they be calling him?

Bobby took his test up to Mr. Miller's desk.

"I just finished, Mr. Miller."

Mr. Miller looked quizzical. Bobby was not a trouble kid, but you never know.

"Ok, you need to take your books?"

"No. I'm sure I'll be right back, probably just my mom dropping off my lunch. I forgot it this morning."

It was more than a forgotten lunch.

84

Terry sat, looking at the computer screen, exploring meth production and the supply pipeline from Mexico, when the door opened and Cuthbert walked in.

Oh, boy, what a time to be looking at the computer, Terry thought.

"Just as I figured. Our public servant, killing our tax dollars staring, probably looking at porn and shopping Amazon!"

"Actually, Cuthbert, I'm working on your problem."

"On that thing? Shouldn't you oughta be out catching the crooks? They ain't online!"

Terry couldn't help rolling his eyes.

"Cuthbert, you have no idea."

"I got some really good ideas, but you wouldn't like them."

Terry blew his cheeks as Cuthbert walked out and slammed the door.

85

Hubert was quiet as he drove. Picking up his prescriptions, he'd looked around for Cora. Red, seeing his looks, spoke.

"She's not here, Hubert." Red saw the question in Hubert's eyes. "She's in the hospital."

Hubert was stunned.

"What happened? She ok?"

"Not sure what's up. She collapsed today, unconscious. About three hours ago. Had to call the ambulance. I've got no help, so I can't leave till after work. I'm worried sick."

"Bobby?"

"I expect they called him outa school. Not sure how he'd get to the hospital. Surely somebody woulda taken him."

Hubert turned and stared out of the window. No dad, no grandparents…just nobody.

"Hubert, you want your meds?"

Turning back to the counter, he nodded to Red.

Now he was on his way to Beedersville Community Hospital.

86

Bobby sat alone by his mother's bedside. Tears streaked his face as he held her hand. She was asleep, but looked so pale.

When they told him at the office all he could do was cry. The principal and school secretary drove him to the hospital. He sat quietly in the back seat and wept, staring at his hands.

When he arrived, they wouldn't let him see her. They were running all sorts of tests. Staying by his side, the school secretary explained Bobby's family situation to the nurses and they said they would watch over him. Then they admitted her to ICU and he was allowed to come to her room. She had IVs and oxygen. There were rings around her eyes and she wouldn't wake up. The hospital gown had slipped off her shoulder and he tucked it back. Touching her hair, he dropped his head against the bed rail.

He was scared. He'd been so sad when his dad died, but at least he had his mom. But now…if something happened, there was nobody. And he didn't want to lose his mom. He loved her so much.

Sobbing, he felt alone. More lost and alone than he'd ever been in his life. His heart pounded.

A touch to his shoulder made him look up.

"Mr. Griffin!"

"Thought I'd come see what was going on."

Bobby stood. "I don't know what's wrong. She looks so sick, Mr. Griffin."

Hubert saw Bobby's tear-streaked face and felt his rugged heart lurch as never before. He choked up and couldn't speak for a moment.

"Got to let the doctors figure it out."

"I'm scared, Mr. Griffin." Bobby choked a sob. The tough skateboarder was a frightened child.

Hubert raised his arm and Bobby came underneath, wrapped his arms around Hubert's waist and sobbed against his shirt. Hubert wrapped his other arm around the shaking boy. A twelve-year-old was just a little kid when things like this happened.

A few minutes later, Bobby looked up. His voice was tiny. His eyes were pleading and fearful.

"It's just Mom and me, Mr. Griffin. We got nobody."

Hubert's throat seized up. He was barely able to whisper.

"Yes, you do. You got me."

Bobby hugged him tighter.

"What am I gonna do, Mr. Griffin?"

"Don't you fret. We'll figure it out together. I ain't going nowhere."

87

Eula Mae had been gone for a month. After the incident at the dinner table she'd needed a break. Gruff with each other at times, she and her husband were actually quite close and she only made it two days before she called. When he'd told her about the skateboard and Bobby, she realized something had come over Hubert. She witnessed by phone this budding little friendship and she was actually pleased for her husband. It sure opened their conversations up.

Deep in her heart, she knew Hubert would have been a wonderful father and grandfather. Though unable to conceive, their vows remained strong. Many times she lay awake and just sort of wondered what their lives would be like now if there were kids and grandkids. She felt an empty spot many times. With no kids, they had been able to put away a tidy sum, so they usually went out to eat on Saturday. Still, she sometimes caught her husband watching families as they laughed and giggled when children interacted with parents. A couple weeks before she'd gone to her sister's house, they were in Indy at a Steak n' Shake and she caught Hubert staring off to one side. Catching his glance, she watched what appeared to be a grandparent and grandchild playing pick up sticks with a plate of French fries. She grinned. What a novel idea. Looking at Hubert, she saw the tender look in his eyes. A gruff man to her and many others, Eula Mae knew his inner workings and was fully aware of the incredibly tender side that lay deep within. It showed as he had watched the two laughing and playing. His mouth curved up on one side and he was momentarily unaware of her presence. Her heart sagged a bit. Yep. He would have been fulfilled

- both of them would – with children and grandchildren.

Now, in the airport on her way home and waiting to board, she felt her phone vibrate. Looking down, she smiled.

"Hello, Hubert dear."

"You at the airport?"

"Yep, waiting to board. I'll be in Indy in a few hours. Looking forward to seeing you, my love."

Usually that would elicit a tender response. It didn't.

"I'm not gonna be able to pick you up."

"What's the matter, Honey?" She sensed something in his voice.

"Bobby's mom is in the hospital. I'm here with him."

"Is any of his family there?"

"They don't have any family. Nobody." There was a pause. "No grandparents or nothing." Another pause. His voice cracked. "Bobby needs me, Eula Mae." She heard the choke in his voice and a lump formed in her own throat. It made her heart hurt to know her man was hurting.

"I'll find another ride, Hubert."

"I got you one. Kim from Schmeisser's said she could get you."

"Bless your heart, Honey. Don't worry a thing about me. You just do what you need to do. Which hospital?"

"Beedersville."

"You stay with him, Hubert."

"Okay." Another pause. She could tell he was struggling to speak. "Love you, Eula Mae."

"I love you, too, Hubert. They're calling my section to board. I'll see you tonight. Bye."

She was quiet the whole flight, her thoughts elsewhere.

88

Gavin sat in the metal chair across from Terry at the Cop Shop. Slouching down, he folded his arms across his chest and glanced around the room. He'd been invited here by Terry. They talked quite a bit the night before and had agreed to meet to talk further.

Terry caught his glances.

"Not the fanciest of offices, compared to what you're used to, huh?"

"Actually, Terry, it is far from the worst I've seen. And I have seen some nasty offices. Nice floor."

Terry laughed.

"Hard to keep it clean, but some days it's all there is to do!"

It was Gavin's turn to laugh.

"Law enforcement has a lot more to it than catching criminals, huh?"

They both laughed.

"I just had the floor spotless that Saturday when Cuthbert came in. I could hardly listen to him with the pig crap and mud flying everywhere. I'd spent two hours scrubbing, on my hands and knees, only to see it ruined in about a minute and a half." He paused and looked at Gavin. "You ever miss being out in the trenches? I mean, you were into big stuff, huh?"

Gavin looked at Terry, thoughtful.

"Some pretty high profile cases at times, but that made me high profile also. That puts a lot of responsibility on an officer. I was successful in putting many criminals away and that made a difference to a lot of people. Do I miss it? Not really. But I know what you're saying to yourself: here's Gavin, retired, yet you find me out in a marijuana field with a gun and no authority."

"Well, I might be saying that in a sense, but that'd be sorta like a man in a glass house throwing stones. I'm a small town cop dabbling in something that gets bigger each time I look at it. Sheriff Burris knows what's up, and I'll call him when we get somewhere with this, but I'm not going to bother him every whipstitch. That would make me look like a doofus."

"Why are you even involving yourself? It's really out of your jurisdiction."

Terry told him of the conversation with Sheriff Burris.

He looked to Gavin for a long ten seconds. "I don't mind this job for the most part, but it really is hard to have a sense of purpose or even meaning when you deal mostly with California stops and dogs dumping in neighbor's lawns."

Both laughed.

"Yes, I remember the garbage I dealt with when I first started with the Feds. All the cases nobody wanted."

"Well, Gavin – if it's ok I call you that?" Gavin nodded. "At least you had the carrot of something bigger waving out there. Here in Winston Corner there's not, like, some exciting option I can anticipate. I mean, it's great we don't have major issues here. Don't get me wrong. People are safe and can even leave their doors unlocked. But, there's something in me that wants to have a challenge. A case that will establish my reputation, perhaps? Something that will leave the town looking at me with respect and not just as some long-haired flunky that's a throwback to Woodstock which, by the way, I was not part of."

"Respect."

"Yes, Gavin. I want respect. I want people to look at me and be proud to have me here, to somehow feel safer and sleep better at night knowing I'm here. Not just having some officer here, but having me, Officer Jones, on duty. As it is, I'm just someone to get mad at. I do a lot around here, and I am willing to do more, if I am given the chance. I'm taking night classes on law enforcement. I want to grow in this profession and I want others to notice. For example, Cuthbert's got that truck of his. It breaks all the laws of noise and all. But you and I know that it doesn't matter what I say or how many tickets I write him or whatever, that old man is not going to change nor is he going to put a muffler on. And people tell me, 'You can't get him to do anything, can you, Jones?' I want them to look at old Cuthbert and say, 'Chief Jones chooses not to worry about that, but he's got good reasons. After all, he knows what he's doing.'"

Gavin looked long at Terry. In his own eyes he could see himself years ago – minus the hair – seeking to make his reputation in the Fed ranks.

"Yes, I get where you're coming from. I had a lot of struggles when I started, before the 'powers that be' freed me from the mundane and gave me more challenging cases. I guess I had my Cuthberts, too. And, really, Cuthbert's muffler is an absolute nothing in the scheme of things. In fact, if you forced him to get a muffler, half or more of the town will be all over your case for that, because Cuthbert is the weekend timekeeper here and people need him to get their clocks set right." They laughed. "Sort of danged if you do and danged if you don't."

Terry nodded.

"So I want to break this case. I want to have a major success in my file."

"You want to move into another agency or a bigger one? Is that part of it?"

"No. Not really. I mean, I'm not thinking of that. I sort of like the small town atmosphere. I'm a peaceful man at heart, and I have simple goals. I guess I'd like to settle down, put down some deep roots. But a man can't set deep roots when he's not respected. My dad always told me to keep the name clean. He was able to open doors of opportunity for people by virtue of his name. I find that compelling. But there is this natural progression of life and career, where you move up in the ranks in many professions. I'm sort of behind the eight-ball in some ways, and I guess in the past couple years I have come to see the light and want to be a significant part of my world and put back into it."

"I understand."

"Why did you move here, Gavin?"

"I always promised Jean we'd get away from the big metropolitan areas when I retired. Her grandparents lived here and she always enjoyed coming here, so we came. Has it been easy? No, believe you me. But it is what it is. Jean did a lot of giving over the years. So, it's Jean's turn and I'm following her."

"Then along comes this situation and you are struggling with the boredom and feelings of uselessness in retirement and this gives you a purpose?"

"In a sense." Gavin looked long at Terry. Terry remained silent, waiting. "Terry, I guess there is something I'm looking for, too. There is a need in me to feel productive. If I am to invest in this town, I also need to feel like there's a reason to be here. I know I'm here for my wife, but I have to face it that I have – hopefully – many more years and this is going to be my home. Besides - and I'm being frank here - I was very successful at analyzing evidence. I guess I'm bragging somewhat, but I was - am - good at putting together a case. There was one I lost. A man name of Harrison Tyler. Big drug case. He came up to me in the hallway after court and belittled me to my face. Never left me. Even after hundreds of successful cases it is the one loss that haunts me. So I guess that's sorta why I started into this. For me…purely for me."

Terry nodded.

"I guess we both seek the same thing."

"Yes." Gavin looked at Terry and then spoke softly. "Terry, if we are going to work on this, then we need to keep each other privy to what is up. You tell me what you find, and I will tell you. Ok?"

"Ok."

"And the first thing I need to tell you is something that I cannot substantiate with any proof right now, but it is in my gut. I had a visit a few weeks ago from an old colleague. There is a new development here, centering mostly around Indy as a base, but there is a possibility that this Harrison Tyler I mentioned is actually running some sort of operation out here – expanding. It's not proven, but it's my gut feeling that what we have here is somehow connected. Harrison Tyler is vicious. He is cruel. If he is involved, it's both serious and dangerous – beyond what you might realize. No offense meant, Terry, but this is definitely something you do not want to tackle on your own."

Terry looked at Gavin. He leaned forward on his desk.

"Gavin, my goal is to solve the crime. I will not allow my pride to jeopardize the case or my life. We're in this together. I respect your experience and your skills."

"And I respect the officer you are and all that you are becoming."

89

Birdhouse was busier than he liked! Online orders were booming and he was working long hours. Still, he enjoyed the money. PayPal put it right into his account and it was sort of like magic money. After all, he was going to make birdhouses anyway – maybe not so many – and they would go into his shed for the next show or onto his garage or somebody would come by looking for one. Now, he just kept making them.

He had the Kovacs boy helping him for a while. When he'd seen the dad whooping on him, he understood. For two weeks, Seth helped him in the shop and, though it was grudging at first, Seth was filled with pride after he finished his first complete birdhouse. In fact, Seth made a point of stopping every Saturday to help for a couple hours. It was a Godsend what with all the orders.

Today he was scouring some of the secondhand stores in Beedersville in search of ideas and different objects to turn into unique bird dwellings. In one store he picked up a set of Farberware pans and a hollow porch pillar. He'd never made a birdhouse out of pans, but it was worth a try at five dollars for the whole set. The pillar he would cut down into eight 10" sections and turn them sideways, put in a hole and maybe even use a pan lid for a roof. With the pans, he'd fit the pan opening with a wood block with hole and peg. It seemed most anything could be used for a birdhouse. Most of his expense was in hinges. Every blue moon he found a bunch of the right-sized hinges in a bin somewhere. It always paid to look at the junk shops carefully, as a one-dollar piece of junk might have five-dollars worth of hinges on it. He really scored some good deals in clearance sales. It took at least two hinges to make a birdhouse, depending on the cleanout style he wanted.

He stopped today at a north-end convenience store to get a Diet Dr. Pepper, standing frustrated and working not to show it while a man bought lottery tickets. It was like the man had decided he was going to spend fifty dollars and waited till he got to the counter before even thinking of his choices. Birdhouse never bought lottery tickets, feeling that not buying them had not significantly reduced his odds of winning. Besides, he thought, some of these people who are buying so many have been duped into believing they have some sort of enormous odds of winning. He knew lottery tickets were a poor financial decision and that the money best be spent to invest or pay bills or, in the case of this man, to buy a real pair of pants and not go around wearing these all frayed and filthy pajama pants with his rear hanging out.

Then, he glanced to the side and spotted it. An O'Henry candy bar! Why, my goodness, he had not had one of those since he was a kid. He used to love them. Finally the man made his purchase and shuffled out. Birdhouse placed his drink on the counter and grabbed a couple O'Henry bars.

"You like those O'Henry bars, mister?" It was the clerk.

"Used to as a kid. Haven't had one for all these years. Haven't seen one in forever."

"Only one other fella buys those. Comes in every Thursday at the stroke of noon and buys fifteen of them. Like clockwork! Never seen the likes of it. Don't buy anything but that handful of O'Henry bars and a Powerball ticket. He's the only reason we keep that candy bar here. Guaranteed income, the boss says."

"Well, I hope my taking some doesn't mess up his count!"

"Oh, we got another box in the back." He laughed.

Driving down the road a few minutes later, Birdhouse pulled out one of the candy bars and bit off a piece.

"Wow! That's good!" Cramming the rest in, he dropped the empty wrapper on his seat. The other bar he put in his shirt pocket.

90

As Birdhouse drove into Winston Corner, he saw Terry's car, along with another, at the Cop Shop. He needed to tell Terry to come pick up his birdhouse. After all, it was almost a requirement of residency to have a local-made birdhouse somewhere on your property. It'd been a week since he told Terry it was ready.

Slipping in between the cars, he strode in the door, finding Terry sitting across from Mr. Crockett. Interesting. Nodding to Crockett, he looked down at Terry.

"What can I do you for, Birdhouse?"

"Well, I got that birdhouse sitting taking up space. Wondering when you might pick it up?"

"Oh, blast it! I plum forgot. You going to be home this afternoon?"

"Yep, got orders to fill."

"How much I owe you?"

"Well, the double decker runs twenty dollars."

Terry reached for his wallet, extracting a twenty. He handed it to Birdhouse.

"Here you go. I'll stop by in a bit."

"Thanks."

"Been out and about today?"

"Yup. Working the junk shops on the north end."

Reaching into his shirt pocket, he brought out the O'Henry, unwrapped it and took a bite. Looking down at Terry and Crockett, he saw them staring at his mouth and then to his hand and the wrapper crinkling between his fingers.

"What?"

Crockett looked to Terry and raised an eyebrow. Terry frowned and looked at Birdhouse.

"You eat a lot of those?"

"No, and yes I know candy bars ain't good for me. Don't give me any lectures. I haven't had one of these for years. I tell you, though, it's good."

"Where'd you get it?"

"What? Are you writing a book about candy bars?"

"Maybe."

"Well, leave out that chapter."

"You said you haven't had one in years?"

"That's exactly what I said. What is so all blasted important about my O'Henry candy bar?" He looked at Crockett. "You and your wife haven't got one of my birdhouses yet."

"I'll order a double-decker," he reached to his wallet, "and pay for it right now, if you'll tell us where you got that candy bar." He held a twenty.

Birdhouse grabbed it.

"Got a few to choose from. Come by with Terry here and you can pick one out."

He turned to leave.

"Birdhouse?"

Birdhouse turned and saw the questioning look.

"North end of Beedersville, Waverly Street, that little convenience store. But you better hurry if you want one. They told me a fella comes in at the stroke of noon every Thursday and about cleans them out."

Terry and Gavin looked at each other as Birdhouse marched out.

"Sometimes the breaks come out of the blue, don't they, Gavin?"

"Yes, they do. I guess we better go get our birdhouses."

91

Jake coiled the hose as they prepared to leave the field. This field was farther from the creek than Cuthbert's, and the hose had to snake through some brambles. Bub always protested when Jake handed him the hose to walk it to the creek, but then tucked his head and did as he was told.

Bub was not stupid, Jake knew. In fact, he was smarter than others realized. Simple in ways, but more in the sense that he didn't care. Bub had no real ambitions and was content not to make any extra effort in thinking things through. He chose not to argue and quietly allowed Jake to be in charge. So, if Jake told him to take the hose through the brambles, well, it wasn't that terrible after all. Over time, there was actually a path through the thorny stems and it didn't make any difference. It all paid the same and Bub was always happy to get his envelope.

Tonight they had checked the patch carefully, using the lights a couple extra times. There was the sign of some sort of animal coming through the patch and partly knocking over some of the plants. A search of the ground showed deer prints. Jake kept the light flicker brief and did not tell Bub what else he found.

His eyes widened warily and he squinted into the darkness.

92

Cooter was enjoying his newfound Apache heritage, and found himself out early on Saturday morning, exploring and sneaking amidst cornfields and woods. The temperature was mild, so he wore only his breechcloth and leggings. His one modern concession was the rustic pouch on his belt holding his cell phone in a beaded hard case. Though he'd seen a few people craning their necks in his direction on other forays, he wasn't fully aware that he'd been positively identified and rumors were spreading about his activity.

This time he was out beyond Cuthbert's and cutting across a drainage ditch in Hobart Smith's cornfield when he remembered the old Anderson place. It sat back in the trees of a small, but overgrown woods. Abandoned for at least thirty years, it was easy to drive by the two-rut track and not even notice, but Cooter thought back and realized he'd not heard mention of it for as long as he could remember. Old Robert Anderson had died of cancer all those years ago and his son, who lived someplace out West, cash rented the place to three or four area farmers and nobody even used the remains of the home place because it sat too far off the road.

Wonder what the old place is like after all these years? Cooter mused.

Cutting between fields, he found himself turning more somber as he got closer to the remote farmstead. Reaching the woods, he remembered exploring these woods as a teen hunting squirrels. The woods were overgrown now with wild grape and almost impenetrable.

Skirting the edge of the trees and cutting through the corner of a cornfield, he found himself staring at another marijuana field. It was a good-size plot, and he stood still, just observing as he felt his ancestors would have done.

"This is a long ways out." He spoke aloud and immediately sensed the way his voice would carry in this quiet place. He put a hand to his mouth and looked around. Walking around the edge of the trees, he went only twenty yards further before he saw the old rutted track to the Anderson place. He knelt and felt the grass.

The grass was dewy now, but it was obvious there had been a vehicle here within a day or so.

Who would be out here?

Reaching to his belt, his fingers grasped at the handle of his tomahawk, feeling an ancestral comfort with a weapon in this situation. Then, crouching, he slowly headed into the lane as it curved through the woods.

Mosquitos were finding him and Cooter cursed himself for not having a shirt on. Pretty soon he was doing a constant slap walk. No matter what he tried, he couldn't reach all of his back and tried shrugging and twisting.

It took him ten minutes to wind his way slowly through, noting how someone had pushed and hauled fallen trees out of the ruts. Whoever it was had not used power equipment, probably to not attract attention.

The old house stood as a lonely, overgrown sentinel in the midst of what was once a clearing but now was but a broken remnant of its former self. Wild grape and other ivy grew in and out of windows and covered the mostly collapsed porch. Anybody who felt that humanity had destroyed nature needed but to see the effects of no humanity for thirty years to realize Mother Nature always won in the end.

It was eerie, scary, and Cooter had to remind himself of the courage in his Apache bloodline as he followed the vague tracks beyond the house. There, in a small cleared area, was a place where multiple vehicles had parked. The grass was worn down and a path cut through to the former kitchen area, where a tarp covered the roof.

Cooter looked carefully around and, seeing nobody, crept up the steps and to the door, which swung loosely on ancient hinges. The door was unlatched and held by what appeared to be a dog chain clip. Carefully, Cooter undid the clip and eased the door slowly open.

93

Out on a walk with Kim, Terry was on a long monologue on evidence collection, for which he'd just taken a test. He felt his department phone vibrate and heard it chirp at the same time.

"This is Officer Jones."

"Terry? It's Cooter."

"What's up, Cooter?" He could hear something in the man's voice and his brow furrowed. He glanced at Kim. They kept walking.

"I found something you need to know about."

"What's that?"

"Well, I'm out at the old Anderson place – you know where that is?"

"Heard about it one time. Fact is, I'm actually just about a mile from there, I think. Never been there."

"Well, I found another field of pot plants near here and tire tracks, so I decided to come over to this place. Hadn't been here since I was a kid. Found something else inside the house."

"What is it?"

"Boxes. Lots of them. Like with drug names and such on them. Looks like Red is setting up shop out here."

Terry stopped walking and turned to Kim and spoke into the phone.

"Cooter, might be a pharmaceutical stash, probably fake drugs. I want you to listen to me carefully. I'm away from my car and it will take me about," he glanced at his watch, "twenty minutes to get there. I want you to get out of the house in case someone shows up. These are not the kind of people you want to mess with. Hang way back somewhere till you see my car.

Under no circumstances are you to let yourself be seen. Understand?"

"Ok."

"And Cooter?"

"Yes?"

"Are you, uh, dressed decent?"

"What do you mean?"

"Well, you know…"

94

Terry slipped the car into the old track he thought was the Anderson place. He'd never actually driven here. Beside him sat Kim. It was against his better judgment, but she had insisted on riding along. On the way, he gave her the lecture of staying in the car and such. Kim listened and nodded.

He slowed as he drove into the long, wooded lane, and seeing that fallen trees had been removed and noting the tire indentations. The grass grew long in the road, which would hide the tracks from all but truly observant eyes. Before he drove up to the house, barely discernable in the trees, he paused to look around.

A knock on the window put his heart in his throat and his hand to his Glock. Kim jumped and let out a short, chirpy scream.

It was Cooter. She watched as the man, half-dressed, slapped a couple mosquitos, then a deerfly.

Terry powered the window down.

"Doggone, Cooter. Like to scared the life out of me."

"Ain't nobody showed up. Them boxes are around the other side of the house. I'll show you." He started to jog ahead of the car and Terry followed, driving slowly.

Kim stared at Cooter.

"I heard rumors about the Apache stuff, but this is the first time I've seen it."

"Me, too."

Ahead of them, Cooter swatted again, twisting and turning like someone having a seizure. Kim shook her head.

"I guess those outfits were ok on the Great Plains, but the

bugs here are all over him."

Pulling up beside the house, Terry reminded Kim to stay in the car. He followed Cooter to the porch, noting the condition of the house, the old tattered tarp on the roof, the overgrown woods, but mostly the isolation. Anything could go on here and nobody would ever know. If it weren't for Cooter's mean-derings in the countryside in pursuit of his elusive heritage, anything happening here could go on for years.

Terry saw there was no clear way out other than the way they came in, meaning whoever was using this place preferred it that way. He loosed his pistol.

Cooter spoke into the strange silence, sounding odd. It was as if the ancient trees and overgrown woods and dank, moss-covered porch stifled all sound.

"Feels better having you here, Terry. Kind of eerie when I was here by myself."

Cooter led the way in and Terry stood in awe at the boxes stacked throughout the room. He wandered back and forth.

"I count fifty-three various cartons and boxes. Cooter, you really nailed it here."

Cooter stood tall with pride, then slapped another mosquito.

"They're gonna bite you to pieces. I got another t-shirt in the car. You better put it on."

"I appreciate it. I didn't plan on being in these old woods. The bugs are thicker than the buffalo used to be on the plains."

Walking to the car, Cooter close behind making slapping noises, Terry unlocked the trunk and lifted the lid. He rum-maged in his bag and tossed a D.A.R.E. t-shirt to Cooter, who hurriedly pulled it on.

"Oh, man, that makes a difference. Thanks."

"They're still thick here, but it'll help." Terry slapped a cou-ple on his face. "I better let Kim know what's up."

Walking to the passenger window, he stopped, wide-eyed.

Kim was gone!

95

"Kim?" he hissed into the heavy silence.

Cooter pointed at the ground.

"She went that way. See? Her steps have scuffed the grass and it's laying down in spots."

Terry pulled his gun as he followed the scuffmarks. Rounding a bush, he found the entrance to a trail.

"Kim?"

From a short ways ahead came a response.

"Over here."

They found her a few yards up the trail. She slapped a deerfly. Terry replaced his Glock.

"Come see what's around this bend," Kim said.

It was a small clearing. Terry noted a plastic table was set up with all the accessories.

Meth.

"Ok, so the plot thickens." Then, looking to Kim. "You scared me. I didn't hear you get out of the car."

Terry pulled out his phone and snapped some pictures of the mess. Cooter slapped at two mosquitos over his left eye. Then he stiffened.

Kim saw the movement.

"What is it?

Cooter crouched and waved the others down.

"I hear a motor."

They crouched and Terry crept back down the trail a ways, then called back.

"It's ok. Come on back."

The Jeep Rubicon came around the bend. Both Cooter and Kim recognized Crockett's vehicle. Cooter looked to Terry.

"I called him, Cooter."

96

Terry made a quick video of the area while Gavin looked around.

"This is big time, Terry. You've hit the jackpot. These are fake pharmaceuticals. I'm sure of it. It's time to contact Sheriff Burris. He'll need to get a sample and make a decision on this. It's likely meth from Mexico or maybe even Fentanyl."

Terry nodded to Gavin, then looked at Cooter. The man looked like a throwback from the Indians in a John Wayne movie.

"Cooter? You need to understand the seriousness of this situation. These men will kill. Stay away."

"Yes, sir."

"Kim? Understand?"

"Okay."

Gavin glanced around again.

"Terry, we need to leave here. Make sure we drive in the existing tracks. We don't want a double set. After we get back to town, you and I will meet at your office."

Terry nodded.

97

"Something in my gut is telling me this is all connected, Brian."

He could hear Brian's wheels turning in the pause. Even though his friend was on speakerphone, they knew each other well. Terry leaned back, listening.

"Your gut feeling has been mostly accurate in the past, Gavin. Wow, this would mean that Tyler is in deep. Pharmaceuticals, too? With the laws on pot changing so much and so unpredictable, he's going to grow his business down into the trenches with the lacing. He'll grow and mix in the rural areas, then take the product to the cities, to the condensed customer base. The pharms we won't know the full story on until we get a sample. I'll arrange for the sheriff to join you to get it – more official for the books. It might indicate a major shift in his base of operations. He's been away from Philadelphia a lot. Indy. That's interesting. I wonder if he's going to move his operation lock, stock and barrel. The more I think about it, the more convinced I am."

"Terry already contacted the Sheriff. They're heading out in the morning to get a sample."

"Excellent."

"Got a spare bedroom at the house, Brian." He paused. "But it would be more discrete staying a couple exits away. Franklin. We could meet at the McDonald's at the exit in between."

"I'd love to stay with you and Jean, but you're right. Small town, not much get's missed and who knows where the talk will go. But let's make a point of having dinner when we can in Indy."

"Okay. Let me know when you get here and want to meet." He looked to Terry. "Got a good man here, Brian. Terry has the makings of a top-notch officer."

"Terry? Can you hear me well?"

"I can, Brian."

"Thanks for what you're doing. I know this is a stretch in your responsibility. I hope there's a time when we can talk a bit more."

"Look forward to it."

98

Hubert stood in the hospital with Eula Mae. Bobby was close by his side. The first night Eula Mae came straight to the hospital, and they'd taken Bobby to his house to get some clothes and he did so in complete silence, looking lost. They took him to their home for the next two nights, spending the days at Cora's bedside. Cora awoke the second day and Bobby stayed until visiting hours were over, lying in the bed snuggled with his mom.

Red had been by every chance he could, and expressed appreciation that Hubert and Eula Mae were keeping steady watch. Others from town had been by or kept informed at Schmeisser's.

Late that evening, after Bobby was asleep, Eula Mae started to bake blonde brownies. Hubert wandered in from his chair and refilled his cup. Loitering a mite long, Eula Mae knew something was on his mind. Besides, he had been sitting and staring at the skateboard magazine without turning pages for at least an hour. She heard him set his cup down and lean against the counter.

"Shame about Cora."

Eula Mae nodded and measured flour.

"Yes, it is."

"Don't know what they'll do." He reached and gave his cup a half turn on the counter with one finger. "Don't hardly have anything and then she'll be too worn out to fix supper or do the wash or anything."

"What do you think needs to be done, Hubert?" She did, indeed have an idea where this was heading, but she wanted him to speak his heart. Continuing to stir, she waited.

"Not sure."

"No idea?"

"Well, Eula Mae, they…uh…need a place to stay where she can get good food and rest. And she'll need to be able to get to the doctor and Bobby will have to get to school. A bunch of stuff." While he spoke he stared off at some unknown spot on the kitchen wall.

"I see." She stirred the batter again and poured it into the pan. "Do you have an idea?" She slipped the pan into the oven. If Hubert had looked, he would have seen her moist eyes.

Hubert turned and looked to his wife of so many years. His eyes also showed moisture. She looked up and saw his eyes. He never cried. A tear ran down her cheek.

"What do you think of them moving here for a bit?" He choked.

She did not hesitate.

"I think that's what we need to do."

They held each other a long time.

99

It had taken a bit of explanation and questioning by the medical staff in addition to Red's vouching for them, but the staff now knew Bobby's unique situation and accepted Hubert and Eula Mae as temporary caregivers. Such situations were ethically difficult and took judgment calls in today's litigious society, but exceptions had to be made at times.

Leukemia. When the doctor said the word, Hubert couldn't speak right away. They were in the hallway. Finally, he asked, "What are the treatments?"

"Well, Mr. Griffin, this is Chronic Myeloid Leukemia. It is difficult, but..." He paused and glanced at Bobby. "But not impossible. We'll have to do further testing on various issues. Research indicates bone marrow transplants do well in many cases."

Hubert paused. Bobby reached and grasped Eula Mae's hand.

"So what do we do now, Doc?"

"Well, we've already told Mrs. Hernly, and she knows some decisions will need to be made. Right now, we will begin medications to build her strength. She's got a strong spirit, and that will help her. Depending on tests, treatment will proceed from there. Unfortunately, it's sort of a waiting game until the tests are all in."

Eula Mae spoke up.

"Will she have to stay here the whole time?"

"She might be strong enough to go home in a few days, Mrs. Griffin. There may be a wait until a marrow match can be made. She'll need lots of care."

Bobby cried and spoke feebly.

"Who's going to take care of us?"

Hubert choked. Eula Mae took charge. Putting her arm around Bobby, she looked him in the eyes.

"You'll be moving in with us. We'll take care of you and your mom."

Bobby held Eula Mae's hand even tighter.

100

Sheriff Burris accompanied Terry and Gavin through the woods to the old house late in the morning, after the dew dried. Nobody was around, but there was evidence of activity. Extra tracks now scarred the area.

Sheriff Burris frowned, whispering as they started for the door.

"We may be too late. This many tracks is not good."

Burris pulled his Glock as he eased the door. Terry and Gavin held their pistols also.

They stood for a moment and stared.

101

A week after she was hospitalized, Cora was strong enough to go home or, in this case, to Griffin's.

When Eula Mae and Hubert held hands at the hospital and told her they wanted her to move in with them, she had burst into tears, which, in turn, caused Eula Mae to reach for her Kleenex and Hubert to rub his nose with his sleeve. Cora looked at them both and whispered.

"I didn't know what to do. God told me to not worry. You're an answer to my prayers."

Hubert, uncomfortable with emotion, looked at Bobby and smiled.

"I been called a lot of things, like grumpy and such, but I've never been called an answer to prayer."

Bobby wiped his eyes and grinned.

102

A package from Amazon. From the shape and size, it was clearly a book. Lisa set it on the counter, pursing her lips.

The night before, wondering what Cooter'd been up to after dinner, she went out quietly and peered into the shop window. Her husband was sitting on a stool sewing on the teepee. With rawhide strips. He was dressed in his full Indian regalia.

Preparing a nice dinner, she pondered Harvey's words. It was true, Cooter never hurt her, and he went to work every morning, rarely calling in sick.

So what if he acted crazy sometimes.

In the midst of rolling chicken in flour, Lisa heard Cooter's truck round the corner of the house. A minute later she heard the front door open and Cooter came in. Strolling over, he kissed her and set his lunchbox on the counter. Opening it, he put the Tupperware by the sink and the Igloo block back in the freezer. He started to ask about her day, but stopped in mid sentence as his eyes caught the package on the counter.

He reached for it, then eagerly grabbed the tear strip and pulled. His eyes glowed when he pulled the book out. Glancing over, she saw the title and winced. *Once They Moved Like the Wind: Cochise, Geronimo and the Apache Wars* by David Roberts.

It'll be a quiet evening, she realized.

103

"It's neat that you live way out here."

Eula Mae grinned.

"It's kind of different from right in town, huh, Bobby?"

"There's so much space!"

They lived right at the edge of town, their property bounding Winston Corner and surrounded by trees. They'd bought the house forty years ago. Built in 1906 and almost falling apart at that time, they loved – and spent – to bring it back to life. Replacing first the roof, then plumbing, electrical, ductwork and a host of other things, they refused to paint over old woodwork, wanting to keep the charm. Remodeling delighted them but, after all these years, some of those remodels were ready for remodeling again. Hubert just didn't look at it the same, though. Back then he had a sort of excitement and felt in a bit of a rush to ready the house for kids. After about ten years and the realization there would be no children, the house took on a different perspective and slowly it became the home of two people without the Crayola drawings, without toys, without little toothbrushes and, in fact, over the years there had been very few little feet through the doors. All their nieces and nephews lived in different states and Hubert's gruffness seemed to increase without youth in residence. Visitors were generally limited to their few friends dropping by or someone stopping to borrow a tool or get Hubert's help on a project. Until retirement, his life focused only on work and Eula Mae, who remained the light of his life, despite his grumpy nature. Perhaps it was only she who understood the deepening of Hubert's moods as childlessness gripped their lives. Still, he had married

Eula Mae, not the concept of children, and he held to his commitment.

They had a considerable nest egg, with Hubert working much overtime and them both being stashers. Hubert's sock drawer could have kept a small bank afloat. Eula Mae knew it was there, but knew they also were well set at the bank and in investments. She knew it gave Hubert comfort to have cash, so she let him be. In his own mind, he thought she knew nothing of his stash – but she did.

The house did have character, thanks to Eula Mae. She delighted in a tidy kitchen, up-to-date with the tools of her hobby. Prominent were her red KitchenAid mixer and the collection of Pyrex mixing bowls and a crock filled with spatulas and wooden spoons and other tools. Last spring Hubert surprised her with a set of Pioneer Woman acacia and olive wood spoons. He'd smiled as she put them lovingly in her crock, but she couldn't part with the old reliable spoons, some with handles warped by her own mother's loving hands. When Hubert was around to see, she used the newer spoons. When he was not, she used the old reliable ones she loved.

Hubert's corner of the house was in the living room, where his chair area was piled with books to read and pens and a coaster and miscellaneous Post-it notes and such. There was always a cup on the coaster. He spent hours reading and researching various areas of interest. A skateboarding magazine now rested atop one stack.

104

"This is a gold mine, Terry. This is big."

Wall to wall boxes. All wrapped in plastic.

"Is this bigger than usual, Sheriff?"

"Not like they might find in a big city, but it's incredibly big for out here in the middle of nowhere. What I don't understand is why it is left unguarded."

Gavin pondered.

"Confidence. This old abandoned and overgrown place sits out here and they know nobody comes around. The less activity, the less chance of being noticed."

Terry nodded.

"They come at night. Nobody to see anything out here. Use covered headlights, let the dew fall over tracks and it all stays a secret."

Sheriff Burris smiled.

"Good, Terry. You're a quick learner. Ok, let's get some samples. Down at the bottom and the backs."

105

Hubert and Bobby had worked hard the last few days to clean out the rooms. One was fairly clean, being the official guest room. It even had its own bath. It was never used and held piles of material and winter coats and such. It was the second room that made Bobby scratch his head. When they first opened the door, a solid wall of boxes confronted them, with a slight passage to the left side leading into the rest of the room. Bobby whistled.

"Wow! Talk about lots of stuff. Where're we gonna put this?"

"Good question. Have to take it out to the shop."

"Is there really a room here, Mr. Griffin?" Bobby chuckled.

Hubert grinned.

"Somewhere behind all this is a bed and everything."

Eula Mae came by with an armload of towels for the other bath, pausing briefly to look over their shoulders.

"Looks like a Goodwill trip to me."

"Eula Mae, these are my books!" Hubert was indignant.

Eula Mae looked to Bobby and winked.

"Bobby, there are books in there that are dead from lack of air. All but petrified, they are. There's a lot of people might love to get their mitts on them and bring them back to life, but Hubert just can't part with the relics of his past."

Hubert glared as his wife continued her task. Earlier she had given the bath a thorough going over, finding spiders in every corner. It was amazing how a clean but unused bathroom could get so dirty.

Bobby just stared at the boxes.

Finally, Hubert reached for the first box.

"Well, it's not going to clean itself. But I don't know if I can lift these things."

By the time they got the third box to the shop, Hubert had to stop and rest against the truck parked by the house. Bobby said nothing, overwhelmed by the task ahead. Hubert looked from the house to the shop to the house and to the shop and then rested his eyes on the truck. Rubbing his jaw, he looked to Bobby. Then, backing up, he reached and pulled down the tailgate.

"I hear Goodwill calling."

Bobby grinned.

Two full loads to Goodwill in Beedersville and Bobby almost sensed hatred on the part of the Goodwill employee at the drop-off door. Almost every box was books and even with the hand truck the employee looked about at wits end. She was just carting in the last box of their first drive-by when she watched them drive up again. The first glance was to her watch.

Driving out, they turned the wrong way and Bobby threw a questioning glance. Hubert, sensing the glance, looked straight ahead.

"Want to check on something."

A few minutes later, Hubert began looking at his dash and tapping. He looked worried.

"What the matter, Mr. Griffin?"

"Something wrong with the truck."

He pulled into the Dairy Queen parking lot.

"Guess it just needs a rest." He turned and winked at Bobby. "Might as well get ice cream while we wait for old 'Betsy' to rest."

"You call your truck 'Betsy'?" Bobby stared at him.

"That or 'Nellie Belle'."

Bobby grinned and chuckled.

"That's silly!"

"It's something my dad did and I've just carried it on. In fact, he used the same names."

"Really."

"Yep, they're good names. Stood the test of time."

"A truck oughta be a boys name."

"Like what?" Hubert turned to look at Bobby.

"I dunno…'Fred'?"

Hubert adjusted his hat.

"It might take me a spell, but…ok. 'Fred,' she is."

"Fred is a he."

"Oh, right. This may take me a bit to get used to. Have mercy on me?"

"Deal!" Bobby reached his hand out to shake.

They did an exaggerated shake and drop-pulled apart.

Both grinned as they exited and headed towards the order window.

106

Bart Pederson trundled in, slapping his hat on the rack. Pratt and Dinky simultaneously looked to their watches. Bart nodded.

"I'm a little behind."

Kim, walking by, glanced down at his posterior.

"More like a big behind!"

Dinky guffawed.

"Hey, Pratt, she beat you to the punch!"

"She's on the ball this morning."

Kim smiled to herself. She was in a very good mood this morning. She and Terry spent three hours alternately sitting and walking in the park the evening before. It was supposed to be just a few minutes, but the conversation flowed so smoothly and it was dusk before they both suddenly realized the time. What she really liked was his openness, and they even covered the all-important-early-on-dating question: he told her he was not even going to try to kiss her. He told her he was not looking for a casual encounter. True to his words, when they got back to her house, he reached out and took her hand to sort of awkwardly shake, and spoke rather shyly.

"I really enjoyed talking, Kim."

"Me, too, Terry."

Both enjoyed saying the others' name. Terry held her hand for a couple seconds extra.

"Well, maybe we could, like, go to a movie this weekend?"

"I'd like that."

Terry had grinned. It warmed her heart to see a man have joy at the thought of seeing her. And talking. Just talking.

And that was that. He'd left, as he said, without trying anything. That meant more to her than he could ever imagine.

Reading before bed that evening, Kim kept seeing Terry's face, his smile and the way his eyes sparkled when she shared something funny and then how they changed to caring when she was serious. He was quite deep, with dreams and responding best to words of kindness and encouragement. It was so easy to talk to him.

"Hey, Kim?" Jarred to reality, she looked around to see the Liar's Table grinning.

"What?"

"You just dumped a load of coffee grounds in the water pitcher!"

Sure enough, daydreaming about Terry, she'd put a filter and grounds in the top of the water pitcher!

Greg looked over from the kitchen.

"You ok, Kim?"

"Yes, I'm ok. I guess I was daydreaming." Actually, she was red-faced.

"Well, coffee ain't cheap. Try not to waste too much."

Pratt found it proper to chime in.

"I bet I know what was on your mind."

"Ok, Pratt, oh great mind-reader. What was it?"

"Well, last night I was coming home from the Quick Stop and I swear I seen you walking with Terry. You all a'dating now?"

Greg was staring at her along with everybody else.

"No, Mr. Nosey! We are not dating."

"Well, just now you were off somewhere in la-la land. At your age, that usually means something."

Carrying a pot of coffee over to the table, Kim put a slight tilt of the pot over Pratt's lap

"Let it go, Pratt." Her face was still red.

Raising his hands in surrender, Pratt conceded. Though he didn't think she would really do it, there was a touch of doubt. When someone is poised over your lap with a hot pot of coffee, unconditional surrender is always the best option.

"Topic closed – I promise, Kim."

She gestured with the pot.

"Better be. Or I'll change the topic."

Bart laughed aloud and then stepped in to help his friend.

"I think we need a joke, Dinky."

Dinky rubbed his jaw.

"I was up to Beedersville at the store, and the cashier was having problems. The register ran out of paper, the scanner malfunctioned, and finally the cashier spilled a handful of coins. When she totaled my order, it came to exactly twenty-two dollars. Trying to soothe her nerves, I said, 'That's a nice round figure.' She was still frazzled, and glared at me and said, 'You're no bean pole yourself.'"

Laughter filled the room.

Pratt smiled, the pressure off. Looking over Bart's shoulder to Kim, he saw she was not laughing. She appeared to be day-dreaming again.

Leaning on the serving counter, she was, indeed, daydreaming. Kim found herself wondering: was she dating Terry?

107

Cuthbert stomped in again. It was as if he had radar and knew that Terry just finished washing the floor. Not hog stuff this time, but mud clumps mixed with corn and straw skittered across the floor. And, of course, though busy all morning, the man had come in during that very short stretch when Terry was leaned back in his chair, thinking of the pot field.

"Got the crime solved, lazy boy?"

"Working on it, Cuthbert."

"I can see that! Well, I can see why people want a tax cut. It's quite obvious they all know you ain't worth what you're paid and so we don't need as much money in the till. And we ain't gonna find anybody with any REAL talent to work in this podunk town."

"Cuthbert, you are a real breath of kindness around here."

"Well, you sit here doing absolutely nothing, and all the while somebody is growing maryjewanna in my field. In fact, they was there again last night. Seen lights."

Terry sat forward.

"They were there again?"

"Boy, ain't you a treat! I just said 'they was there again' and you didn't hear me and had to ask again? Boy, have we drug bottom on the brain issue."

Terry rolled his eyes.

"What time were they there?"

"Long about two in the morning."

"What were you doing at two in the morning?"

"Well, if'n you need to know, Mr. do-nothing, fella my age has a bit of difficulty, so I was out on the porch. Glanced up and seen lights flicker twice in the field. Stared for a while and then seen car lights snap on quarter mile away and head north."

108

"The plant is a part of American history, with hemp used in old times for the making of paper and, ironically, the printing of Bibles. Washington, Jefferson, Franklin and so many others are said to have grown it. It was a cash crop for the longest time, but in the historical accounts, what's missing is what idiot was the first one to say to himself, 'Let me chop some of this up, smoke it and see what happens.' Probably some tobacco merchant looking for another crop. But no matter how it happened, hemp is a part of our history. In WWII a lot of hemp was planted to provide for rope needs."

Sharing this information with Terry, Gavin looked over to see the town officer smiling.

"What?"

"Your career has filled your mind with a lot of interesting facts."

Gavin chuckled.

"That's only touching the surface. I could go on and on about the formation of the Food and Drug Administration around 1906 and the reasons behind it at the beginning. Concerns for the overuse of addictive painkillers is not a modern problem. Morphine, opium and cocaine are not new issues. Nor will any kind of legislation make them disappear. Washington has tried to outlaw, fight and now legalize. None of them are a solution. Look at the overflowing prisons and the rarity of effective addiction treatment programs. See how even in prison drugs are commonly available and people will take incredible chances and stash them anywhere to get access. Marijuana will remain a cash crop in many circles and maybe we'll take marijuana off the main watch list, but it's already becoming rather tame compared to all the opioids. That's why people like Harrison Tyler can get so far. He operates on a part of the radar that has been sort of tossed to the shadows in the quest to deal with opioids. Still, his syndicate is powerful, and he is still a target, but he puts money into pockets to get the focus elsewhere. There are those who wear the badge but slip the word to him for a cash retainer. He's still raking in a fortune and, with the fact he's lacing it with crystal meth and other things, he's crossed a line in my mind. He's not dealing just in some sort of hallucinogen; he's creating a poison that is killing. He doesn't care, as long as he keeps his lifestyle and power."

"Sounds like there was a bit of unfinished business when you retired."

"Eventually Tyler will do something and get nailed."

"But it would be nice to be in on it and look the jerk in the face as they slap the cuffs on?"

Gavin looked to Terry, a sort of sad look on his face. He nodded, fingering the cuffs at his belt.

"Let's head up to town. Where was that convenience store?"

109

"Terry, this is how it's played. Birdhouse said the man comes in exactly at noon, so you go in at five minutes till and buy a fountain drink. Either stand and make small talk with the cashier or look at newspapers. When the man comes out, you follow him out the door. Hold your drink in your left hand if he bought the O'Henry's. I will have the car parked out here and will snap a few pictures. You should walk - not hurry- to the car."

"Understood." Terry wore his street clothes and a Carhartt cap.

Terry got out of the car and entered the store. Taking a minute to fill his Diet Dr. Pepper, he slowly moved to the counter. The clerk looked at him and said, "That's a dollar."

"That's it?" Terry asked, as he put a dollar on the counter.

"Yep, right on the money."

"I bet you sell a lot at that price. It's like at least $1.49 anywhere else."

"We have a lot of regulars. I think some will spend the extra gas just to come here and hand me a dollar bill." He looked at the door. "Here's a regular now."

Terry glanced to the door as a man walked in.

Tall and sporting a scraggly beard, he wore an old t-shirt over a pair of frayed pajama pants. He went to the fountain machine, grabbed a giant cup and filled it with Mountain Dew.

"Can I help you with something else, mister?"

Terry looked up at the clerk.

"Uh, not sure. I'm trying to decide if I want a candy bar." Terry had noted the location of the O'Henry bars. Bottom shelf.

The scraggly man came up and paused, glancing at Terry. He spoke in a way that revealed several missing teeth with the remainder brown and beyond salvaging.

"They got good candy bars here." Terry thought either the man is on meth or he's had too many candy bars.

"I'm tired of my usual PayDay. Got a suggestion?"

"Nope." The man set his drink on the counter and then used both hands to grab a double handful of O'Henry bars. Placing them on the counter, he reached to his pocket and pulled out a $50 bill. The clerk bagged the bars and made change.

Terry thought quickly. He shifted his drink to his left hand. "Well, I'm outa here. Thanks and have a good day."

"Okay. Come back for another cheap drink."

Reaching the door, Terry paused a moment and then opened the door, stepping aside and politely gesturing for the other man to go ahead. Shrugging, the man shuffled out, turned and headed to a car parked across the street.

Inside his car, Gavin noted Terry holding the door as the man exited with a bag. He'd seen the old Monte Carlo park off to the side of the building and saw the man exit the passenger seat. As discreetly as possible, Gavin snapped a few pictures. Zooming, he snapped several more. Terry came around and got in.

"Good pictures?"

"Yep, clear enough to show this isn't the type of character you'd want a daughter bringing home to meet you."

Terry chuckled.

"That guy could keep a dentist busy for an entire career."

"Meth does that, and users just plain don't care. Brushing teeth and flossing is never on their short list."

"Gavin, it seems strange that pot is legalized in special forms for medical use. But Indiana has not done that. The Feds have sort of left it alone, leaving it to the states. What bothers me most is the quantity of pot, combined with the meth and pharmaceuticals we are seeing. This is not a small operation. And, if Harrison Tyler is involved, as you think, he is lacing it and people will die. Poison is and always will be, illegal. It's called murder and manslaughter."

110

By the time she was in the house, Cora was exhausted and they put her to bed, covered her with a quilt made by Hubert's mom and quietly shut the door.

Later, while Cora slept, they sat down to eat dinner. Bobby's eyes were bright as he surveyed the table. There were green beans, baked pork chops with bacon, mashed potatoes and rolls. Then, when Bobby thought dinner was done, Hubert wandered to the kitchen to break out the ice cream.

"Wow! This is the best meal!"

"I bet your mom is a good cook," Eula Mae said.

"She does real good, but…"

"But what?"

"Well, Mom says we don't have a whole lot of money to eat fancy. I love her macaroni and cheese. She gets the little boxes."

Eula Mae glanced at Hubert. Their eyes met for a brief moment.

"Partial to pork chops, myself. You eat them much?" Hubert asked the question casually.

"Not in a long time. Usually we have hamburger. Mom calls it 'mortgage meat.' She says we have to pay the bank for us to live in the house."

Eula Mae and Hubert said nothing for a few moments. Bobby was finishing his ice cream, making elaborate swirls and seemingly going to scrape the bottom off the bowl in his quest to get every smidgen of ice cream. Then he stopped and looked at the bowl.

"Mr. Griffin?"

"What?"

Bobby choked up. Tears shown in his eyes and his voice cracked.

"Is my mom going to get better?"

"She'll need lots of care. It's going to be hard for her."

Looking to his lap, Bobby's eyes closed and he began to shudder as the tears flowed.

Eula Mae stood and walked over to his chair, put her hand on his shoulder.

"Come here, son. We're going to say a prayer for your mom."

Bobby stood and wrapped his arms around her and sobbed into her apron. Hubert and Eula Mae were unable to talk.

111

Cooter stood in the bushes.

Curious about the strange car, he began tracking it, hiking through the brush at the roadside to see where it went. Wearing full Indian gear, he slid through the brush as he imagined Cochise would do in tracking a wagon train or a cowboy.

First, he learned it only came by every third night. Second, it must be some new electric car, almost completely silent. Third, the driver was sort of scraggly, with a wispy beard and gaunt features. He knew this because, after the first encounter, every time the car drove by his mailbox he saw the driver crane his neck down the lane. Three nights ago, the driver's face was illuminated by his phone and gave a clear picture to Cooter.

Now, as he carefully pushed his way through the tall grass and brush, he once again worked his way to Cuthbert's field. Just before he reached the other side, he saw a car in the distance flash on its brights. Cooter chuckled a bit to himself as he pictured the driver, who tended to slow a bit at his mailbox each time he passed, trying to explain to anybody about seeing an Apache Indian in the road!

Sure enough, the lights stopped a ways before the field. But he knew the car was still running. Creeping to the brush across from where the car went off the road, Cooter waited a good ten minutes before crossing the road. Bent almost double, he followed the tracks till he came to the car. At the same time he heard voices ahead, so he knew the car was empty. He came up to it and peered through the darkness.

It was one of them Smart cars. Silent as can be.

Creeping along the tall grass and weeds, he stayed on the trail of the two men ahead.

112

Terry was scrubbing the floor again when the Cop Shop door opened. Without looking up, he spoke.

"Be with you in a second." He was in the worst corner, behind the water dispenser. Besides, he thought, serve the community well to know all the duties of a police officer.

A chair creaked. He put the brush back in the bucket and sat back on his heels and looked over.

"Kim!" She looked awesome in a lavender top and skinny jeans. A lot of people wore skinny jeans hoping against hope they would work. Kim had a slender figure that didn't disappoint.

"Hey. I see you can be domestic."

He laughed.

"I'm a man of many talents." He liked the way her hair was down on her shoulders. So often it was tied in a bun for work. "Your hair looks really nice like that, Kim."

She smiled.

"Thanks."

"What brings you by?"

Here it was. But it was something she needed in her heart to say.

"I just wanted to see you." She paused, knowing his response would be telltale.

He smiled. Tenderly, she thought.

"I really wanted to see you today, too, Kim. This is really nice."

She relaxed and smiled, then asked, "You really wanted to see me?"

He talked like he had a frog in his throat.

"I did."

"Why do you like to see me?"

"Because you..."

Kim raised her eyebrows and waited.

"Because I really like being around you."

"Why?"

"Well...I like to talk to you. I feel like I can be myself. I feel like you don't judge me."

"I like being around you, too, Terry. A lot."

"That's nice to hear, Kim. Um...can we get together tomorrow afternoon?"

"How about after we close up tonight? Pizza sounds good."

Terry smiled.

"Deal! I'll pick you up."

Kim stood, smiling. She could see happiness in his eyes. It made her feel real good.

"See you then, Terry. I'll make sure I'm out promptly."

"If not, I'll wait."

Kim paused at the door.

"Terry?"

"Yes?"

"A question came up at work. There was a rumor that you and I were dating."

"Really?"

"Yes, and I guess I'm just wondering...are we dating?"

Terry smiled.

"Yes."

"Cool." Kim's step had a spring to it.

113

"Usual, Gavin?" Greg hollered from the kitchen.

Holding a thumb up, Gavin found his seat and settled in to look at the headlines.

He found himself looking forward to the times at Schmeisser's. There were more glances his way and he looked more deliberately to the Liar's Table.

Dinky, glancing at Renner and Pratt, then quickly at Gavin, started his joke. Gavin noted how seriously Dinky took the responsibility to tell a joke. He imagined the man pouring over joke books to find just the right one.

"So, this lady takes her husband to the doctor…"

The door slammed open and Bart strode in, turning his body to face all three directions and take in the group. He nodded to Gavin.

Renner berated Bart.

"Hey, look here! You're running behind and it's affecting all of us. Dinky was startin' his joke and you barged in. Now, let's just sit and hear the joke."

Feigning surprise, Bart held his hands up, then sat and folded his hands on the table and looked at Dinky, exaggerated in his anticipation.

Kim grabbed the pot, but paused as Dinky began again.

"Ok, so this lady takes her husband to the doctor. She waits outside the room while her husband is with the doc. After about ten minutes the doctor comes out with his stethoscope in his hand and has this real concerned look on his face. 'Ma'am, I just have to be honest with you. Your husband just plain don't look good.' The lady looks at the doc and says, 'I agree with you, doc, and he's not very bright either, but he's really good with the kids.'"

Groans from the table.

Gavin spluttered his coffee and laughed. Dinky looked over appreciatively, and then pointed to Gavin as he spoke.

"There's a man knows a good joke!"

Kim couldn't leave it untouched.

"Dinky, you telling this joke about yourself?"

Now there were chuckles all around. One after the other chimed in.

The door opened as Terry came in. He heard Bart comment.

"Your looks ain't got any better over the years, Dinky."

"Had to tie a bone around your neck to get the dog to play with you!"

Dinky slapped off Renner's hat at that comment.

"Is that your face or did your neck throw up?"

"Don't be so rude. There's a lady present."

"Where?"

Terry stopped. He looked perturbed. He pointed to Kim.

"She's right there pouring your coffee. She deserves your respect."

"Oops. Sorry. We didn't mean nothing."

Kim stared at Terry.

Terry walked over to slip in across from Gavin. Terry glanced at Kim and gestured with the cup, then lipped the word "please."

Carrying the pot over, she filled his cup.

"Thanks, Kim."

Kim smiled and then looked to Gavin.

"Warm-up, Mr. Crockett?"

Once again the formality.

"Yes, please, Kim. And thanks."

Gavin couldn't miss the lingering look between Terry and Kim before she went to the kitchen. Then he spoke to the deputy.

"We know of several fields. They're well cared for and spread out. We know there's meth. We also know of the pharmaceuticals. This is much bigger than small-time. I want you to pay attention to me. If I tell you to do something, I want you to do it without question. Understood?"

Terry nodded. Though part of him bristled at being directed, he knew Gavin had serious experience and it wasn't time to be territorial or bull-headed. He actually valued Gavin's willingness to take him on. It was like taking a class at an academy and having an experienced retired agent showing him the ropes. And it felt good to have a partner.

Gavin, on his part, knew that Terry was willingly allowing him to take the lead. It was a sign of maturity and wisdom in the younger man that spoke volumes for his character.

Terry leaned over to Gavin and spoke softly.

"Burris called this morning. The Pharms are actually heroin and meth crystals. Faked for transport."

"Tyler's going big in the Midwest. I can feel it."

"How do the pharmaceuticals get to market, Gavin?"

Gavin glanced around. The Liar's Table was preoccupied with some sort of carburetor issue for somebody's 1967 El Camino, incorporating napkin drawings.

He spoke softly.

"It can be various ways. And it depends on whether the drug is a fake of the labeled drug or whether it is an opioid or other narcotic that is merely being transported in the form of another drug for the sake of concealment. Word gets around as it does in all those circles that if you order a common med from this website in, say, Canada, what you'll get is the hard stuff you want. The deception is constantly morphing. Fake pharms can be sold through websites that show origination and payment in other countries, but mailed from wherever in nondescript flat rate boxes. There are some doctors on the edge who knowingly buy fake meds, then sell them in their offices with no records. Then there are the lower level dealers who sell at rotating parking lots from the trunks of their cars. There's honestly no way to totally stop it. But every source stopped is lives saved. In fact, the Liar's Table was just talking about the '67 El Camino.

The bed of the '67 can be lifted up to transport contraband. Can be decked like a classic for the car shows, but serve a dual purpose."

114

After Gavin left, Terry ran a lot of things through his mind. One of them was Kim. Glancing over towards the kitchen, he watched Kim laughing with Greg.

Her abilities were important to Greg. She was reliable, didn't need to be supervised, and was able to keep everything straight out front so Greg could focus on the cooking. Greg relied on her. Kim did not call in sick unless she was about to die or felt she would expose others. She had a sense of humor. In fact, she wore a maroon t-shirt today with the slogan, "I ain't your mother – clean up your own dishes." Terry smiled as he watched her balancing dishes and taking them to the tub by the kitchen.

Finding himself sort of giddy when he thought of her – which seemed to be all the time – he wondered what about her so attracted him. Was it how cute she was? Certainly he enjoyed looking at her. Was it her eyes? They were just sort of drawing him. She was easy to talk to, and he found himself comfortable sharing things with her. And she seemed to feel the same way. And, yet, she also seemed to understand there were times he just needed to be quiet. It wasn't that there was something wrong – he just needed to be quiet.

He didn't feel controlled by her. With some women he'd dated, they seemed to want to know where he was at all times, or would ply him with twenty questions about everything. Kim wasn't like that. Maybe it was her own experience and her maturity that kept her out of funky relationships. She had a reputation of not dating very often and rarely going beyond a date or two. He asked her about that last night. Her response somehow didn't surprise him.

"It is quite easy to tell what a man is after. When he wants a kiss as some sort of reward for an evening out, then it tells me something. And there are those who seem to think that a date is payment for an expected frolic in the sack. It's all a game to some. I'm not looking for casual. I'm beyond that, Terry. I've made mistakes. I also have regrets. Don't put me on a pedestal. I'm looking for a lot more than I used to. I guess it puts pressure on a guy, but I'm not a cheap fling and I will not ever be one." She then had looked at him tenderly. "It means a lot that you didn't try to kiss me the first time we went out."

He grinned.

"I've still not tried to kiss you."

She laughed.

"When the time is right, you will."

He did not miss the fact that she said 'when' and not 'if.'

Now, sipping his coffee, Terry was still in his own thoughts when Kim slipped into the seat across from him.

"Hey," she said.

"Hey. All caught up?"

"For a few minutes anyway." She fidgeted awkwardly. "I wanted to thank you for what you said earlier."

"No problem."

"They didn't mean anything, really, but you saying that meant a lot to me, Terry. A lot." He saw a tear in her eye.

"You ok?"

Kim nodded. Terry waited.

"This is something I've never told you." She glanced around the room to make sure things were ok. "Last time I seriously dated was five or six years ago. A fella from Indy. We were at a burger joint when some of his friends came in. We'd had good conversation, and then suddenly these friends of his came to the table and looked at me and he didn't introduce me for a few minutes. It was real awkward. After a few minutes, one of his friends looked at him and pointed to me and said, 'This your main squeeze?' I was appalled when he looked at me, then up at these friends and winked and said, 'Yep, my main squeeze.' I felt like I was a nothing. I vowed I would never be involved again with someone who didn't give me respect." She paused. "It felt really good when you said that to the Liar's Table, Terry. It may seem like a little thing to some, but it was huge to me. To hear you say that made me feel safe. Protected somehow. And…valued."

Terry reddened.

"I do have a lot of respect for you, Kim. I won't let anybody belittle you, even in jest. And I guess you make me feel good about myself."

Kim smiled and looked at her hands.

"Terry, I need to get back to the kitchen, but I want to ask you a question first."

"Shoot."

"Why are you so interested in this case? Couldn't you just pass it on to the sheriff?" She was not speaking accusingly, but with curiosity.

"Yes, and rightly I should pass it off, but…" He looked her square in the eye. "All I do is hand out tickets and take calls about dogs in other people's yards. Not exactly meaningful stuff. I think half of the town looks at me as a flunky. Now here comes this case that really is – well, Kim, it's looking bigger all the time – and I have a chance to build a solid reputation. I have been keeping the sheriff in the loop. He's given me his blessing to check this out. The samples he sent in came back. In fact…Gavin and I are meeting with a friend of his from back East and the sheriff tomorrow. I think it's beyond any one of us. It's a team effort."

Kim nodded.

"I need to tell you something, Terry." She looked at him, then reached over and placed her hand over his. "I believe in you. And I'm proud of you. No matter what. And I want you to play it safe."

"Thanks, Kim. That means a lot." He curled his hand around hers.

Kim smiled.

"I mean it, Terry. Don't get hurt."

"Ok."

115

Robert was sick of the dog. In fact, he was sick of the whole situation.

He spent a lot of time rolling his eyes and scratching his head.

The other day he'd gone to the garage – barefoot - when he suddenly stepped in something messy. Even before he looked down, he knew what it was as it squished up between his toes. Stumbling over to the side of the garage, he walked on his heel and then leaned against the siding and looked down.

"Dadgummit!"

Bending down, he retrieved a stick and began to scrape the stuff off his foot. It was up between his toes and he contented himself with getting the major chunks off, then continued into the garage on his heel to where he kept a bag of old undershirts. Grabbing one and turning a five-gallon bucket over, he sat and fumed as he wiped his foot. He knew he'd have to go in and sit on the edge of the tub and stick it under the faucet.

Darla walked in, heading to the car to go to work. Dressed in her favorite blouse - a mottled brown and orange with puffy sleeves over dark brown slacks, he normally might have commented about how nice she looked. But he was in no such mood. She glanced down at him and crinkled her nose.

"What happened?"

"Stepped on a land mine! Daggone dog! Third time this week."

"Oh. Maybe you should wear shoes."

"I been going barefoot for years. Why should I have to change because of some stupid dog? Besides, it wouldn't change the effect of the land mines. I'd just have to sit and pick it out of the shoe treads with a toothpick."

"Maybe you should go around and pick up the…stuff… with a shovel."

"And what am I supposed to do with it?"

"Put it in the trash can."

Robert was exasperated.

"Lord have mercy! What has life come to, Darla? It's quite clear the saying is wrong! It's really 'man is dog's best friend.' We house 'em, feed 'em and clean up after them. And now I'm supposed to walk behind the dog and flush the toilet for it! They got it made!"

Robert detected a trace of a smile on his wife's face as she went around the car. He whined to her retreating back.

"Wish I could go to work and you got to stay home with your dad…and the dog."

"Sorry. You're retired."

"He's taken over my recliner. He uses toilet paper like it's going out of style."

"You talking about my dad or the dog?"

"Oh, you know very well who I'm talking about! This…dog is another issue."

"His name is Cuckoo."

"The dog or your dad?"

"Now you're being funny."

"I'm serious as a heart attack, Darla. The dog is more than cuckoo. The dang thing is nuts. It seems to think I'm the next thing to its mother and it wakes me up in the morning by trying to kiss me. It happened again this morning. I had my mouth open and woke up being French-kissed by a dog! I about puked by the time I got to the bathroom and grabbed the mouthwash. Had to brush three times before I felt clean again! And now I can't even walk across the yard without having a land mine blow up between my toes. All he does is go in and out, in and out, and these land mines are killing the grass."

"Bye, honey. I got to go."

"Yeah, right. Enjoy your day." Suddenly he smiled. "By the way, hope you got a lint roller at the office. You musta sat on the couch. You got globs of hair all over those nice pants."

Darla looked down.

"Where?"

"On your rear. You look like Sasquatch back there."

"Dadgummit!"

"Great having that dog, huh?" His sarcasm was thick.

116

Terry kissed her.

It seemed so natural. They'd gone to Indy and decided to walk along the canal. Couples and families enjoyed the walkway and some rode bicycles. Nobody was around the moment they looked at each other and kissed. It was a sweet, lingering kiss, transitioning to a hug. Standing on the walk, they held each other quite some time, kissing again and again.

They were two happy people.

Starting to walk, they had their arms around each other. It was hard to get their feet in rhythm. Terry stumbled.

"Kind of hard to walk with our arms around each other."

"That's ok, Terry. I want to learn how." Looking up, Kim felt a change. Terry was peering ahead. "What is it, Terry?"

"Those men up ahead. The group over at the side of the path up there?"

"Yes?"

"I think one is involved with the fields of marijuana."

"Well, don't stare and we'll walk by. Get a closer look without looking like that's what you're doing."

Terry held Kim's hand and looked at her as they passed the men. Just a quick glance affirmed that one of these men was at the convenience store that morning buying O'Henry bars. Same scraggly beard, rotten teeth. About to avert his eyes, the man met his glance and gave a questioning look. Terry looked away and drew Kim closer as they walked away. They rounded a corner and came to steps. Terry led her quickly up the steps.

"Let's get lost somewhere, Kim. I think he recognized me."

They crossed the street and entered the Convention Center,

where an assembly of churches was being held. Swarming with people, it was easy to be lost in the crowd. At the top of the first escalator, Terry glanced back to see the man looking across the crowd. They disappeared into the moving throngs.

He called Gavin on the way home and told him what had happened. Gavin questioned him extensively about the other men.

Riding quietly the rest of the trip, both in their own thoughts, Kim glanced over to see Terry obviously deep in thought. She reached over and grasped his hand – tightly.

As they kissed that evening on the step, headlights approached. And slowed.

Terry reached for the gun at the small of his back as he stepped in front of her.

"Get behind the post, Kim."

117

Bobby laughed as they played "Spot It!" It was a frustrating game for Hubert, but Bobby sure was tickled. With all the different sizes of the pictures, Hubert stared forever before he'd find a match. Finally, he won a game and pumped his fist. Bobby said it was the rage at school, making its appearance mostly at lunchtime.

In the kitchen, Eula Mae sat talking in quiet tones with Cora, who had slept much of the afternoon. Bobby looked around the living room.

"How come you don't have a TV, Mr. Griffin?"

"We do have one. We just don't pay much attention to it."

"Where is it?"

"Right over there." Hubert pointed to a corner, where an ironing board held piles of towels on one end and a selection of glass vases on the other. Sure enough, Bobby spotted the top of the screen behind it all.

"You ever watch?"

"No."

"Why not?"

"Couple reasons. One, most of what is on is really mindless drivel." Bobby stared at him with a questioning look. "That means it has absolutely no meaning and it's a waste of time. Then, second, it is all packaged as objective – meaning not taking a side – but they only give you the pieces of the story that support their view. They're all liars."

"Oh."

"I guess there's a third reason. That's the fact that I can sit here and watch it and I find myself all upset, then I get all irritated and it affects everything I do and say. So I find it best to just not worry about anything that I can't do anything about."

Eula Mae looked over.

"Don't let him fool you, Bobby. He's an old grump already. The TV just makes it worse." She chuckled.

Hubert frowned. Eula Mae had sonar ears. She could pick up a conversation from a mile away.

"Your turn, Bobby."

Cora coughed. She lowered her voice as she spoke.

"Eula Mae, do you have any children?"

Eula Mae spoke softly.

"No, we never had any."

"Hubert is good with Bobby."

"He is. He's really taken to Bobby. Really surprised me when he first mentioned him. Truth be told, Hubert tends to be tight with a dollar. Used to be it took the grinding of rusty pulleys to get it out of his pocket! When he bought the skateboard and shoes I was shocked." She leaned on the counter and put her chin in her cupped hand. "Fact is, he's absolutely enjoying having both of you here at the house. It's like having a child and grandchild of our own. Sort of bringing life to the house."

"I wondered. I don't want to put you out of sorts with our being here. You're used to the quiet and doing your own thing."

"Oh, Cora, you do not have to worry one bit about putting us out. Fact of the matter is, you've brought so much to our lives over the past couple weeks. More than you could ever imagine. I'm having a blast cooking for more than the two of us. I'd forgotten what the large pans even looked like. And look at Hubert – sitting on the floor playing that card game. Go figure! No, Cora, you and Bobby have brought a lot to this house. It has given a reason and purpose to our days that was really lacking. I saw a change in Hubert when he said he watched Bobby at the skate park. He's always been grumpy. Well, not always. Perhaps a bit taciturn, but he slowly went into a shell of sorts after we tried but couldn't have children. It was like a veil was pulled over his life – and mine. He became more morose.

Oh, I've never doubted his love for me. We did, indeed, marry for better or for worse. But there has been a certain joy lacking for many years."

Hubert's laughter resonated from the other room. Bobby laughed, too.

Eula Mae smiled.

"Oh, what a beautiful sound."

Cora spoke softly, looking wistful and distant.

"Well, it's been a blessing to have Hubert take an interest in Bobby. We have no family and it just seems we plow our way through, but always without anybody to lean on. It's always different on holidays where people gather with their families and we are by ourselves. It's given us an appreciation for each other and a bond that many mothers and sons might not have. Bobby loves me and would fight for me. But Christmas and Thanksgiving are quiet. I guess it's been good for us, and good for Bobby to have independence, but I want him to need others in his life."

"Well, I guess we have ourselves a mutual need group here, Cora."

They laughed. Hubert and Bobby looked at each other in the other room. Hubert glanced up and whispered to Bobby.

"Womenfolk are getting along well."

"I can tell Mom is feeling better. Thank you, Mr. Griffin, for letting us stay here."

"You're welcome. You really never had a pocketknife?"

"Huh? Oh. Nope."

Hubert reached into his pocket and pulled out a brand new Buck knife.

"Here."

"You letting me borrow this?"

"No. I'm giving it to you."

"Really?"

"A boy needs a pocketknife."

Bobby got up and ran to his mom.

"Wow! Hey, Mom! Mr. Griffin gave me a pocketknife!"

Cora smiled at Hubert, then looked to Bobby.

"That's very nice, Bobby. Remember what to say."

"Thank you."

"You're welcome. You think we ought to go to the skate park tomorrow?"

Bobby chuckled.

"So I can work on doing stupid stuff?"

Hubert chuckled.

"Something like that."

"Mr. Griffin, are you a grandpa?"

"No."

"I don't have a grandpa. Mom and I are sort of alone."

"Is that hard?"

"Sometimes I wish I could have a grandpa and a grandma. My friends go to their grandparents' houses for stuff. I always wonder what that would be like."

"Yeah, I wonder some times, what I would do with a grandkid."

"Probably stuff like what we're doing now, huh?"

"Probably."

They both looked at each other.

Eula Mae appeared in the doorway.

"Anybody for popcorn?"

Hubert and Bobby looked at each other and yelled in unison, "Yes!"

118

Later that evening, Cora had the Bible Eula Mae gave her and was reading in bed. Hubert sat in his chair in the living room while Eula Mae sat across the room in hers.

Bobby went in to say goodnight to his mom. He was in his pajamas and snuggled for a few minutes.

"I like it here, Mom."

"I do, too, Bobby."

"I know Mrs. Griffin is taking care of you. It'll help you get better. And boy does she cook good!"

"She certainly does."

In the living room, both Hubert and Eula Mae overheard. They both felt a bit guilty, but looked at each other and craned their ears to hear. Hubert cupped both ears and turned like radar towards the bedroom.

"Mom?"

"Hmm?"

"Does a grandpa always have to be related?"

"Well, I guess not necessarily. A grandpa is more something of the heart. More than a relation, it's a feeling. I guess neither one of us have much experience with it, do we?"

"No." He sounded sad. "Mom?"

"What, Honey?"

"Do you think Mr. and Mrs. Griffin would be my grandma and grandpa?"

Eula Mae looked over at her husband and reached for the Kleenex.

Hubert stared.

119

Terry and Kim relaxed when Gavin got out of the car. He approached them and noted their looks and how Terry's hand was at his back.

"You two ok?"

"Yes, but you sure gave us a start when you pulled up."

Gavin looked back.

"I guess it would have been better if I'd called you first."

Kim walked up beside Terry and held onto his arm.

Gavin looked to them both.

"There's been lights in the field tonight. Thought we might take a look-see."

"Ok. How long since the last flash?"

"Probably half an hour."

Terry looked at Kim.

"Hey, I'll give you a call when we get back." He gave her hand a squeeze.

120

After they got in the car, Gavin spoke into the distance.

"Small of the back can be a bad spot for a gun. Man gets knocked down it can be hard to reach. I prefer hip or appendix. Ankle can be good, too. Just a thought."

"Thanks."

Terry and Gavin parked a quarter-mile away from the stand of pot in Cuthbert's field, having driven carefully with lights off. Of course, they couldn't kill the engine sounds completely.

"Terry, my alarm bells are ringing and my scalp is prickling. It all adds up to be careful. These folks aren't like the rest of the people in town. They will have no respect for a badge or anybody telling them to put their hands up. They only respect a gun. And sometimes the men working at this level of the game can be lit up half the time."

"I'll be careful."

"That fella that bought the candy bars? He looked like he spent a lot of time lit up, but he didn't look stupid either."

"What do you suggest?"

"We go carefully. Something has to happen soon because these plants are right at maturity. If anybody is out there, we watch and wait. We need to figure out where they go from here. It will do us no good to get the local small fry. We need to find the next step in the ladder. Now, either they will go to another field or they will head home. Maybe somewhere else. I'm not sure how well we can tail them, but that's what we have to do. When I was working, we'd put a transmitter on the car, but that's not an option. So we go back to doing the best we can. We'll approach together at first and split up as we near the field."

The incoming dew helped them walk quietly. Nearing Cuthbert's cornfield, Terry sensed something and slowed. Gavin stopped and looked to Terry, questioning.

"Something's different, Gavin."

Both men peered into the darkness. The plants were gone!

121

Emaline was spitting fire.

It'd been a rough day. It started when she spent a frustrating hour trying to figure out why her order of hair and skin products was twice what she had ordered. Talking to some extremely foreign voice in what was probably the Philippines who gave the incongruous name of Mary, Emaline finally figured out she had clicked the order button twice. "Dumb Internet," she said. You sit and wonder if anything is happening, so you click the button again. She remembered the little note that popped up saying not to click twice, but after a minute she was convinced something didn't take and she'd clicked again. Goodness! It would be six months before she needed more products. Not to mention the double charge to her account. Emaline was convinced this sort of set up was a conspiracy, preying on those who didn't know better.

Now at the shop, she found the lavatory faucet leaking and there was water everywhere. The worst part was finding it the hard way. Stepping into the dark back room, Emaline did a spider dance and managed to grab the corner of a shelf as she fell, dumping seven bundles of paper towels for the bathroom dispenser into the mess as she landed on her bottom and winced with pain. Unable to jump as she used to in her youth, she had to sit in the water for a few moments before rolling to her knees and struggling to her feet. Here she stood, soaked, with an appointment in thirty minutes to give a perm to Dinah Higginbotham, who couldn't come in till evening. A notorious talker, anything Dinah heard she repeated, usually with liberal embellishment. Boy would Dinah have something to take home tonight! A water leak would become a tsunami by tomorrow afternoon.

Walking stiffly to the light switch, she traced the water and heard the leak in the bathroom. Somewhat handy, she shut the water off under the sink and went to get old towels off the dryer to help clean up the mess. It was then she realized the new order of products was sitting in the water and she would have to empty the boxes back here and carry everything out to the front shelves.

Words of varying degrees of color flew around the air of the shop. Emaline was not known to be conservative with her tongue and moments like these brought out her deepest talent. Laying the towels out, she walked over them and then looked into the mirror.

Another burst of oral color erupted as she saw the front of her outfit. She was soaked! Glancing to the coat hooks, she pulled off a lime green smock she despised and pulled it over her wet clothes.

She would have to call Harvey to fix the sink. And quick. What would she tell the people who needed to use the restroom? They wouldn't be able to wash their hands! There were those, like Mabel Fitcher, who came expressly to her shop to use the restroom. Said she was just looking at the products, but Emaline knew she was coming to use the restroom and keep her own clean. But all Emaline could do was smile and say "hello," even though she knew the truth. Every other month, Mabel bought a little four-dollar bottle of nail polish remover. Emaline rolled her eyes. It barely paid for the toilet paper Mabel used.

Harvey would probably charge her an arm and a leg to fix the faucet. Which meant the cost of four bottles of shampoo and three conditioners. How was a person to make a profit?

Coloring the air once again, Emaline glanced at the car going by under the streetlight.

What on earth? She rushed to the window and squinted. It was Jean's Gavin! The car was headed out towards the edge of town. She'd been too busy to think much on what she saw those other nights. Watching further as the car passed under a light, she could tell there was a passenger.

Looking down, she saw water soaking through her smock. Her shoes squished. A brand new pair of flats and look at them! Emaline looked to the clock. Scratching her head and pulling the stray hairs back over her ears, she stomped her foot, spewing water.

Stepping outside into the darkness of the front of the shop, she stepped to the curb to see what direction the car was going. It traveled north and turned east at the far end of the street before disappearing from view. Her car keys were at home, so she could not follow. She just knew there was a major crime and Jean's Gavin had them all fooled.

Turning back to the shop, she chanced to glance south and stopped in her tracks. What was that? It looked like a car, but the distance between the headlights and taillights was too short. While she watched, the car's lights flicked off.

She locked the door behind her. Dinah would just have to reschedule.

122

Cooter wore just the breechcloth to the mailbox that night. He'd gotten caught up in a book and neglected to get the mail till well after 11 o'clock. Making his usual pause at the bushes to look both ways, he chuckled to himself.

He'd been watching for the little car. There was a pattern. Right about 10 o'clock, at a little bend in the road about fifty yards away, they always took it too fast and there was a whisper of gravel announcing their arrival. What made him do it he really could not explain, but last night, hearing the gravel, he jumped to the mailbox and leaned his elbow on the box and crossed one leg over the other, as if he was just contemplating life.

It worked. Headlights enveloped him as the car passed, and it actually slowed, showing two faces lit in the glow of the instruments and a cell phone. Both men gawked and Cooter smiled.

Now, here he was again, knowing he had already missed the little car. Reaching into the mailbox, there was a package wedged in sideways, forcing him to bend over a bit and work at it. The mailman seemed to take undue pleasure in jamming Lisa's Book-of-the-Month-Club package in catawampus. Straining with the package, he was not attentive and a van was upon him before he heard. It was a windowless delivery van. It slowed perceptively at the view of an Apache Indian at the mailbox and Cooter turned, getting a good look at the men inside. The gawking faces in the window were the same two from the little car. They both stared at him with mouths open.

"Odd." Cooter spoke to nobody in particular.

123

It had been a long and busy day for Jake and Bub. Jake had to go deep in the closet to get his real good clothes. He had to look his best. He actually convinced the elderly lady next door that he had a job interview and she offered to iron his clothes for him, so he carted them across the yard and sat and lied to her while she made them look crisp. After all, he really didn't need a job.

He needed a new set of tires.

Tire day came about every other year for him. Aside from the Smart Car provided by the man who paid them, and which was kept in a garage a few blocks away, Jake drove a 2001 Intrepid. The tires were getting pretty worn and it had just reached a point where he needed to do something.

What with the night work, he had enough cash to buy a set, but old habits die hard. Why buy a set when it could be had for free? He had already done the research. Walking used car lots of an evening, he'd pegged some cars with the same tire size and wheel configuration as his.

Now, driving his Intrepid into the lots, he put on his best manners and brought out his fake driver's license to test drive selected cars. He'd found dressing up opened more opportunities for test drives. He drove the cars across town to the alley behind his rented house where Bub awaited. Jake stopped, popped the trunk and checked the spare. The key was speed. Too long of a test drive would make the salesman suspicious, so they worked quickly and then Jake returned the cars with the excuse that the air conditioning was kicking in and out. In two of the test drives the spares were in great condition, so he merely took them and put the cover back over the spare compartments. With the last two drives, he had to get more serious because the spares were pretty worn. Picturing the way the car set in the lot compared to the office, Bub threw a jack under and removed a tire from the passenger side of each car and replaced it with an old one. Then he returned the car and, parking with the old tire away from the direct view of the lot salesman, made his excuses and left. Driving by the house after each test drive, they installed the newer tires on the Intrepid. On the last test drive, Bub opened the hood and found a much newer battery and changed it out also.

By 3 o'clock they had really nice tires, an almost new battery and a brand new looking factory lug wrench Bub kept for himself. He didn't have a car of his own, but he obsessively collected lug wrenches. They lay haphazardly piled in the corner of the carport, with several others leaning against the posts.

All in all, the day brought a smile to Jake and he was relaxed. His dad always told him, "Son, it doesn't matter what you drive, just so you keep good tires on it."

For nearly twenty years, Jake had followed his dad's advice. But he took that advice a step further and never paid for a set of tires. Or a battery.

Yep, it was a good day.

It made the work that night more pleasant.

124

Sheriff Burris was working late. He'd promised Cathy they'd go out this weekend, so he needed to get some things done. Payroll was time consuming, what with the new computer system designed by someone with no common sense. And later there was a budget meeting in the conference room.

Normally payroll was done in the morning, but his meeting down at the truck stop with Terry and Gavin broke up the process. They introduced him to Brian Phillips. This was bigger than he'd thought when Terry first called. What he thought was some two-bit pot supplier was turning into a major investigation. He was actually pleased to have the government man involved, for it made his own role easier. If nothing came of this, the blame was not on him. But if it became anything big, he could emphasize his role. Politics and publicity were fickle things.

Brian was obviously competent and, even though Gavin was retired, Brian's faith in the man and his sort of shadow involvement spoke a million words. This whole thing was a bit unorthodox, but he felt comfortable with it. Terry was under their care and teaching, which was comforting also. So the peripheral involvement of the Sheriff Department was ok with him. Both Gavin and Brian fully understood him. This wasn't their first rodeo. On his part, he'd assured them – and meant it – that he'd lend any help he could when they asked.

Turning back to the computer, he clicked the mouse and rubbed his brow in wonder. Why on earth was there a drop-down box here?

125

Thank God I wore flats, Emaline thought as she hurried down the street. Reaching where she last saw the lights, she carefully peered around the corner, surveying the edge of town. Streetlights were few out here, so darkness enshrouded most of the area. A few scattered houses showed lights in the distance and a lawn care warehouse and office showed a deeper silhouette against the dark sky. This was about all that anchored this end of town. Everything else headed north and a bit west. And there was the old filling station. It used to be a lively place until the Quick Stop came in with six pumps, pizza and chicken strips. Boarded up for years, some expressed hope a buyer would turn the old station into something. The problem was the underground tanks. It would cost a fortune to dig them out.

Scanning the area and realizing there was no sign of a vehicle, Emaline started to turn and stopped.

"What was that?" She clapped her hand over her mouth as she realized she'd spoken out loud. Hunkering in the shadows, she craned her neck and spotted a tiny flicker of light.

"What in blue blazes?" She moved her head around to catch the light again. It was coming from the old filling station!

"Something fishy is going on."

Looking back towards the center of town, Emaline contemplated for a brief instant the thought of calling the Cop Shop, but her cell phone was back in the shop. Besides, Wally was probably in the middle of a John Wayne movie. Pursing her lips, she slipped around the corner.

126

Kim sat nervously on the porch, hugging her knees. She was worried and it felt strange. Of course, she was not emotionally cold and had lots of empathy and sympathy, but this ache in her heart for Terry's safety was something new and deep.

She cared for him. How many years had it been since she'd felt this way? Perhaps never, she thought. Oh, she'd cared for men before, but this was different. She knew he cared for her, too.

127

Emaline tripped on the broken curb, landing on her elbow and whispering color as she struggled to her feet. Straightening her front, she felt a tear in the pocket of her smock.

"Daggone it! This ain't that old!" Though she cursed softly, she clapped her hand over her mouth again. "Quiet, Emaline," she spoke to herself.

Reaching gravel, she stopped and took in the area. From where she stood, there was no light, so she walked back and forth until the little glimmer showed. It was coming from a corner of a boarded window. Pegging the source, she worked carefully to approach the building without being heard. She wished she had moccasins, because that's what they put on in the old western movies so they could move quietly. If she had those she could feel twigs and such and move like a shadow in the night. But then again, she wasn't sure they would go well with her lime green smock and, besides, she didn't have moccasins. Her flats would have to do. After being wet and now trucking down the sidewalk and into gravel, she knew they were toast.

Nearing the building, she stooped to peer in where the light showed. There was light, but she could not see anything but a fluorescent light hanging from the ceiling. There was enough light that she knew there must be at least one other light also. Reaching a finger into the corner, she felt insulation. Somebody had tucked insulation into the cracks to keep the light from showing.

Obviously a man did it because the job was not done right, she mused.

Standing up, Emaline carefully worked her way to the back corner, where she peered around the building.

There was some sort of car parked there. It was tiny! What on earth was it? And why was it parked here? Looking up, she saw the door standing ajar. Scratching her head, Emaline stepped carefully.

But not carefully enough.

128

Inside the station, two men worked, moving the crop around on the drying racks. They had used the van earlier and brought the plants in. Then they'd run off to get some dinner and returned again in the Smart Car.

Jake and Bub worked well together. They first met in jail. Not averse to skirting the law, they were the type who took trouble in stride. Jake was the one in charge when they worked, with Bub content to do what he was told and take the envelope of cash handed to him every couple weeks. Bub figured Jake's envelope contained more than his, but that was ok. Jake had to deal with the big boss.

He wouldn't have been ok if he knew about the extra Jake took out of Bub's envelope and tucked in his pocket.

As they worked, Jake watched Bub pull out an O'Henry candy bar, unwrap it and throw the wrapper in a box by the door. There must be a dozen wrappers in there, he thought. At least enough to rot Bub's remaining teeth, which already were bad enough.

Jake was in charge of cooking the meth. This was the second time they had cooked it. They showed up one night and all the supplies were in the woods, as they had been told on the phone. Jake knew how to do it. Now, the crystals were in the containers in the corner. He tended to take a small bit home with him in a baggie for personal use.

"Jake, how come we got the meth here, too?"

"Bub, don't worry about that." Jake paused, then looked around. "Mixing it with this weed. Gonna pack a real punch. And them other drugs at the house are for the same thing."

"I wondered."

"Just remember you don't know nothing."

"About what?" He paused. "Jake, how do you know if you mix it too heavy?"

"I said don't worry about it."

"I'm done worrying."

Grabbing another green plant, he arranged it on the drying rack.

"Jake, we're running out of space. What we gonna do to get this all spread out?"

"I got to rig up some extra racks with them two-by-fours over there. And don't talk so loud. Never know who might wander by."

Both men paused to strip down to t-shirts in the almost suffocating heat. Propane driven heaters stood in three areas, keeping the entire building hot to dry the plants. They didn't bother with the slow dry that makes for better pot. This was what they were told to do and they found it important to follow orders. Within a couple weeks the crop would be handed off in the middle of the night to a couple of unknown men in a small delivery truck. Jake and Bub would each receive an envelope of cash and then wait till they were contacted again for the next job.

Grabbing a cordless drill and decking screws, Jake took a couple boards and dragged them to the only open spot left. Setting one over the other, he glanced over to the door, and saw it ajar. He shook his head and hissed at Bub.

"You idiot! You left the door open. How many times I got to tell you to pull it until you feel it latch?"

"Oops."

"Idiot!" Jake walked to the door and was reaching for the handle when he paused and his eyes widened.

Someone or something was out there. Lime green was showing in the crack of the door.

129

Sure enough, the plants were gone. In fact, the cut stems were fresh. Harvest had not been long ago.

"Dang, Crockett! We missed them!"

Gavin looked around.

"It would appear so. I wonder about the other patches. We might have trouble getting to the other patches without someone getting suspicious of our lights."

"Are we shut down?"

"Not yet. Maybe we can find where they're drying and storing. But it's probably some distance away. You call Sheriff Burris and let him know what's up. I'll call Brian."

130

Robert was disgusted.

Darla handed him one of those shiny short-handled scooper things – like a mini square posthole digger. He stared at her for a moment and said, "What's this for?"

"Clearing landmines."

"You gotta be kidding me!"

"You're retired. You got plenty of time."

"It wasn't my idea to take in your dad's dog."

"Look, Robert – Dear – I clean up your dishes; I clean your clothes; I clean your dang whiskers out of the sink where you leave them. I do a host of other things to make life nice. Now, I don't think it's asking too much to pick up after the dog once a week. Besides, you keep tracking it in the house."

So today was his landmine day. Never in his life had he ever anticipated such a job would become a routine need.

It was bad enough he was unable to go barefoot anymore. Now the degradation extended to picking "dog stuff" out of the grass. This was not on his retirement bucket list.

So it started. Once a week he went out and scooped, and then put it in the trash can. Last week he peeked out of the drapes as the garbage man stopped out front and tore the lid off the can. Robert knew there was a scooper full right on top and the man must've got a whiff and a view.

Going over to the window, he looked at the yard. Hmmm. Dumb dog did most of them out on the perimeter, instead of the usual patch near the door. Maybe he'd just wait till tomorrow…

131

Jake kicked the door as hard as he could and heard a thunk followed by something hitting gravel. Cuss words sounded from the dark.

He jumped outside. Grabbing Emaline by the arm, he pulled her inside and slammed the door.

Bub, caught off-guard by this sudden turn of events, stood open-mouthed. Jake looked at him.

"Grab some of that rope, Bub!"

"Who is it, Jake?"

"I dunno. But this is a problem."

Emaline sat up, blinking her eyes. The door had given her a solid knock on the head and a goose egg already sprouted on her forehead. She was stunned and blinked at the lights. She managed to color the air as her head cleared.

"Lady, what are you doing here?"

Emaline could see frayed pajama pants and looked up to see the man glaring down at her. He was tall, making him that much farther up. He wore an almost worn out t-shirt and from the way he talked and held his mouth, it was clear his teeth were in bad shape. He had a blue bandana around his forehead, soaked with sweat.

"My name is Emaline Poovy and I was just taking a walk and happened to see the door open. I was going to shut it. I'll just go home now." Starting to rise, she felt his hands shove her back down.

"Not hardly. You expect us to believe that line about taking a walk? First, this place ain't on the way to anywhere and, second, ain't nobody in their right mind goes for a walk wearing that ungodly green thing you got on. Not unless you escaped from a loony bin."

Emaline, a bit stunned, but still prideful, had to respond.

"You talk about me? Look at yourself! You walking around in them frayed pajama pants and a shirt that doesn't even coordinate. Have you no pride? And then you slam a door into an innocent bystander. And you," she looked to Bub, "Don't you have the sense to know that your belt should match your shoes? You two are fashion idiots!"

"Lady…" Jake's voice rose. "You need to shut your mouth. You're sitting here causing us grief and you up and complain about the way we're dressed?"

"Do you guys own this building? I happen to know there hasn't been anybody making inquiries about it for years. It's on the wrong side of town. Besides, my husband will be looking for me. Best I just get along out of here."

"Like I said, lady – not hardly. You ain't going nowhere. Bub, tie her good."

Bub had already tied her hands and Jake shoved her down further and held her kicking legs while Bub tied the rope around them. Knowing no fancy knots, he tied a series of regular knots.

"Obvious you weren't a Boy Scout, Bub."

"Shut up, Jake. These here work as good as a fancy knot."

"Make sure you pull it tight."

Emaline squalled and twisted.

"You're not going to get away with this!"

Pulling the wet bandana from his head, he slipped it into her mouth and tied it behind her head. Gagging on the nasty cloth, Emaline muttered indecipherable cuss words.

"What do we do now, Jake?"

"We get the racks built and get the plants spread out. That's what we do. Got to get this stuff wired up."

"I mean what do we do with her?"

"Just get to work, Bub. We got a job to get done. I'll have to call about this."

He had one contact number to use only in emergencies. He had never called it before. Dialing the number, which was on a small slip of paper in his wallet, he turned to look at Emaline as he listened to the rings. It rang several times before there was an answer.

132

"What?"

"We got a slight problem."

"What have you done?"

"We got a lady here. Found her peeking in."

"Idiot!" The voice was emphatic.

"Yeah, it was stupid of her."

"I'm talking about you."

Jake paused. There was no mistaking the tone of the voice on the other end.

"What do we do with her?"

A pause.

"Sit tight. I'll call back."

Click.

"What'd he say, Jake?"

"He's gonna call back."

"So what do we do?"

"Hang the plants, stupid."

Bub glared at him and reached for a plant. Jake continued to build another rack and was reaching for a wire a few minutes later when the phone rang.

"Yeah?"

"Bring the lady to Greentown in an hour. Call when you get close and you'll get further instructions."

Click.

133

A man wearing an expensive suit stood inside the warehouse door. With timing at a crucial point in the Midwest, he'd made a rare trip to personally check on operations. Staying arm's reach from most levels of his empire, he still found it helpful and essential to make the occasional appearance. It kept local "managers" from becoming too cocky and pondering stealing a cut. When "inspecting," as he called it, he dressed in a tailored suit and always had a bruiser of a bodyguard by his side. It was strict orders never to say his name.

In Indy, he was with the first link of the delivery chain when the local man in charge, named Al, looked at his phone and stepped to the side and answered.

After a brief mumbled conversation, he hung up. He was distracted.

"The field men have a problem. Some lady came snooping and saw them at the drying facilities. They have her tied up. What do we do?"

"This is not good, Al. I entrusted this operation to you, and you were to vet these guys well."

"I did, boss. And they've done very well." He thought for a moment. "They'll have to bump her off."

"No! This is a critical stage. We don't want to create a manhunt right now." He tapped his balled fists together. "I heard you tell them Greentown. I'll come along and decide myself what to do."

His bodyguard glanced at him.

"I know, Simpson. It's getting too close to the action. But sometimes you have to get in the trenches in this business."

His bodyguard nodded and headed for the car.

134

Emaline kicked and cursed through the bandana all the way. The little electric car was a two-seater, with no extra room, so she sat on Bub's lap. Her curses mingled with those of her two captors as she kicked and squirmed.

"Hold her, Bub!"

"She's like a greased pig, Jake!"

Emaline's eyes widened at that comment and she jammed an elbow into Bub's jaw.

"Ow! You stupid…" He slapped her, hard, across the face. Blood came from her nose and she wiped it with her sleeve.

Emaline, with a look of wariness but not defeat, ceased her struggles.

Nearing Greentown, Jake dialed the number again and, getting directions, found himself outside an abandoned scrap metal warehouse in a sort of run-down little enclave in town. Pulling up to a specified door, he stopped the car.

The door opened. A small light shown inside, carefully shielded but showing a silhouette.

135

Terry stopped a moment.

Gavin glanced over.

"What?"

"I got a hunch, Gavin."

"About what?"

"Let's look that woods over a bit more."

"What are you thinking, Terry?"

"Well, if'n I was wanting to be a bit isolated, say for making meth, a woods out here would be a handy spot. There's that water source I told you about, but I just wonder if there's more."

A few minutes later they stood, staring. Now that the pot was harvested, there was little threat of anybody showing up. So, flashlights on, Terry and Gavin surveyed the small dirt clearing. Around a blue-tinged propane tank were several frying pans, miscellaneous coffee filters, empty ephedrine packages and other items, along with a lingering odor.

"Meth."

"Yep, Gavin. I don't understand why I didn't pick up on it the other times I've been here."

"I didn't either. But look," Gavin pointed to the trash. "None of this is covered in dirt, there's not much of it, and it looks to be all recent. I think this has been used just in the past couple days. Sort of a cook-and-run-operation. Used for making small amounts and getting out."

"So likely they're gone."

"Probably gone with the pot, Terry."

"I'll call Sheriff Burris to let him know what's up."

136

Harrison Tyler stood and smoothed his suit as the little electric car pulled up out front. He realized the benefits of these quiet cars. A mere whisper on the roads allowed them to readily sneak around the fields. The method of dotting the landscape with small fields was a new thing. He'd come to the Midwest to avoid the heat being placed on him in the East. Still, his home was back there, and he didn't want to uproot his respectable existence, so he developed a new plan of operations in cornfield, USA. The problem was the distance from home. Still, the building of the organization was progressing.

Two men in the car dragged in a woman wearing an ungodly green smock. Dropping her arms, they stepped back as she kicked out. Curses continued to be unmistakable from around the bandana as they shoved her to the floor.

The man in the suit approached the struggling woman and hissed.

"Shut up!"

Emaline saw the look on the man's face. It curdled her innards as she stared up at cruel eyes.

Al motioned Bub and Jake to leave. The man in the suit glanced at them.

"Go outside, but don't leave." After they closed the door, he turned to Emaline and, grasping his pants just above the knees, pulled them up as he squatted in front of her. "Lady, you have put me into a situation. A bad situation. Mostly bad for you. Sticking your nose where it doesn't belong has brought you only one thing – shortness of breath – in a sense. I cannot let you go."

Emaline's eyes widened. She mumbled a prayer.

"Al, keep her here until I tell you what to do. Is there a store-room you can lock?"

"Yes, boss. She'll be locked tight as a drum."

"And do something about that ugly green thing. I've never seen anything as detestable as that."

Emaline struggled and managed to speak around the bandana in a way to be understood. It was more of a mumble, but the man in the suit understood enough.

"Who are you?"

The man looked around, taking in Al and Simpson. He knew his rules, but this woman would soon be no more. He smiled at Emaline.

"Harrison Tyler."

137

In the storeroom, the cold seeped clear to her bones. Before shoving her roughly into the small room, Al untied her hands long enough to remove the green smock. Taking it to the door, he tossed it to Jake.

"Get rid of that."

A small crack below the door allowed the tiniest glimmer of light to enter the otherwise pitch-dark room. Squatting to look under, she saw nothing but the bottom of a wall. Feeling around, she found no other doors or windows - just a small vent at the base of one wall.

Emaline sunk down in a corner, hugged her knees and cried.

138

Jake and Bub left later to check on the drying of the crop, then drove home in silence to get some rest. Both were tense with the issues of this new development. Both had been in jail; both willingly committed crimes and had no qualms about stealing; both expected to spend more time in jail. Nevertheless, neither had ever been involved in such a situation as this. They read the look on the face of the man in the suit.

"He gonna kill her, Jake?"

"Dunno."

"I ain't never been a part of nothin' like this."

"It ain't our concern, Bub. They'll probably threaten her and make her promise to keep quiet, then set her free."

"You really believe that, Jake?"

Jake stared ahead at the road. Best not think at all.

139

Pratt kept looking to the door.

"Who you looking for, Pratt?"

It was Dinky.

"Nobody. Just looking."

"Yeah, right. I'm not as dumb as I look."

It was approaching 9 o'clock and Greg was cooking up a storm. Several extras were in today and he was hoping lunch would be the same.

The Liar's Table was in full swing. Dobbs, Pratt, Renner and Bart all leaned back and talked of nothingness.

Dinky cleared his throat, making sure all turned to him.

"So…A young boy just got his driving permit. He asked his father, who was a minister, if they could discuss the use of the car. His father took him to his study and said to him, 'I'll make a deal with you. You bring your grades up, study your Bible a little and get your hair cut and we'll talk about it.' After about a month the boy came back and again asked his father if they could discuss use of the car. They again went to the father's study where his father said, 'Son, I've been real proud of you. You have brought your grades up, you've studied your Bible diligently, but you didn't get your hair cut!' The young man waited a moment and replied, 'You know Dad, I've been thinking about that. Samson had long hair, Moses had long hair, Noah had long hair, and even Jesus had long hair….' To which his father replied, 'Yes, and they walked everywhere they went!'"

Everybody but Pratt laughed. Bart noted this and couldn't leave it.

"Pratt, what's on your mind? I think you got the hots for jabber-jaws!"

"Yeah, Pratt, I seen you look at her the other day when she was in."

"I seen it, too. But he was looking more at her walk!"

Pratt didn't deny the allegations, which made other heads turn. He raised his hand.

"It's strange. I was out walking last night and saw her shop lights on. Walked by and there was no sign of her." He shook his head. "Ain't like her to leave the lights on and just leave. No lights were on at her house either. I went back by before I came here and the lights were still on in the shop."

"Might be with a boyfriend!" Dinky ribbed Bart and winked as he chuckled.

"Yeah, right, Dinky! Like that's gonna happen."

Eyes glanced at Pratt, who looked worried.

Renner spoke.

"When did anybody last see her?"

All the joking stopped. In Winston Corner people looked out for their own.

Kim, who heard the conversations, spoke.

"I saw her in her shop last evening. Saw her putting stuff away."

The bell jangled as Gavin walked in. Heads nodded and he nodded back as he went to his booth. Kim brought his coffee.

"Thanks, Kim."

"Welcome, Gavin." She turned away as he looked up in surprise. The bell was jangling again and he looked to see Terry come in. Kim smiled and swooshed over to him, surprising him with the offer of a kiss. He accepted. Even the Liar's Table was distracted by this public display. In Winston Corner, it was a public declaration of possession.

Terry smiled at her as others commented. He realized the implications and it didn't bother him.

"Whoa! Did you see that? Our trusted public servant has been kissed right here in Schmeisser's."

"I seen it! We got witnesses!"

Greg looked on from the kitchen. Kim kissing Terry? Well, he'd been wondering.

Distracted, they all played on.

"Do we hear wedding bells?"

"Kim? You gonna quit when you get married?"

Kim glanced around and smiled. Grabbing a cup, she poured and delivered it to Terry, who scooted in across from Gavin.

Kim waved to the room to quiet them.

"Settle down, fellas. We got important issues going on."

Gavin glanced up questioningly. She looked at Terry.

"We're wondering about Emaline. Pratt saw lights in her shop late last night and nobody was there. No lights at the house either. Then in the middle of the night, still lights at the shop, but no Emaline."

Terry glanced at Gavin.

"Something's not right."

The door jangled again. It was Hubert and Bobby. Finding a table, they caused some long looks, but most knew the situation.

"Coffee, Hubert?"

"Please, Kim."

"Bobby?"

"Chocolate milk, please, Kim."

"Have it there in a minute."

Terry spoke to the room.

"Is her car still at home?"

"It is." Pratt took off his cap and rubbed his head.

Glancing to Gavin, Terry squinted.

"Anybody seen anything strange the last couple days?"

Renner looked around with a questioning look.

"What do you mean by 'strange?'"

"Well, anything out of the ordinary. Anything."

Bart rubbed his jaw.

"Well, seen a strange van over that side of town last night. Just lost and driving through, I figured."

Greg yelled from the kitchen.

"Hubert, want breakfast?"

Hubert raised his hand and waved.

"Over easy, Hubert?"

"Yep."

"Young fella?"

Bobby smiled.

"Scrambled, please."

Terry and Gavin looked at each other. Each grabbed their cups, took a swig, put them down and stood.

The others watched as they went out the door.

140

In the middle of his eggs, Bobby stopped, fork halfway to his mouth. Hubert saw him.

"What?"

"I just remembered something strange I saw a while back. I should have told Terry."

"What was it?"

"Looked like somebody had been in the old filling station. There was a new lock on it. And tire tracks."

"Let's go find Terry."

A few minutes later they drove by Emaline's shop. Terry and Gavin were inside. It had taken but a moment to jimmy the lock, and they quickly went to the back room, and then on through the back door to glance around the alley.

Both men looked up as Hubert and Bobby walked in.

"Terry, Bobby needs to tell you something."

Both men looked to the boy.

"A few weeks ago I was going by the old filling station and saw a new padlock on the back door and tire tracks in the back."

Terry looked at Gavin.

"That place has been shut down for years."

"And a new padlock. Best we go look. First, though, let's drop by her house."

"Thanks, Bobby."

A few minutes later they slipped the latch at Emaline's home again with a credit card and made a search of the house. There was no sign of her. Terry found the cat food and fed the crying cat while they were there.

141

Approaching the old station and walking to the back, Gavin and Terry both stopped for a moment. Gavin looked up and whispered. "Smell that?"

"I do. Marijuana. Lots of it."

Gavin touched one of the boarded windows.

"Warm, but not from the sun. There's a lot of heat in there."

Both men glanced and saw the tire tracks.

"Might be somebody here, Gavin. But likely not. My guess is they will only come at night. Besides the lock is secure."

"Instead of using the door, maybe we can go through one of the windows."

Walking carefully, they heard nothing. Finding a loose corner of a board, they pulled and succeeded in springing it out a few inches. Then, with a crack, the nails slipped, exposing a large hole. Both men jumped back and waited.

Nothing.

Looking at Gavin, Terry stuck his head and shoulders into the hole.

"Dang! Here's the drying operation." Pulling the board further, they opened the hole wide.

Crawling in, both men stood and surveyed the arrangement of racks and hanging plants. The heat was stifling. Gavin looked to the three heaters.

"Quick dry. Loses quality, but gets it to market sooner."

Looking to some containers in the corner, Terry walked over and peered inside.

"Gavin?"

Walking over, Gavin peered down.

"Crystal meth." He paused. "Whoever is doing the drying is multitasking."

Gavin turned silent. It had been three years since he'd been on such a scene. Then the disappointing court outcome. This was exactly the same type of operation. Could it be his old nemesis? His gut was speaking to him. It had to be. Right here in small town U.S.A.

Terry, walking around the room, suddenly stooped to the ground.

"Gavin!"

Reaching down, he lifted an earring.

"Is that Emaline's?" Gavin asked.

"Likely. Who else would wear something like that?"

"Yes, she's a nosey sort and must have seen something and decided to look into it."

"They've got her...or..."

142

Carefully crawling out and fitting the board back in, they made plans to be back after dark to try to catch whoever was working here.

They knew they needed to catch the men seen at the filling station in order to find Emaline. And they also knew without saying that it might be too late.

Gavin was quiet.

"What are you thinking, Gavin?"

"As far fetched as it seems, I know it in my heart – this is Harrison Tyler's operation."

143

Cora napped much of the morning, but felt good all afternoon and evening. She had been undergoing treatments and had taken time off work. Red hired a temp out of Indy and told Cora she'd have a job waiting. While Hubert and Bobby were outside, she sat on the couch and talked with Eula Mae, who sat across the room in her customary chair. In the time they had been here, Cora felt well cared for, and saw a difference in Bobby. He was more content, smiled all the time and couldn't get enough of Hubert. Constantly praising Eula Mae for the meals, Bobby dearly loved the blonde brownies so often present on the kitchen counter.

"Eula Mae?"

"Hmmm?"

"Thank you."

"For what?"

"For making a difference in our lives."

Eula Mae was a bit slow to respond, fighting her emotions. There was a dab of moisture in her eye.

"I think you've made a difference in our lives, too, Cora."

"I don't know what Bobby and I would be doing right now if the two of you had not come along."

"God works in mysterious ways. I think it was God who brought us together."

"I guess I've always believed in God, but not really paid attention."

"Well, Cora, God loves you and is always waiting for you to turn to Him. He never pushes. But there are times when I believe God just sort of says, 'I'm going to do this' and works a little miracle in somebody's life. I think he did that in our lives."

"You think God wanted us to need you?"

Eula Mae smiled.

"Who needed who?" Eula Mae glanced around the room. In just a few days there were changes. A pair of socks lay, inside out, on the floor. Two different pairs of shoes lay by the door. Bobby's skateboard leaned against the wall. All around there was a new zest in the house. "Cora, I want you to look around this room. See the socks? The skateboard?"

"Yes."

"Well, it's more than simple things like that. In the kitchen there are cups on the counter and bowls in the sink, Cocoa Puffs in the cupboard, Twinkies in the pantry. There's a different kind of clutter than there used to be. It's the clutter of an active house. But there is something deeper. Look over there." She pointed to a skateboard magazine opened on the floor. "Hubert bought that magazine! He has taken interest in new things. In the past, he would be sitting in his chair with his nose in some book. Where is he? He's with a young man out in the shop, working on who knows what."

"He's really good for Bobby."

"It's more than that, Cora. He loves Bobby. I know the look I see in his eyes." She paused, unable to speak for a long few moments. "We...both of us...love both of you. God gave us a special gift, just when we needed it."

It was Cora's turn to be tearful. She reached for the Kleenex. Looking down at her lap, she spoke softly.

"I never knew my mother, Eula Mae. I have always been alone. It has been hard for me to be close to anybody. There was never a mother to put my arms around, or to hold me. I wanted to hear a mother telling me I was loved. It's like something has been missing all through the years." She paused. "I always wondered what it would be like to have one." Her voice cracked and she looked up at Eula Mae. "Now I know."

Cora began to sob, years of struggle and missed dreams

welling up to the surface. Eula Mae couldn't speak and tears flooded her vision. She wiped her eyes and put her book on the end table. Still hardly able to see, she arose, walked over and sat next to Cora. Reaching one arm around Cora's shoulders, she pulled her close.

"Come here, baby girl."

Cora wrapped her arms around Eula Mae and sobbed. A tiny voice choked.

"Momma."

Cora cried for the years the locust had eaten. Eula Mae was blinded by tears of the silent prayers uttered over the years and now answered beyond what she could ever hope for.

144

About to come in to the house a while later for a refill of coffee, Hubert peered in the window first and paused.

Eula Mae sat on the end of the couch; Cora was curled up under a fleece throw with her head in Eula Mae's lap. His wife slowly rubbed Cora's hair and it appeared they were talking softly.

Hubert stood for a few minutes, careful not to make any noise. He watched the look of love on his wife's face, the little movements of her lips as she spoke tenderly to Cora. He knew the look of love, but he'd never seen it quite this same way.

Turning carefully, he went back to the shop.

145

Brian Phillips rubbed his chin that evening. It felt like sandpaper. Packing to fly to Indy, he forgot his usual Harry's razor with the precision German blades. On the way to the hotel, he stopped at a discount store and bought a bag of ten disposable triple-blade razors. Ten for two dollars. This morning was rough. With the first scrape he knew he'd made a mistake. It was like trying to shave with a bent screwdriver with a jagged edge. Wincing, he'd grabbed for the toilet paper to stop the bleeding and gave up shaving for the day. Somewhere he would stop and get a better razor. There was no sense in voluntary torture. Throwing the rest of the razors in the trash, he grabbed his shirt. As he knotted his tie later and snugged it, he felt his whiskers catch the collar and chuckled.

"Brian, you tried to save a couple bucks, and now you just threw two dollars in the trash. Once again you learned it pays to buy proven quality."

It was only two dollars lost, but he did the human thing and berated himself for quite a time, having imaginary conversations with the manufacturer. It had been his routine in life never to buy the low end, rarely the top end, and settle somewhere in the middle. His mom taught him that and it was she who gave him the year's subscription to Harry's, based on what she'd heard and seeing the shaving rash on his neck. Although he argued with her that this was violating her principles, she stuck with her guns and insisted he needed to step up. He was amazed at the difference.

Driving the rental Avenger and looking to the left to pass, he craned his neck to free the whiskers from the collar. It had been a frustration all day. He still hadn't stopped at a store; the case took precedence over comfort.

Now he was headed down Interstate 70 with a sense of urgency. The intense orb of the setting sun rapidly crept into the horizon behind him, like a floodlight pointed into the rearview. Early that evening he'd gotten the tip he'd been waiting for. Harrison Tyler was headed to one of his very rare forays into the field. Knowing the history of the case from Gavin, it was clear something was up for Tyler to get his hands that close to his supply line. But it was the last bit whispered to him that set his neck hairs on edge. His informant swore someone was stuffed into the trunk just before Tyler headed towards the fields.

Brian tried to reach Gavin, but there was no answer. Earlier that day he'd had a brief phone conversation with Sheriff Burris to let him know he might be investigating things in Buckner County that evening. A courtesy call. At the time, he had no clue he would be there so soon. The sheriff had mentioned meetings all evening at the office about the next years' budget, so Brian did not call ahead, trusting to instinct that the sheriff would be around. Saved a lot of issues when communication was conducted face to face.

Following Google maps, he pulled into the sheriff's office. Exiting the car, he went to the door and entered to find several deputies and a couple polo shirts sitting drinking coffee over a sheaf of papers. Brian looked over and met the eyes of the sheriff, who rose.

"Brian?"

"Yes, something's happened. Can we talk privately?"

146

The door slammed open as Bobby came in the back door. He was laughing. Behind him, Hubert came in the door, grinning from ear to ear.

Eula Mae looked up. She and Cora were making a breakfast casserole for the next morning. Both smiled as Bobby trooped into the kitchen.

"Grandpa says we need to have ice cream!"

A tear formed in Eula Mae's eye.

Cora choked a bit.

Bobby didn't notice, opening the freezer door.

"There's none in here, Grandpa."

Hubert walked silently into the kitchen, looking at his wife. Unable to speak, he recovered quickly.

"Probably need to run to the store."

Cora looked to Eula Mae and smiled sweetly. Returning the smile, Eula Mae touched Cora's shoulder.

"You seem to be feeling better. Would you be up to a quick dash to Dairy Queen?"

"That would be wonderful! If I can stay in the car, I just need to throw on a sweater and my shoes."

"Cookie Dough Blizzard, coming up!" yelled Bobby.

147

Jake and Bub came in early that evening about 9 o'clock, slipping quietly in through the back roads. Usually arriving more towards ten, they knew they had a lot of work to do. Wasting no time, they didn't say anything when they went in. Each had their jobs and went at them. Both wore ear buds and listened to music. Bub was getting ready to move some plants when he happened to glance down. Yanking his ear buds out, he let them fall.

"Jake?" There was no answer as Jake's head bobbed to the music in his ears. Bub knew Jake liked heavy metal with his favorites being Slipknot, Iron Maiden and Metallica. He walked to Jake and slapped his shoulder. Jake jumped and ripped his ear buds out.

"What?"

"Come here."

"You got to do it yourself. I got my own stuff to do."

"Forget that. Just come here."

"Why?"

"Just come here."

Jake walked around the rack, dragging a couple plants. Bub was staring at the ground.

"What?"

Bub pointed.

"Look."

"Ok, so it's a footprint. We've been walking all over. Quit being stupid. We got a lot of work to do."

"It's not one of our footprints."

Jake stopped. Looking down, he glanced back up at Bub, who was looking around.

"It's a cowboy boot toe. Neither of us wears cowboy boots."

Jake, the only one armed, reached for his gun.

148

The audible sound of a Glock slide caused Jake to stop in mid reach.

"Police! Hands up!" Terry saw hesitation in Jake. "Don't even think about it, mister. In fact, it'd be a real good thing if both of you put your arms into the air real careful."

Both men slowly raised their hands. Neither had heard the door open.

Terry stood in the doorway, then quickly stepped in further to allow Gavin to enter, revolver in hand. Walking to Jake, Gavin slipped the man's gun from its holster and then frisked both men.

Terry's phone rang, but he had silenced it earlier. He was unaware it had gone off several times.

Gavin held the earring where both men could see.

"Where is the lady who belongs to this?"

Bub blurted out, "She weren't…"

"Shut up, Bub!" Jake spoke harshly. Looking to Gavin, he hissed, "Ain't never seen that earring and we ain't seen no lady."

"Kidnapping is a federal offense."

"We didn't kidnap nobody."

"Then where is she?"

"We took…."

"Shut your face, Bub!" Jake slammed a fist into Bub, who fell backward across a drying rack, scattering plants and the rack across the floor.

Hearing a noise from behind, Terry's heart lurched as he spun around.

149

"Seth! Whatcha doing here?"

Birdhouse was getting ready to put a second coat of paint on a line of wren houses he and Seth had built. He had them all lined up, setting on an old paint and varnish-covered pine board with 16d nails sticking through to set the birdhouses on when painting. They could do the other sides while the houses sat on the nails. It kept them from sliding and they could paint that bottom side first. The points would not mark the paint much.

"I knew we needed to get that second coat on. Wasn't doing anything important. Just watching the dumb TV. Thought I'd just wander over and help."

"Well, grab a brush. You want to do the red?"

"Sure."

They painted a few minutes. Birdhouse watched Seth and realized his painting needed work, but really wasn't too bad. Besides, he was learning.

"You're getting better all the time, Seth."

"Thanks. And I was wondering if I could make a special birdhouse for my mom? Something with a little fanciness to it?"

"Got a birthday or something coming up?"

"Her birthday is next week."

Birdhouse stared for just a moment.

"Seriously?"

"I know. Not much time. But I just thought of it."

"I guess we best choose the wood tonight. Start tomorrow. I think I'm all set for the bazaar on Saturday."

"I was thinking of that bazaar. I got nothing big planned for Saturday. Was wondering about maybe going along."

"That works." Birdhouse beamed inside. "You want to go with me to deliver a house tonight?"

"Sure. I'll need to call Dad first."

150

Kim was home, sitting on a kitchen chair, waiting for water to boil for a cup of tea. Bengal Spice, her favorite. Truth be told, she just wanted something to do to keep her mind occupied.

Terry had been gone all afternoon and was not answering his phone. She knew he and Gavin were out and about investigating and she was worried. Such a strange feeling to care.

Funny in a way that she didn't care whether Terry cracked any big cases. But she knew it was important to him, and Terry's feelings and needs were important to her now.

It felt good to be concerned about him. The feelings were confusing, yet somehow gave her a sense of peace and happiness.

Working for Greg all these years, she'd had her share of glances, but there was never any real reason to reciprocate. Focusing on the job, she knew Greg relied on her and she knew he was looking to the future with her and the restaurant. She'd sat on the porch more than once, thinking of ideas for the restaurant, even sketching out ideas for a seating change and researching ovens and coffee pots. Now, here she sat, not thinking about anything to do with Schmeisser's. Instead, her mind was filled with Terry's face and the way he looked at her. And the way he made her feel inside.

The teapot whistled and it took a moment to break her thoughts.

151

Terry, wide-eyed and gun ready, faced the doorway.

It was Pratt! In his hands he held a green smock. There was blood on it and a smoldering anger filled his eyes. His voice cracked.

"It's Emaline's. It was in the back window of their car."

"Dang, Pratt! You're gonna get yourself shot!"

"Something's happened to her." Walking up to Bub, who had just gotten up, Pratt slammed him across the mouth, knocking him back to the floor. It was enough to jar Bub's cell phone from his pocket. It skidded to a stop under the drying rack. Pratt stooped to hiss at Bub. "Where is she?"

Terry grabbed Pratt.

"Hold it, Pratt!"

Pratt threw him off and, red-faced with rage, grabbed Bub by the shirt collar and yelled in his face.

"Where is she? What have you done to her?"

Gavin and Terry both grabbed Pratt and managed to drag him off.

"Pratt! Stop it!"

"So help me…!" Pratt shuddered.

152

The despairing whimper was heard by no one. In the oppressive darkness of the car's trunk, Emaline lay and cried. When Tyler ordered her to be tied and put in the trunk, the look on his face told her more than she wanted to know. The last humiliation was the duct tape over her mouth.

The night's darkness enshrouded the landscape as the sedan made its way toward Winston Corner.

"Al?" Tyler had turned to the man sitting next to him.

"Yes, sir?"

"We have to get this crop dried and sent to the mixing facility by middle of next week. The heroin is set to be ready then. That will allow for a couple days to mix before we get it to market. If this all pays off, I might move you to the mixing facility."

"Yes, sir. I thought it was meth this time. The boys have been cooking it."

"Doing some of each, some with both. Seeing which brings the best business. It's called market research. Might even try rat poison. I hear that gives a unique twist." He smirked and the glint in his eyes was that of a man concerned only with market share.

Al nodded. "Probably gives a good high. Are you worried it'll kill somebody?"

Looking blandly at the man, Tyler watched Al uncomfortably look to his lap.

"Profit is the only thing, Al."

Tyler lapsed into silence, deep in thought as Simpson drove. This was a serious problem, this loud-mouthed lady in the trunk. She could not be allowed to go free. He was not afraid of such necessities, and there had been others in the past. It was a rarity, though, for he knew that drug production was one thing, but the police tended to pursue more closely when there was a murder. Not all murders, but of people like this Poovy lady, who was a member of a small community. Not like some alley-bound bottom of the barrel hireling. This lady's absence would be noticed.

He knew he'd have to figure this one out himself. It was how he started, as an enforcer for a kingpin. Ambition took hold and he literally enforced his way to the top. The trappings of the top he enjoyed were beyond his wildest dreams except for the constant vigilance needed to stay there. There were others wanting what he had. Constant jockeying kept him searching for those with just enough ambition to be useful and reliable - like Al - but without the drive to overtake him. He valued intelligence, but more in the sense of street smarts rather than anything. Al was smart, but seemed to lack in the area of hiring men for the grunt work. Still, there were no previous issues, but this one in particular had the potential of taking down this whole new wing of his realm. If he had to, he could just cut the links and let it go. In this case, he could take Al, on a moment's notice, and just drive away. There would be no ties to follow. But this was a crop virtually ready for market. Just a couple weeks and he would have a shipment ready. The quick-dry method decreased quality, but it really didn't matter with his market. For the low-end customers it would sell quickly and he would clear a tidy sum.

After the drying process it would all be trucked out in the night to a temporary facility in Ohio, where it would be chopped, mixed and bagged. Then, another quick night drive to a parking lot in the back of the independent truck stop in Pennsylvania where there were no lights. Several small vehicles would arrive over an hour's time. Each would take only two minutes to load, engines running, and the product would be off to end-line suppliers. At the end of the hour, his enforcer would drive by and the money would be transferred in moments. He always paid his enforcer well in cash. This ensured loyalty and efficiency.

So he needed to take care of this lady. To make her disappear would incite a search. He wanted it quiet, if only for a few days. So the only reasonable option was to take her back to her home and find some way for her to have an "accident." As much as he didn't like to be this close to the action, it was where he started and it was essential to get this load to market. He was also expanding on the East coast and needed the product and the cash.

Glancing at his watch, Harrison Tyler knew he would have to move quickly in order to be well away by dawn.

His mind worked on a plan for Emaline Poovy.

153

Walking through the dark fields that night, Cooter had seen the Smart car head towards town. Then the lights went out. He just happened to be in a line between trees and corn where he could see the lights shut off at the edge of town.

Lisa merely looked at him over her book earlier as he headed out, wearing his Indian garb. It was accentuated tonight by his latest purchase – a turquoise necklace with wolf teeth. It was all fake but looked real. And it was the difference between three hundred dollars and a mere thirty.

Walking out the door, he knew Lisa was deliberately staring at the pages of her book. She no longer rolled her eyes at him, but he knew she thought he'd gone off the deep end. Stepping off the porch, Cooter looked back to the windows and then made a beeline to the shop. Skirting sideways around the teepee lying across sawhorses, he reached under a tarp in the corner and, smiling, held up his ash bow. Slinging a quiver over his shoulder, he grunted in what he assumed was Apache talk. Then, looking to the workbench, he paused. A look came to his eyes as he solemnly reached under the vise and brought out a box.

Opening the flaps, his eyes glinted. Reaching carefully along the sides to the bottom, Cooter – Dancing Wolf – slowly and carefully drew out a full Apache war bonnet and placed it upon his head, tying it to fit. Tilting his head to look in the mirror over the workbench, he smiled broadly and, grabbing the bow, slipped out the door.

Keeping in his mind the location where the lights flicked off, he headed, bounding and howling quietly, towards town.

154

It was his cautious side that caused Harrison Tyler to order Simpson to stop a hundred feet from the boarded up station. Never having seen the sight before, he sat for a few minutes just watching. The little Smart Car was nestled behind the former gas station. All seemed quiet and well this evening. Nobody appeared to be around. But the back door stood ajar, allowing a shaft of light to cross the gravel and beckon to anybody looking at the right angle.

"Idiots. Al, give them a call."

Al pulled out his phone and dialed.

155

"That tastes wonderful!" Cora said.

Sitting in the back seat as they savored their ice cream, she looked around. What a wonderful evening. The fresh night air added to the already deep sense of peace and happiness in her soul. Bobby put a giant bite of "Cookie Dough Blizzard" in his mouth and shoved his spoon in his cup for another.

Hubert grinned, a butterscotch shake in his hand.

"You're eating that in record time, Bobby."

Cora shook her head.

"I always tell him he should slow down and savor it."

Bobby grinned over another bite.

"I am savoring it! I'm just savoring quicker than you do!"

Eula Mae laughed, looking out at the night.

"Hey, what say we go for a little drive around town and see what there is to see?"

156

"No answer, Mr. Tyler. But I've ordered him to keep it on mute unless they're in the car. Don't want any passerby to hear anything."

Wise, thought Harrison. How many times had he been suddenly distracted by some stupid ring tone across a restaurant? Still, he was a careful man.

"Simpson, check it out."

"Yes, sir."

Simpson pulled his gun, racked the slide and opened the door.

"Simpson."

"Yes, boss?"

"Any shots will be most unwelcome for our situation. We don't need any attention. Too many people in these areas carry guns."

Simpson nodded and quietly shut the door behind him.

157

"Ok, I know your name is Bub." Gavin helped the man up.

"That's all you're gonna know. I ain't gonna tell you nothin'. Jake don't know nothin', either."

Gavin couldn't help but smile. He looked to the other man.

"And we know your name is Jake."

Jake glared at Bub.

"That was stupid, Bub."

"What was stupid?"

"You said my name."

"I did not!"

"Yes, you did!"

"Did not!"

"Did, too!"

Terry waved his arms.

"Stop it!" Both turned to him. "Where is the lady who belongs to this...this...green...thing?"

Bub looked to Jake, who looked to Terry.

"We found it here. Don't know nothin' about a lady."

Pratt advanced again, restrained only by Gavin.

"It's Emaline's! She wears it in the evenings at the shop when she's cleaning up. She never wears it outside. You're lying, scumbag!"

Gavin looked to Pratt.

"How do you know all that, Pratt?"

Pratt blustered.

"Well, I see her. I mean...I...sort of...watch over her. She's there alone."

Terry looked at him.

"Does she know you're watching?"

Pratt looked down.

"No."

Gavin looked to Jake.

"Ok, we know you're lying. What can you tell us? Kidnapping is a federal offense. Best you talk." He didn't want to say out loud what his real fear was. He met Terry's eyes and knew he was thinking the same thing. What if it wasn't just kidnapping?

158

Simpson heard voices as he approached the door. Stopping to listen, his eyes widened and he turned to the sedan. His steps were too quick and he slipped on the gravel, sliding to his knee. The voices inside quieted.

Harrison Tyler, conversing with Al, looked up in time to see him go down. Alarms went off in his mind. He knew his bodyguard and the look on Simpson's face said something was amiss.

Recovering and hurrying to the car, Simpson slid behind the wheel, put his gun on the seat and spoke, breathlessly, "Something's going on inside, Boss. Sounds like the law."

"Let's get out of here!"

Simpson slammed the car into gear.

159

"I wonder if the fireflies are out tonight?" Cora was enjoying the outing, but already there appeared tiredness in her eyes.

Hubert nodded. They were enjoying the night and had all the windows down.

"I saw a few earlier, Cora. We'll just take a spin out towards the edge of town and take a look off into the fields. Times I've been there you could see thousands. By the way, there's a skateboard competition in Indy in a couple weeks. Eula Mae and I will spring for the entry fee!"

Bobby was incredulous.

"Thanks! Mom?"

"Absolutely, it's ok."

"Wow!"

At the edge of town the fireflies were numerous. Bobby stared.

"If you put all those in a big jar it would be a huge light."

"It sure would be. Maybe we should get one of Eula Mae's canning jars and try it."

"Maybe another night, Hubert. I think Cora is getting tired."

"Ok, we'll make a quick lap and head home."

Bobby leaned on his mother's shoulder as they came to the fields. Looking ahead to the turn, Hubert squinted and peered ahead. In the dark he saw a small shaft of light. There was activity at the old abandoned filling station. Headlights glared and there was the sound of tires spinning gravel.

"Something's wrong!" Hubert yelled to himself.

160

Gavin carefully approached the door and heard receding footsteps.

"Turn off all the lights, Terry!" He pointed to the surge strip on the floor with extension cords running in various directions. Shoving Bub and Jake to the ground, Terry reached and flipped the lighted switch. Gavin hit the switch by the door. All was in darkness.

Allowing a few moments to let his eyes adapt, Gavin slipped the door open further as he heard a car door shut. He saw the dark sedan reverse, slam into gear and start to turn.

He stepped out into the darkness.

161

Hubert also saw the inside lights go off. Turning that way and flicking on his high beams, he saw the sedan backing out and an illuminated figure leaving the back of the old gas station followed by another. Squinting, he tried to make them out. It was Eula Mae who first yelled.

"It's Terry and that Mr. Crockett! I think they're after that car!"

Hubert hit the gas.

"Hold on!"

162

Simpson found himself boxed in by a couple of defunct light poles, one broken and hanging doubled, the globe almost touching the ground. Hitting the brake and slamming the car into reverse, he gave it the gas and turned the wheel. Not accustomed to wearing a seatbelt, Harrison Tyler held to the strap over the door as Al, also unrestrained, tumbled into his lap, groping to right himself.

"Get off me, you idiot! Hurry, Simpson!"

Slamming it into drive again, Simpson started to give it the gas when a four-wheel drive truck suddenly appeared in front of them. Simpson braked desperately. Tyler and Al both slammed forward into the seat in front of them. Raising his head and cursing, Tyler saw a grim old man's face in the headlights, looking down from the driver's side of a truck. There was no place to go. Glancing behind, he saw two men running in his direction. Both had guns drawn.

"Slam into him, Simpson! Push him out of the way!"

"Boss, that's a big truck! It ain't going to push!"

"Well, do something! Get us out of here!"

"Nowhere to go!" Simpson was panicked.

"Every man for himself! Run!" Tyler threw open the door and hurriedly disappeared into the shadows.

Simpson caught his sleeve on the inside door handle and wrenched it loose, giving time for Gavin to leap into his path with revolver in hand. Seeing the look on Gavin's face, the big man stopped and threw his hands in the air.

"Don't shoot!"

"Don't move!"

Terry dove at Al, catching him around the waist and knocking him to the ground. Reaching for his cuffs, he saw the third man disappear into the night.

Gavin put Simpson against the car. Chancing a quick glance to the night, he knew Harrison Tyler had once again escaped his grasp.

163

Fifty yards into the field, Tyler heard no sounds of pursuit. Still walking quickly, he dialed his phone. He'd make arrangements for someone to pick him up by GPS beacon. What he needed now was a place to hide, near a road but away from prying eyes. Stepping in mud, he realized his suit and shoes were likely ruined. Didn't matter, though. The important thing was to get away.

In the distance he heard the struggles and vague voices.

"Terry – you got extra cuffs?"

"No."

"That was Harrison Tyler! He's getting away."

164

Hubert jumped out of the truck, firmly instructing the others.

"All of you stay in the truck!"

Reaching behind the cab into the corner of the bed, Hubert grabbed a bundle and trotted to where Gavin had Al against the car, reaching for the handcuffs behind his back. Gavin was startled, but quickly recognized Hubert.

"Don't shoot! It's me, Hubert."

Terry spoke.

"What are you doing here, Hubert?"

"Looking for fireflies. Gavin, here's some zip-ties."

"Awesome, Hubert! Hold him against the car while I tie him to the door handle."

Then Hubert went over to help Terry. Securing Simpson's legs, they both rose.

Gavin stood at the edge of the field, staring into the darkness. Terry rushed over.

"See anything?"

"No! And he's not a man you want to chase in the dark."

165

Without any warning, a shadow came out of the night and Tyler was tackled by something akin to a giant feathered bird with arms. Hitting the ground hard, his face plowed the dirt. Feathered wings covered each side of his face and Tyler shuddered with fear. With the bird on his back, he was unable to move. Struggling and in a panic, he was able to reach a hand up and brush feathers aside. Twisting his head to glance upward, he was shocked into immobility with a glimpse of history. On top of him was a man in full Indian attire. Bending to make eye contact, the Indian began hooting and whooping. Reaching to his belt, Dancing Wolf pulled his tomahawk. Tyler panicked and tried to claw his way through the dirt to get away.

166

Turning to the sedan, Gavin spun as he heard sounds in the distant darkness.

"Over here! I got him!" Dancing Wolf hollered.

Terry waved.

"Go, Gavin!"

Rushing into the dark field, Gavin followed the sound of struggle.

"Help! Indians!"

Gavin smiled. It was the unmistakable voice of Harrison Tyler. Pausing barely an instant when he saw Cooter's garb, Gavin knelt and put a knee in Tyler's back as Cooter carefully stepped back. Pulling the handcuffs from his belt, Gavin dangled them before Harrison's face and smirked, "I've been saving these for you, Tyler." He slapped them on and glanced to Cooter.

"Little far from home for that, huh, Cooter?"

"Well, I was out and about. Not a word, ok?"

"Just get out of here. I'll contact you tomorrow for a statement."

"Promise, not a word?"

"Promise. Now, get!"

Cooter bounded off through the field with a barely suppressed war cry of victory.

167

Back behind the old station, the crossing of headlights created a confusing and surreal light. Depending, a person was either a silhouette or clearly visible, and alternately seemed to be walking through a strobe.

Taking advantage of the happenings outside, Jake and Bub took a dive for the door, knocking Pratt violently to the ground where he lay momentarily stunned. The two then jumped into the Smart Car and accelerated around the corner – where they promptly ran out of battery.

"What's wrong, Jake?"

"Out of power! Didn't you charge it last night?"

"I can't remember, Jake. Oops!"

"Oops is right! Knot head!"

Jake leaned on the wheel.

"Let's get out of here, Bub!"

Both men crawled out and ran down the street.

168

Terry looked into the darkness of the field.

"Gavin? You got him?"

"Yes, I've got him."

"Who's out there with you?"

"Nobody."

"I thought I heard someone yell. Sounded like Cooter Wilson."

Gavin stumbled into the headlights from Hubert's truck, pushing a man in a dirt-covered suit. Terry glanced into the darkness and then to Gavin, a question in his eyes. Tyler, squirming, raised his head and looked into Gavin's eyes.

"Crockett! You got nothing on me. I was just driving through the area and stopped to take a leak behind this old building."

"Why did you run?"

"Well, if you saw men running toward you from the night, wouldn't you run? You see…you can't get me, Crockett! I'll be out of this tomorrow and I'll have you for harassment." The man smiled and looked back into the darkness. "And I'll have that Indian, too."

Terry smiled and looked to Gavin.

169

Pratt ran over to the sedan.

"Where is Emaline?" He yelled at Al.

Al, still reeling from what had just happened, only stared at him.

Running around to where Simpson was cuffed, Pratt slapped him.

"Where is Emaline? If you've hurt her…" He smoldered, fists clenched.

Inside the trunk, Emaline listened intently to all the muffled goings-on, not sure what was happening. When she heard the worried voice of Pratt, her eyebrows raised. Then she heard Jean's Gavin.

"Where's the lady?"

Turning to her back, Emaline raised her bound feet and kicked the wheel well.

"What was that?" Pratt asked.

Terry glanced around, searching for the source.

Bobby, sitting in the window of the truck, pointed.

"I think it came from the trunk!"

Another kick and a mumble.

Terry tried the trunk. Locked. He went to the driver's door to find the latch. Going back and lifting the lid, he smiled broadly.

"Here you go, Pratt!"

Pratt, turning to peer into the trunk, suddenly looked elated and reached to pull the tape from Emaline's mouth. Peeling it gently as possible, he reached to untie her legs. Helping her out, he kept one arm around her as she wobbled.

"I heard it all." She pointed to Tyler. "He has fields all over, and I know where his other facilities are." She looked to Tyler. "I could hear everything you said to Al." Trying to squirm away from Pratt's arm, she looked at him as he spoke.

"Not sure you're steady enough, Emaline."

"Oh, I'm steady all right." She looked at him strangely. "You were really worried about me, weren't you?"

"I was."

"I'm feeling unsteady again. Maybe you ought to hold me up a mite longer." He returned his arm and she perceptively leaned towards him.

Gavin looked to Tyler.

"Kidnapping, drug trafficking, and I bet we can find your mixing operation. Oh, yes, Harrison. There's enough evidence this time."

Gavin smiled.

Terry looked into the distance where loud barking was heard.

"Gavin, give me a hand getting these fellas locked up. Then I need to go after the other two."

Sheriff's cars suddenly dashed from the north and slammed to a stop, casting their headlights into the mix. Gavin glanced over to see dark silhouettes change into Brian Phillips and Sheriff Burris and a couple deputies.

"Brian!"

"Perfect timing! I see you did all the work and I get to pick up the pieces."

"It's Harrison Tyler, Brian. Kidnapping, drugs. I think we've got him this time."

"Correction, Gavin. I got him. You're retired and according to the records I'll be the agent in charge, but you and I know it wasn't me that got him – YOU got him. It'll help my career, and make a difference to your peace of mind."

The three men were being guided by officers into the back of Sheriff Burris' Suburban.

Walking over to Terry, Gavin and Brian, Sheriff Burris shook hands all around.

"You guys did a great job."

They all turned their heads as a ruckus sounded off in the distance and then drew closer.

170

The shouting grew louder and within a couple minutes both Jake and Bub appeared around the corner with their hands in the air. Behind them marched Robert with a shotgun. More zip ties were used as Robert related his capture.

"Was in the garage with Birdhouse and the Kovacs boy. They brought a wren house. I looked up when the dog was barking. Dang dog barks at everything, but this time it was different. I looked out and these two strange fellas I never saw before were running through the yard. Next thing I see is them both laying on the ground. Well, I grabbed my shotgun – I always have it by the door – and cornered 'em. Seen all the activity and marched them straight over here."

Terry scratched his head.

"Robert, why were they laying on the ground?"

"One of them probably walked into a landmine and slipped! Took the other one out, too. Good 'ol dog!"

Terry stared for a moment before the realization hit him and he looked at Gavin and smiled.

"I'll never complain about those calls again. Sort of puts it in perspective!"

171

Cooter made his way home that night. Stopping at the end of the drive, he retrieved the mail. Detouring to the shop, he took off the war bonnet and left the bow and quiver. A few minutes later he walked in the front door. Lisa looked up.

"Honey, are you ok?"

"Yeah, why do you ask?"

"Well, you're filthy and your knees are scuffed."

"Oh...well. I took a bit of a fall. Tripped in a mole hill and did a dive."

She stared at him. He could tell she was trying to decide whether to pursue it further. Finally, she spoke.

"Did you get the mail?"

"Yup."

Lisa looked back down to her book.

Cooter headed to the shower.

172

The next morning, quite a crowd gathered at Schmeisser's. First shift waited expectantly as people trickled in. Kim knew there'd be more arrivals a bit later. It was the way of things in Winston Corner after any big event. Greg's profit rose as people gathered to hear details. It was the obligation of all living in Winston Corner after a big event to come early to Schmeisser's for an informal question and answer session. It was the small town version of a press conference.

In fact, Greg pulled out extra bratwurst when he heard the first snippets of news from Kim and the early fellas. Eggs were in good supply, and would be needed today. And he had plenty of donuts. This would be a good day.

Dinky strutted in the door, glanced around and saw a bigger crowd than usual. Having been late watching a football game over by Indy, he was unaware of the happenings of the night before. Seeing opportunity, he launched into his morning joke, relishing the increased audience.

"Fella named Dallas heard that his father, grandfather and great-grandfather had all walked on water on their twenty-first birthdays. So, on his twenty-first birthday, Dallas and his big brother Damon, headed out to the lake. 'If they did it…'" Dinky stopped in mid sentence, something rare.

No one was paying attention. Renner stared at the door. Bart did the same.

It was Pratt, coming in with Emaline. Eyebrows raised as only in a small town.

"Morning, fellas."

They stared as Pratt led Emaline to another table and held

her chair. Emaline looked up at him.

"Thank you, Ben."

The Liar's Table all gaped silently with shock. Not only did Pratt and Emaline come in together, but she used his first name! The men's eyes were big as Emaline looked their way. She glared back and snipped,

"Whatsamatter? Never seen a man be polite before? Wouldn't doubt it! And staring is rude!"

Pratt sat opposite her.

"Coffee, Emaline?"

"Yes, thank you, Ben."

Ben Pratt raised his hand to Kim.

"Two coffees please, Kim."

Busy brewing extra pots in readiness for what she knew would be the rush, Kim stared at Pratt. She smiled inside at the two of them.

"Two coffees coming up." Then, as an afterthought, "Cream and sugar, Emaline?"

"Yes, please."

Oh, my word, Kim thought to herself. Then, aware of the routine, she noted Dinky's struggle.

"Go ahead, Dinky. We're listening."

Dinky smiled and adjusted his seat. Looking around to make sure eyes were on him, he began again.

"Fella named Dallas heard that his father, grandfather and great-grandfather had all walked on water on their twenty-first birthdays. So, on his twenty-first birthday, Dallas and his big brother Damon, headed out to the lake. 'If they did it, I can too!' he insisted. When Dallas and Damon arrived at the lake, they rented a canoe and began paddling…"

The door opened. All heads turned. Dinky was perturbed, but turned to look.

It was Hubert and Bobby, followed closely by Birdhouse. Nods and greetings came from all around.

Greg smiled and put some extra bratwurst on the grill, up in the right corner where he kept the heat lower.

The atmosphere was hesitant, anticipating.

Dinky scratched his head.

People nursed coffee and Greg was busy with hollered orders. Kim emptied a pot into another.

Dinky was confused.

173

Birdhouse took a seat.

Next came Terry and Gavin. They headed to the table in the back. Gavin stopped short as Renner spoke.

"Morning Terry. Morning, Gavin." Gesturing to chairs at the Liar's Table. "Join us."

All around were echoes of, "Morning, Gavin. Morning, Terry."

Gavin smiled. His first name!

Kim brought the coffee. Dropping some creamers by Gavin, she reached into her apron and pulled out a handful of Splenda packets and placed them in front of Gavin, pausing just a moment to catch his look. She smiled.

Dinky look quizzical.

"I missed something?"

Renner reached for the cream.

"Yep, you did. Big happenings last night. Terry and Gavin busted the biggest crime ring this side of the Mississippi."

Terry looked up.

"I don't think it was that big of a deal."

Gavin glanced over at Terry and smiled to himself.

Pratt looked at Emaline and spoke to the room.

"We got no worries with a man like you around, Terry. You saved Emaline."

Nods of affirmation appeared across the room.

"Gives a man peace at night knowing we got a good man around."

Terry smiled and caught Kim's eye. She was beaming.

Birdhouse looked to Gavin.

"Gavin, I got a special birdhouse for you and Jean – bring it over later today."

The door opened again. Max walked in, followed a moment later by a man most had never seen before. Gavin looked up.

"Morning, Brian."

Brian was clean-shaven, having stopped at a Walmart on the way home last night. He felt better.

"Make room, fellas."

Chairs scraped.

Brian sat next to Gavin.

"You said something about the food here, Gavin. Thought I'd try it. What do you recommend?

"Bratwurst and eggs."

"Bratwurst? This early in the morning?"

"Nothing like it. Greg makes the best."

Greg smiled and cracked eggs.

Brian looked over at Gavin, then to his back.

"No handcuffs, Gavin?"

Gavin smiled.

"Yep, no handcuffs. Retired now."

Terry smiled at Gavin and spoke over his coffee.

"Kim and I are heading to Indy for dinner tonight. We'd love to double with you and Jean. You don't leave for your cruise 'till next week, do you?"

Gavin nodded.

"Next Tuesday. We'd love to go to dinner."

Max looked over at Gavin and commented, "Looking a little shaggy, Gavin. Best come by later and I'll fix you up. It'll be on me."

"I'll do that. But I'd rather pay."

"Ok."

Renner grinned and shook his finger at Gavin. "You missed your chance."

Gavin nodded his head, then looked at Dinky.

"What's the morning joke, Dinky?"

Everybody quieted and looked to Dinky.

Dinky smiled.

"Fella named Dallas heard that his father, grandfather and great-grandfather all walked on water on their twenty-first birthdays. So, on his twenty-first birthday, Dallas and his big brother Damon, headed out to the lake. 'If they did it, I can too!' he insisted. When Dallas and Damon arrived at the lake, they rented a canoe and began paddling. When they got to the middle of the lake, Dallas stepped off the side of the boat... and nearly drowned. He was furious and embarrassed. He and Damon headed for home. When Dallas arrived back at the family home, he asked his grandmother for an explanation. 'Grandma, why can't I walk on water like my father, and his father, and his father before him?' His sweet old grandmother took Dallas by the hand, looked into his eyes, and explained, 'Because your father, grandfather, and great-grandfather were born in January. You, my dear, were born in June.'"

Laughter erupted! Uproarious, tension-releasing laughter. Belly laughs. Kim leaned against the wall. Emaline guffawed. They all laughed together.

Dinky grinned from ear to ear. It was the best response he'd ever had!

All was right in Winston Corner.

About the Author

This is Mark's first venture into the modern. Always sensitive to the weird and absurd, this drive down the road to Winston Corner allowed him to indulge in some character creation with the humor that so freely flows from his heart and mind.

Spending his high school years in small Sandpoint, Idaho, and then later moving to Spiceland, Indiana, he finds many character ideas in the people of his life and community. Mark holds a B.A. in History from Boise State University, Boise, Idaho, and a Masters in Counseling Psychology from Ball State University, Muncie, Indiana, and is an ordained pastor. He has experience as counselor, seminar speaker, adjunct college faculty, pastor, hospice chaplain and now author.

Follow him on Facebook

69608121R00183

Made in the USA
Columbia, SC
22 August 2019